Helen Marten (1985, Macclesfield) is an artist based in London. She studied at the Ruskin School of Fine Art, University of Oxford, and Central St. Martins, London. In recent years she has presented solo exhibitions at the Serpentine Gallery, London; Fridericianum, Kassel; CCS Bard, Hessel Museum, New York; Kunsthalle Zürich and Palais de Tokyo, Paris, among others. She was included in the 55th and 56th International Venice Biennales and in 2016 won both the Turner Prize and the inaugural Hepworth Prize for Sculpture. Marten's work can be found in public collections including Tate Collection, London; Guggenheim Museum, New York and The Museum of Modern Art, New York. She has forthcoming solo exhibitions at Castello di Rivoli, Turin and Kunsthaus Bregenz. Marten's artwork is collected in three recent monographs and she works with Sadie Coles HQ, London, Greene Naftali, NYC, and König Galerie, Berlin.

The Boiled in Between

Helen Marten

In loving memory of MAK, for all the birds
and the ducks
and
for Frances, may your world be always open

The Boiled in Between

When the fog casts a shadow, one puts on a coat.
Lyn Hejinian

In the dark times will there also be singing?
Yes, there will also be singing.
About the dark times.
Bertolt Brecht

Nothing helps scenery like ham and eggs.
Mark Twain

MESSRS.
EXTERNAL &
INTRODUCTORY
Traffic

MESSRS.
EXTERNAL & EARTHLY
The Somebody Logo

MESSRS.
EXTERNAL & BODILY
House and heart

MESSRS.
EXTERNAL & MANLY
Ethan, for a man

ETHAN
New tenements

MESSRS.
EXTERNAL & CRUMBLY
Cellophane

PATRICE
The Age of Obsession
Full of face

MESSRS.
EXTERNAL &
MELANCHOLY
Birthday

ETHAN
A pair so famous
A godless herding
Canals
Old soup
Oats

MESSRS.
EXTERNAL & STILL
Milky way

ETHAN
This Tudor trifle
P.S.

PATRICE
Darkling

MESSRS.
EXTERNAL & SLEEPY
Coffee all coffee

PATRICE
Hortulan Greenth

MESSRS.
EXTERNAL & FALLING
Ducks, electric

MESSRS.
EXTERNAL & HOMELY
1,094 bones

PATRICE
Margarine
Bowl and box (storage)
Must your hot itch

MESSRS.
EXTERNAL & WEARY
Rainbows

ETHAN
An occult alphabet
Farmyard pH

MESSRS.
EXTERNAL & GRASSY
Spirit levels

PATRICE
Divining the dog

MESSRS.
EXTERNAL & ANIMAL
Café calling

PATRICE
Time

MESSRS.
EXTERNAL & WOODY
Glue

PATRICE
Cherries, newly

MESSRS.
EXTERNAL & HEAVING
Dust

ETHAN
Specific antibodies

MESSRS.
EXTERNAL & SULTRY
In a fool's coat

PATRICE
Table of excluded dishes

ETHAN
A kneaded clod
Monster
Terms in crumpling
Natural sweets

MESSRS.
EXTERNAL & SUNNY
Open sky situation

PATRICE
Little mushroom

ETHAN
Maltworm
Heavy metal
Cardinal directions

MESSRS.
EXTERNAL & COUNTING
To grasp a fish

ETHAN
No fixed address

MESSRS.
EXTERNAL & YELLOW
Two flowers

PATRICE
Busy (future perfect, feminine)

ETHAN
Boon (future perfect, masculine)
Sousing the nappy

MESSRS.
EXTERNAL &
COMMUNITY
Invent the underworld

MESSRS.
EXTERNAL & BLUE
Shorts, early

ETHAN
Th Dyssy
Science (old magic)

PATRICE
Happiness
Great is wickedness
On more wizened dismantling tools

MESSRS.
EXTERNAL & PEATY
Rotten earth

ETHAN
A tobacco zone

MESSRS.
EXTERNAL & SORRY
Witch grass

ETHAN
Ichnos frog

PATRICE
Jogging to the sister library

MESSRS.
EXTERNAL & WATERY
Sailing alone

ETHAN
Chopped hands

MESSRS.
EXTERNAL & STRICKEN
Memorandum

PATRICE
Luxury
Dead Badger

MESSRS.
EXTERNAL & WEALTHY
Always Christmas

ETHAN
Browned off
Delicates
Customs and declarations

MESSRS.
EXTERNAL & BREEZY
Old wind

PATRICE
Hot shells
Lobster, a season in red

ETHAN
A wretched macaroni

MESSRS.
EXTERNAL
& DARKENING
Fishing

MESSRS.
EXTERNAL & SALTED,
OPTIMIST & OILS
Out

PATRICE
Big sky

ETHAN
The farewell head

PATRICE
Home

PROLOGUE

MESSRS.

All the broken windows and propped doors are where we left them. The snapped twigs pointing the way back are where we left them. It smells of cooking and non-poisonous paint. Legs inert, legs wide apart, legs striding. It's all there inside the head. Calmly floating on shadows. We comment, not complain. You could speak about the colours where we left them too, but perhaps that wouldn't reflect a commitment to the truth.

ETHAN

I offer this brain to you like shedding orange peel.

It comes to you soft in the shape of a face and says here, welcome, have my skin, my looks, my point of view.

It has the oblique body of a paragraph slanting down on the page.

It has committed feet, with momentum, like a half moon hell-bent on getting full.

On getting off.

PATRICE

The absolute honest truth frightens me. There are misguided souls who find its essence in a bowl of washed spring greens, with nuts and olive oil licked about. But when that dish is knocked by flies, made erratic, buzzed and opened up to wind, the simple circumstance of it changes. Brusque access of feeling, too, might seize you and there is often some confusion, some fraudulence. There are peanuts thrown in wild disorder.

MESSRS.

We are like a plastic hawk dangling from an olive tree, our movements tracing a shape to inform fullness, swaying through the blaze of sun. The olive tree, grey and stoic with observation, is always there. And when in those glorious new days we are not the hawk – neither body nor air, but a silent streaming of temperature – we can see it all from a dissolving point of view. There is no code or sin, but translation.

This is the grand scramble, the boiled in between.

Some day edibles will run slim and the fat holding us all together will sizzle off or flatten out dried as paper. When we reach that point, even a bit of poison proves useful as glue. A malignant strain at least provides direction.

Who will care about the facts and faces then? When bodies are just bulbous costumes with cobbled information. When proper pronouns and their coordinates blink out leaks.

What use is all that when the action is striking out, keeping going where we don't usually care to look?

MESSRS.
EXTERNAL & INTRODUCTORY

Traffic

It is sometimes said that tears are shed over disappearance. It is sometimes said that the maximum figure of domestic entanglement, without reduction, is two. Human solicitation sometimes means an unzipping of one face and the absorption of another, of many different smiles piled on, glued over with specks of unspeakable matter. This is the threadbare business of men and women and babies. All their animals, the plants, the packaging, milky linen and a stomach filled with mulch.

One might lie awake until morning, left fist balled against the wall, thumping out sheep or the minutes remaining to lever the right fist out of fury and into a hat or jacket, into an appearance of readiness. Sometimes there is an uncovered head, bald, or perhaps an umbrella, broken. Sometimes there is rain and its wetted roads. There is something in the very poise of a hand, its clipped nails and signals sent flying off under the sky that speaks of the grammatical problem of having a body. The birds arrange themselves on telephone wires; they spell it out; they are writing a play. There are people in the world who appear not as primary objects, but as incidental specks or spots on objects. They too are writing a play.

We all have our audiences, our front row voices ready to whisper us into an unspeakable afternoon. The neighbours lend an ear, extend opinions, but never a hand. We love and murder at the same decibel. And together we scream or softly pace out the words that end in mortgage or divorce, in a nice bracelet or a quick trouser-down fumble under the stairs. We sit in our cars with the radio too low, holding our poor tails between sore legs until a shadow blows across the road and enough time has passed to feel new. To feel tenderly indifferent. We send a lasso out onto the air and feel the dead souls catching in its loop. We torment ourselves with all their commentary that gurgles and raves beyond our curtains. We twitch and lose our lip gloss. Voices leak. We invent them, footnote and file away. We get hot and strong and fall over our shoes with laces long undone. *We're on the verge of ruin!*, we say to each other and it feels nice to speak. *Let us have the moon and some steady flower to plant in our buttonhole, a rich rosebud stuffed in a jar and pickled to sludge next to biscuits and dog food! Let us have porcelain and paracetamol! Let us slam our heads first into each other and then against a wall! Let us be body and building, for both have a heart and a spine!* We are floor plans and footprints, little rats and private jokers. We run around in twos and fours, singles seeking girls and boys and a birthday in between.

We accept the situation. We don't like any politics. We shatter religion and family. We are the squashed beetles still breathing on the bottom of a shoe. We are smelly beige and full of beer. We are hair-spray, atomised, chemical, vanilla.

All those organic habits of the house are inscribed in us at organ depth. All our feet on the ground are just more examples of vehicles moving in sunlight – a diagram of function. The little empty attic of a brain, stocked with lumber and broken furniture. The kitchen with its earthquakes and fires. The bottom of yet another heart with all its accidents pushed back and forth, a large pendulum in aluminium foil. We remember the thousand little acts that took us to present day, the chopped onions and tears that ran down. It is impossible to find a permanent view. Nobody eats until they starve to death. Until they roll over and die or do a dance, kiss a lover quietly – the most solemn things a life can do.

Clothes look like weather and weather like a sheet to wrap closely about. Do we know what expires in daylight? What privileges of modern living or names carved into trees heal up and mean nothing in vast silence, without even the wild birds whose old seasons are a new delusion? The puddles of deserted gardens are left alone to swoon with their soggy reeds. We do not understand the technicalities of life, so instead we get comfortable with the thresholds, with the buildings where we can camp down and behave with national manners. A body in a bin bag, after all, is a figure in a landscape. We spread butter on our bread or eat an apple and it is the first apple, the first bread, the first butter. There is something in the quality of stillness, in the sadness of beauty giving in to the sensation of *being* that turns everything into a prototype.

We Messrs. are always here. Our grips and turns, our fingers, our lips over body parts we barely dare to poke a finger into. We are always here and never here. We are a fiction. When we raise our hands or our voices, we launch a little banner. We are something like a cluster study of half a dozen surfaces pressed together, not against glass, but the general transparency of day, of a routine Monday way of looking at things, a Thursday way or a Sunday. We are several minds. We are male languages and female languages. We will look to the man and call him. We will look to the woman and call her the same. We are the breath, the stutters that fill it. We are dog languages carrying rhythm like water. We are built languages with glimmers of structure and a little trouble finding our way to the front door. We will concentrate on essentials: how is your health? Your happiness? Your heart rate? We will find a shape in the chaos. We are here and there. The voice of tepid regret. The punctuation of accident. Wheat germ and same day dry-cleaning. It is our job. Our function to talk above all. Not a mockery, but a patience. Hands that rake over shoulders or open wide to absorb the impact of myth. We will tell you that you are a little brave, a little determined, a little sloppy and wet around the edges. We will watch you fuck and cradle your head in our arms. We will tell you that you'll chase a serpent map to its cursive end. We won't say stop. There are long years of scraping liaisons together, normal and expensive, pushing and scraping, sad or unusual tasks, always scraping, performed simply to declare *I miss you*.

Don't take for granted that characters here make their meals or meanings with regularity. It occurs to us that we, personally, have told you nothing. That our merciless proceedings show neither a future nor a past. We offer ourselves like a rope to hang onto. A flag, hoisted to signal the acts. We tell of Ethan and Patrice, the major chambers of their lot. We are not shamed by the power of love and its atoms that cling gathered about. We have no business affairs invested, no supposedly damaged heart. We are collective and all at once nobody at all. We say man or woman and mean not husband or wife but everything in between. We shall settle our voice on the veranda. We shall settle oddly, obstinate, above it all.

MESSRS. EXTERNAL & EARTHLY

The Somebody Logo

We cannot remember much of our origins. Namely only a jumble of things, of objects past: hands emptying jars with an economy of movement, touching indulgences in drawers, avoiding the drunkard papers slow with small print, the dapple-bellied plates all old jam and crumbs, whole chicken in one pot, coarse hairs and the pleasure of self-love beneath the covers. We had a knack for the resuscitative energies of matter. How the bloated belly of the cathode TV on one mother's counter quite merrily matched the lens of another covetous eye and its dilation over bright squares of clothing on the neighbour's line. Things not to be assessed by their own causality for our feelings are indigenous to place.

There are so many things we want to tell. But perhaps we have forgotten. How to conjugate the verbs to describe varicose veins and the dull defective clunk of bedsores or bunions. We've forgotten or never knew the celestial essence of industrial psychology, and why the hot sweet gush of milk before bed does something thick and rich to our bodies' proteins to make us sleep well. And isn't that nice, because out there with the counted sheep and the zzz's it's possible to breathe into one another, to feel unfixed and light not dead with heavy kidneys and a flooded heart.

There is one way to start – with the furniture – worth noting the degree of polish, the certain grade of skill in turns around the legs. Or start by flinging out a voice, by sticking your fingers in the sockets, bumping into walls as someone falls down the stairs just trying to orient up from down. Wet shoes. Somewhere thereabouts lie all the beginnings that happen and end, cryptic and forlorn, blowing about in the lawless territory between fact and fiction.

There's always one set of hands – or many – fiddling with laces only to come up holding weeds that scorch a rash across the palms. Just tying shoes to move along. And often, because it's rained in this country as it always does, there's a sudden consciousness of having feet, having *wet feet* on *wet sod* that mutually weep beneath us. Having feet being a symptom of self that gets you back to basics. Gets you moving again.

Learn to deal with it, families used to say. *There'll be much turning*, they said, and how was anyone to fathom what was meant by that? Were we complicit or affected? To nod our heads endlessly with theirs, those nods constructed upon the very absence of affirmation and us moving our thick skulls up and down only to avoid words or keep warm or busy? Was it to be *that* kind of turning?

We knew that weaving through the rocky diagram of living, above oozing noodles of worms and tree roots, under blown glass skies, just looking for where you came from, was only one part of the bitter progress. But we didn't know the complications. That the where you came from and the where you belong might change with every limping day. All the moves in the world, forward and back, seemed told in a poor broken semaphore performed half from memory and the rest signed out with only mildly burning twigs so the general rhythm of instruction was first confused then ultimately collapsed. We lost our category.

Remember the wise maternal function of family? The good and bad objects, the nurses and lovers, the crumbs and morsels, pools and positions of speech and support? People are simply a collection of individuals shaken and salted, sometimes strapped uncomfortably together. Everyone performs their dynamic process of labour: they judge and are judged. The audience has always been a point of reference against which theatre defines itself.

Some folk might tilt their chins and say *there are no stones in the sky, so no stones can fall from the sky!* We disagree. Each infant arriving in this world makes its entrance in a rush of wind. The child breaks things and then things break the child. Sometimes wind arrives like a rodent thought and knocks you hard about the head, shatters an alphabet of new feeling inside your skull. Cars accelerate, bones are broken, soda belched and blown away. Stick your tongue out in a thin haze of rain and you taste the ash of the city, its fried fish, its petrol, its joints rolled up and spat hot in burning greens back out into the air. This is the circulation of circulation itself. A breathing set of people and their places. Some wind singles you out. From the first flicker of a leaf you know it points directly at you. It says your name and spoils poetry with reason and conjecture. When you are touched by wind, by the forces that bend the trees and scatter dirt hard and fast against windows, this is communication. We tend to underestimate the power of wind. We are something of all these flickers: not individual listeners in any front row or figures red faced on a stage, but rather the soft mist of expectancy that settles slowly about the ears and refuses not to be heard.

We are the Messrs. The instruments of psychic observation. We are not the moral function of behaviour, neither analyst nor pulse. We are spectator, servant and clown. We are animal, vegetable, mineral. Our flight takes us everywhere. We are interested. We see broken men and women, and cast the spaces in between. We found these two, Ethan and Patrice, and bedded down to watch them squeal.

There is Ethan. The King of beers and chicken fingers. His beard is desiccated, meaning passions take weeks to grow through secrets and skin. There is Patrice. The Queen of hearts and ripping them out. Her fingers are cut and have bled down into the soil. They eat at the table of what they have left unfinished. They are amazed individuals in skirts and shorts, rolling their shoes over curb stones, gravel in their soles. Their thoughts are of bed and warm socks, not the absurd dirt of other people. The abstracts of other people. They are bodies in need of chemically better living. They don't reveal their focus is money, they tell you they're after happiness. They are silhouettes to follow and unfold. They are full of blood, which alongside other people always acts thick like a thief. It understands itself as a molecule amidst structure. It is hands in the kitchen, peat on the riverbank. It is rubber on the asphalt and any number of cosmologies under the nail. It sets down its load in the veins of cats and the boxes of storage centres. If the critics are staggered with definition, spare a thought for the people. The awkward and virginal people, when it comes to facts.

So show us a house, we'll draw you mustard
nags panting.
Show us a barn, we'll tell you a myth.
Show us a tent, we'll assess the erotics of its pitch.
We Messrs., after all, are busy setting a tilt.

MESSRS.
EXTERNAL & BODILY

House and heart

What happens here goes on for some time. Has gone on for some time. Trees used to grow with wood so hard it lined the walls of all the capable buildings in town. Sometimes the sky is so black it looks cleaner than anything could ever be. Now it's rather sheep and puddles and stomachs never in need of a laxative push.

The allotments are cracked and studded with broken buckets. Space is marked and people do their best, but somewhere somebody made a false prophecy for the land that is roasted by degrees of heat and sun, washed up in weather and nobody tames it. We're all out measuring weather's weight, factoring the pulse of weeds against the waft of rooms that stink of pancakes, steak and orange juice.

Today it is mud. If it were flooded with water, you might row around in a wide loop with little ducks everywhere because we love them. Instead some leaves shuffle by with indecision, others suck up the breeze, scooting past the plastic rims, licking their rounds before bedding down to nestle, stuck in wet straw. That is the bottle's play of plastic light, how it flits like a tiny disc in all the hollow things, like a clock or a memoir or the moon.

Prudence plays a small role in the conduct of this place – there is grass that seems able to converse with everything – with the rabbles of dogs and rabbit hutches, with the new trains and their slick blitz, the older ones all mechanical clang in the air's draft – puffed out – and further across the earth just a big sleepy ventilation. This one is a landscape sold on the merits of all the other landscapes, on the nice horizontal sketches of museums and the peculiar power of invented lives that look very much like our own.

The animals know more, we think. They happen upon their information in the manner of the barn with its sure cocks and happy roosters. They know the remedy for this mental trick is buried in another trick, the joke of substance in absentia. He tells us so: one bird with his squawk, yellow beak sideways, no blinks, mocking the other birds for even thinking about landing. Whole suburbs are founded on these gestures of claiming territory. On claiming inconvenience.

In the year when there was snow all over and only the beakers and a few stalks cracked a path through the whiteness, people brought their horses here and pounded their pubics around on brown leather saddles. There was no dust to settle in, no ridges of mutual support for the overlooked physics of dirt. It was wet and white and a little green, like salt or coriander.

People lost their keys from pockets and the losers would scrabble around, fingers frozen, realising they could no longer justify their margins of existence, their fragile positions of simply being a breathing vessel on this giant blue planet. The creases and stains of other people roughed up the land. A time of frozen plenty. Feet shod dirt on carpets. Worms fattened, buried deep till summer. And with all the necessary authority of it coming, weather went off again, falling right off the edge of the Earth's sinking bowl. Rarely did anyone stop to note even a finger or a foot, and if we did, we were not factoring in the occurrence of the shared skin and creases, the truth that all this same stuff covered each of us, stopped us leaking out, held us soft and terrible like fragile enamel.

Like a single sick giggle, everything was doomed with early disillusionment. What happened was whole cycles of people feeling murderous about one another. What happened was pale bodies full of cheap wine. What happened was cultural shoes snapped at the heel, men and women run ragged whipping their heads and exposing teeth and hair to the sky for breaking. Most people in their small houses got through each day simply by hating their neighbours. Days clocked up and it was hard to tell if we were charmed by time or the weather.

It was a season of communal malaise. Of narrative struggle. People looked how the seasick look at maps and dream of land. How the hungry see a wrapper, a skeleton fish and trace the edges of their own bones with a slow finger feeling morose and giddy-eyed.

Many people in towns grew fat, whilst those in the country stayed thin in apology to nature, their bodies a solemn alignment of the dignities of careful growth, clever promises made to make the trees carry on with buds and fuzz and lichen. In the town there were idle feet, often centigrades rocketing to one impossibility or another. It was slums and edifices, murky sky and gin palaces; it was idle land, fresh air, bright sunshine and no public spirit. Infidelity kept them warm and cold. Couples split and rearranged, with mouth-first landings somewhere moist and unusual. There was always somebody half naked, congested in their cubbyhole homes like so many shrews and voles and mice.

In the country they'd never fell a tree and make an axe handle. They were reverent and slow-fingered. In the towns, they stuffed anything that would burn into their fireplaces and carried on breathing the rotten air. The table was laid and they were divorced in time for tea. They didn't look after their bones and would do anything to escape the house. People paid each other to keep at a distance, living out their own gloomy ironies of feeling connected via transaction. They humped their sofas and each other, mislead in their conception that heat meant empathy and therefore intimacy. When fingers got stuck in bottles and limbs stood grey-clothed in empty bathtubs they wondered whether this was the plunge of great erotic feeling, of unparalleled velocity.

We acquire our own versions of happiness. We pick them up at the chemist. We will meet the daughter of a pharmacist, a magician, the unwitting farmers, the florist, dusty curates, all of them touched by the blow of a fortune teller. Which body belongs to the future mother? Which tousled hot head to the boy with the battered bottom? The big hands and squeezed hearts belong to the busted marriage pair, their molars hanging out unhinged, their intestines blocked with impotent sludge, spud skin and unzipped flies. Once the sore of domestic morbidity cracks, it tends to spread at speed.

There is a house in the distance. A few all around. It's big like a town. Some buildings with their backs ripped off send staircases sloping right out into air. They're covered over with boards and belts of warning orange, but people go in and out, their decisions predicated, naturally, on conditions of weather. We stay put and look up at the trees and the blocks of buildings overlapping them, taking little time to calculate the degrees of calibration offered by either god or architect. There is no looking at the corners with their nice bricks or cornicing, thinking how neatly one inorganic block folds into the bright breast of natural things. No. Not that. We drink coffee and gallop from building roof to tree canopy, barely noting the difference between slate or leaf.

From where we can see it now, the view is stretched out. If we lie on our side or close one eye the view feels heavy, looser on the edges. We can angle our own choice perspective. What should feel like pollution feels rather like a suggestive hanging on, as though all these silhouettes of everything and nothing that float on by in layers could be caught and dragged back into a shapely form. We could pull time from the top or bottom and should choose a landscape suitable to our condition.

The sun whips the railway into little shards. The smell of hot tracks, their groan in the heat. We watch the train lines black and unmoving and make chromatic rhymes with the mashed-up flies and spiders of autumn, black too but talcumed now in the dust. We could imagine ourselves packaged aboard those trains, finally chopping the scene to bits in escape, seeing anew something ravishing, some palomino horses in a field or cement in factories with their piles scooped and troubled like concentric hairdos. Those troubles not designed to trouble us, or not yet anyway.

Anachronistic heavens, we all stood under them. The HaHa house stands too in rubble like some murderer in ruins. We called it that when the two top windows fell out and in absence of a door or in fact any certain relationship to soil or sky it sagged downwards in a crudely propped guffaw. Each step around the house had a different hue of desperation. And each brick, with all its acid brothers and acid sisters of mortar and their uniquely aggregated pity, had its own melody.

Golden Gingko used to blossom all around. Grass bent as it shouldn't, snapping off in the wind. Grass turned to hay, sweet straws, battered-blown across the land. Only recently some amicable nobody folded plastics over the windows, coarse ridge-sewn plastics – banners for breathing – and now all the condensation hangs in the bottom edges with weed decks thudding and daily unravelling threads so you can't pick window from wall.

They used to be touched by light, the windows; not broken by it, but opened up, polished. The house was named a wonder with its hyacinths, sloping grounds and happy rush of folks about. Not a burglar's dozen like now with the copper wrenched out and carried away for cash. Something of structure had made an invisible leap out the window with those burglars, its own soiled body visible for just a moment as water had lurched out where the copper was sawn and the radiators rang themselves cold against the wall in alarm.

We wondered whether the house mourned for a repossession of indoor and outdoor space, or yins and yangs and all the half-hidden parts that no longer got their shapes to rhyme together. That rather just rested in a foggy doze.

In times of rain and wind, the house accommodated for mood by flinging tiles off its roof, a cascade of roofs, onto the ground, the roof garden. The physics of the roof with its mimicry of the physics of breasts was always on a slow downwards fall. In summer – a hoppy brew – it stank of ferns; the only yeast of subversion. The little place sat there in weather taking its whacks.

We have been watching for some time. May we be forgiven. We Messrs. with eyes all over. When we took a jug with both hands and scooped its heavy bottom up to pour, the weather flowed out of it. We looked at the water in our glass, observed the specks and their impossible swirl and knew answers lay in an observation of closeness that sometimes meant staring at nothing much at all.

MESSRS. EXTERNAL & MANLY

Ethan, for a man

He has a face that is splintered, Ethan, like the oak he lays in houses that will never belong to him. If this is about glue, we should speak of glue. Of glue. He has it often under the nail, on his fingers, trails also on the small metal pins that suck and jangle air into his canvas pockets. The glue stays for so long, a whole building disappeared into a body. It is a false map those fingers of his, first blueprint, quickly bitten off, mouth erased, chis-elled away sometimes with the ring pull of a Coke can. When he sees squirrels by the curb, laid out geometrically, blown open like skirts or bogged down in a porridge of blood, he remembers the privilege of living and feels sad for the wounds on his hands.

He had a wife once. Her fine body with its small hips that pulled fabric close around her bones and pressed, almost painfully hard against his thighs, her frightening stillness at the moments when he came, rattling fast and strange. Those blue panties were little puddles to fall right into. To jiggle his feet as some people twist their hair was a move towards alleviating anxiety in ever-smaller increments. Her small chest veined green and blue, hitched up and down, cupped by a hand that would never do it any good. He'd study one part of his headache, realising he could not relocate the pressure but rather reassert the existence of entropy in his noisy little life. They'd lie together and watch for birds. Watch for the particular bird, orange feathered, limbs stalking all bossy. Could have been a cantaloupe on a fork. In that landscape misty with dust, with the white woolly smoke of planes and the brown woolly smoke of birds, all of them shadow evidence of the great velocity of real outside space.

She was Flora. Flora Dorothy Lily Patrice. A long and struggling vine. That she was named after a collective taxonomy for which she had no patience enraged her. She was poor with grasses or lavenders. She hated green. Her friends called her F, a friendly mitigation. But she felt more like a T, arms out at either side of her elongated frame, no breasts, no bumps, just a serif hardness. She was a stable line when she chose it.

He had known her first as Dorothy. Passed her before the checkouts with his canned beans and her plastic apron flashing slick with fish guts. The hairnet pushed back on her crown like a mandarin's hat. He didn't even know what you'd do with octopus. With those rubbery arms, suckers gasping on the blue. The fish always flopped back and stared. *I could pop your eyeballs with a pin*, he would think. Their bladders and their hearts.

And he'd feel something clasp in his spine, feel how the air sticks to everything, just like that as he'd raise his fist up through space to scrape at his hair.

He made visits daily. *You're going to be a famous poet*, he'd repeat to himself before stepping into the cool sludge of the supermarket. But when he'd reach the fish counter where she'd be, only grunts would come out. As though a hole had been made in his throat. Him grown in a city drainpipe, his words tangled tapioca. He'd buy his fish, looking for a cheap trim, skimming coins across the counter. Her anchored and upright like all small fine things to the Earth. The two of them lengths of comparable feeling. Flora Dorothy Lily Patrice. Such height in names. Stacked tall. The two of them warped figures reflected in the chewing-gum bubble at the neck of the toad, bulging, not bursting. That stupid ceramic frog sitting there on brushed steel with its taped-on tip card in downward curves: *thank you for caring, your coins count*. He'd drop a penny into its mouth, not look at her as red flamed about his collar. The stress of structure was heavy over them both. Swimming rather than walking. Even the journey home would mean growing older, more tired. He'd put his bag of fish in the freezer and wash his feet right there on the carpet, thinking about her flat boy's body, imagining laying it out over a great basin filled with ice and water, covering it all with his mouth and a white sheet.

And that was it, how it came to be that he valorised shampoo, validated conditioner above a life lived freely. One to cleanse and one to cream. Him a gentle boy with hair in his soap, with worries at night that hurt his stomach. The crowning mirage of all those supermarket visits, all those petty plastics scooped in and out of transaction just to make contact. Shouldn't he be laying floors and laying women and spreading out children in beautiful family allegories? That was the anthropological view and *what is love and where anyway*, he would surmise, not expecting the universe to answer but hoping for a peremptory twitch to at least reset his compass. His index of secret postures didn't include her at all. It wouldn't be awful to be thrown out of bed. It wouldn't be awful to roll on his knees in the soil, to follow temptation down the corridor and right out the door.

Dorothy became Dot to him. A shortened affirmation of property, precise and graphic. Clean. Whoever you are, out there, looking, washing, folding the laundry, your name begins with X or Y, maybe something other. So many letter-functions it takes a practised tongue to roll through it. Dot to Dot. Hair puffed like a mushroom, a ripe meadow mushroom. A black spot. *You are the world's rarest mineral in a storm*, he would tell her, tell himself, as he clicked a photograph. Her silhouetted in their garden, graded against the sun, limbs more spent than the peach tree whose roots beckoned to nothing but knotted earth burst apart with boredom.

Some things fitted well into his landscape. He'd have a few dirty thoughts aroused just by handling the butter on the table. Pink fingered dawns and pubic hair spiked in knowing that everything in this very present world curves back to the pleasures of the apple, the sins, too. Remembering her face and blending it into another, feeling the plunge of a cheekbone settled into the wide vinegar hollow by his hips. Always hips, those aching contours, pulling pleasure out of your coat like lovers.

What came for them wasn't plague, which would have been easier. On cold brilliant days when the geese honked overhead, he knew they mocked him. Rained laughter right down at him with their goose vowels and grammar dropped somewhere across the Atlantic. *Make a wish*, they seemed to say: *We are waiting, We are waiting, We are waiting*. It became *Fuck you*. So much to rattle him. He could simply fall off the edge of the Earth in defeat. The endless barking dogs that might tear his whole face off, the dogs whose bones he might break and kick to seizure. He is not fatalistic but one day those dogs will eat his birds and he will shoot them dead. Even the senseless chicken shit in the yard rings him into rage, all those natural things that intimidate the city, and the fury only intensified as he yanks at his jeans, rubs himself raw and spits his face away in the soapy mirror. That third dimension only adding to the clunk of inner emptiness.

ETHAN

New tenements

Where do the people go? This I have often thought on a busy street, myself hunched to nil, limp dick pulled out, trickling an emergency down a broken wall. So much traffic and feet, then suddenly fewer and none. As though I was once the owner of one complete thought, it ready to share, but know nothing more now than how close the smell of my hair and penis feels in this blowing weather. The state of my teeth and wardrobe goes little way in the manner of reassurance. Even near the lurid tinge of a car park littered with pink plastic bags and fag ends. Even near the mechanical payoff, the plastic glitter of a shopping centre, I feel myself not quite invited.

I have moved often. Towards the closing out of nature with its costly drainage, palatial edifices and well-lit streets. Towards an abundance of water with its need for reform, fresh-air-low-rents and lack of amusement. Towards bright homes and gardens with their flow of capital and no sweating. These are my three magnets: town, country and town-country.

Since I do not want to keep changing direction while I walk and do not want to spend my whole time recalculating the best direction of travel,

I arrange my walking process in such a way that I have picked a temporary goal – a clearly visible landmark – which is more or less in the direction I want to take. I shall walk in a straight line towards it for a hundred yards, and as I get close, pick another new goal, once more a hundred yards further on, and walk towards it. I shall do this such that in between I can talk, think, smell the spring, without having to measure my direction every minute. These are my paths and goals.

Or I shall simply kid myself with quiet fallacies and march knowingly down a familiar route. Past the bags of coal softened by rain, their lumpy boulders turned to a river of column grey, past a tiny hand grasping at something pornographic, past two cathedrals, pert and soaring, past freckled maidens and any building defined by a precise relationship to numerical signs – past all of that – there is a room with thirty-five wooden panels.

I am here for pleasure, to buy something or meet someone. I am here for service. I sense already the kind of grievance that men playing poker have when the game slides away from how they would like it to be. When the colour of money seems all but a scent soon to blow fully off the grease on their palms. Even the miserable colour of sweat can't trap it. I am here to purchase myself into invisibility.

The wooden panels are covered with black cloth. They lean against the walls, edges overlapping, and you need only to cast one ruined fugitive glance towards them and the signs become clear: how to pay, where to fling the hellos or the clothing. Running a hand over the boards, like a professional arranging the feeling of approaching power, you can hear the groaning shuffle of sex.

Purchase is straightforward, a payment of notes tacked to the boards, nestled in with the many uncaptioned images that have been pecked at with coloured pins. A calendar three years out of date. It's a cosmology of abuse. Across the pins, long laces join pictures of single people, prices, portions of time, weights and hair colour; chaos string-shapes that look like letters in an oversized sentence. The relationships between people and the more stable facts of architecture – the corridors and carpets here – are uneasy.

I would like to throw out a protest of innocence, that I came by mistake, but my hands are practiced and tacking cash to the walls I notice specks of deliberate dirt that make my trousers harden.

The walls are obsessively touched, dotted with roundish flecks of a dried substance I know through intuition would not have been brown when fresh. The marks look like rusted roses, but miniature, mocking the baggy hugeness of the strings in their refusal to expand.

The bodies in the pictures are incredulous, as all bodies are when unclothed. Something strange about nudity that seeing a nipple or bulge usually smoothed over and hidden by linen or elastic does nothing but draw focus to the twitches of identity that hover around the mouth and eyes. The bodies are clean and tight, each of them framed in a sympathetic light. Nobody looks various like ham or cold cuts, but quietly specific. I admit the wall stains are more troubling, although the blood – I'm certain it's blood – could have run from a single snagged nail, mussed all over by other busy fingers. I clutch at a twinge in my right knee, mortal stone whining in its socket. There is crumpled paper in the litter basket on the floor, some charred foil claiming elemental rights as the first shiny mineral in the place, the first gem. All these pilings of aggravation. I put up with the spooky collisions even though I am frightened of this house.

The trick with the panels is squinting, the images presenting the wisdom and welfare of many despicable facts. It is difficult to pick out a single figure. I note the faces and forms that excite me but the equality of error in placement means they all look like a family, a sordid arrangement of shared qualities that seems more a portrait of troubled humanity, more something to disturb the soul than pique an abstract pleasure. I can taste them on my tongue. I could bite off a little piece of cheek and chew it with all the casual obliviousness of lost property. There are men and women and neither and both. There is plastic, loud and soft. There are things to marry, harmonious and uniform, honest roles and barbarisms I blush to disclose. But the catalogue of possible expletives bolsters me.

And as it rains outside and the sky is plunging, purging itself of facts and dirt, there is time to look around. With so many minutes cushioning fatly around the Earth, the revision of these subjects and my method could become infinitely more extensive, more elastic, more complex. Should I regard myself as the victim here and flee without delay or, with real life being one giant sieve to shake myself through, does this promise of an occult practice of illumination mean I should continue with cheer? My money is down. My trousers, almost. I feel I may be sliced through the neck. I'm ready to turn pink and flush through my imagination. I'm ready to out-manoeuvre the imagination.

I trail the length of the room, always remembering to start on the edges and work slowly to the centre. I examine more fabric and note blotches and runs in the weaving. I think of my tongue against it all. I think often of my tongue, corrupted and dizzy by its natural urges to bite or lick. I wonder if the panels offer a moral lesson. If they are proud yet obstinate attempts to make the world an enemy by pointing out all the routes of connectivity it doesn't yet understand.

Once after a road accident I was advised by professionals to file away my own blood serum, like an assiduous gardener for the trellises of my future form. A little clinical lesson in moving beyond, preserving, but with emphasis on sequence. I liked that idea in the same way the miracle of cellophane around shop objects fills me with a chemical kind of happiness. A collision of shiny second skin that pleases all my vitreous fantasies for inside and out. I frequently feel a tiny fizz in the brain in these instances. I smell it like cordite, whilst endorphins and opiate receptors bang out against each other in the analgesic hot tub of my head.

This building with its panels is pursuing a similar obsession for glass. The dystopian perversion for making everything clear and thus cold and also breakable. When I first glanced its roof rising saw-toothed through the grass, I expected something utilitarian. Something inside concerned with products and their happy packaging. But time here hangs heavy and lost like a casino. Some of the windows have been covered over with bin bags. The skylights are closed and I think transparency is often an unhealthy climate to live in anyway. I know it is full of people, but it is never what it seems.

I wondered if my aura of careless spiritual lethargy would be legible. If I offered as much personality and reassurance as a crumpled newspaper. The bland visitor, me, with my silly curls falling. I wouldn't want to waste any time with strangled sensibilities for manners. I could hardly be regarded as a house guest, although this, after all, *is* a house. A happy house, a knocking house, a shop, an abode thumb-greased and clinging to classification. For there are bodies all about but no shoes left tidy by the mat.

I opened a small door onto a shy slip of a thing. Onto many things. Figures with lips and chins, a tangle of colour and coordination. They stared out from the edge of a green. I'd begun this depressing excursion and now everybody seemed made minute by their own careful single names for themselves and the acts before them. Girls and boys from the images, already introduced with an uncanny sense of preparation, now moved in real-time versions of their previous likenesses. This was the outside but inside. The carpet was plastic grass. The gapes in stockings its plants. I wanted to point back to my notes on the wall, my money a faint persistence that I was a decent figure, that in this real landscape my own mud was simply part of the natural shaded patch of universal desire.

I was surprised that the lack of privacy alarmed me. Not even a curtain. All these bodies performing the assigned duty of touch. But like machinery, like a bored peeler of potatoes who, whilst engaged in the act, shows you how much they know about peeling potatoes. I could smell blood and salt. I could see undone shoes and public exterminations. Ejaculations. So much frank cohabitation. So much sexual beauty, instability, eloquence. People as patterns. Form in its truest sense: naked structure. Madness, I thought.

Some were finished or waiting, biting their fingers, shelling nails off their thumbs. I hoped they might bite a woollen specimen from my own trouser leg, an *I love you* of willing mouth against my own being. Maybe they would peel off my skin, it standing unflowered in their weird woody den, and wring it out, squeeze it like a rotten blackberry. There was nothing abnormal to be discovered beneath my clothes. Just something small and mean and squashed together.

I unbuttoned my shirt and picked a coarse blanket from the floor. I would have liked to seal myself into it. To measure space. An alien tent and me a cloth doll about to be flung around. At least I physically exist, I fathomed, feeling liquid in my nostrils, noting a dent in my shoe. The blanket was rough on the skin of my neck, something synthetic and grey, little letters wobbly and stitched by hand on the corner that brushed my ribs. N-T. I wondered at a possible meaning, a first and last name spoken fast or in a hush: *Nice Time*, *New Tenements*, *No Town*, *No Talk*, *No Tears*, *No Trouble*.

My pelvis stuck out in a new way. I couldn't say quite why or fit the tenderness with medical adjectives so perhaps just being here was my beautiful new take on nature, me moving more slowly through it. The saliva in my throat moved too like it was grieving. I swallowed it. Something thick and the air which smelled of thyme, although there were no bushes or small shrubs about.

I could feel a tremble rising. I looked at my hands. I solicited my hands with their fingers clasping. As if they could tell me how to hold myself, how to seek safer surfaces or recoil without declaration. They don't look like they lack experience, but they don't look like they write interestingly either. Down a pair of trousers? Well they look practiced enough in the imitations of perfunctory passion to produce a smile, but not as though the shocks of pleasure they'd tweak into the groin would be either long-lived or excessive. They look like hands that have touched leather and blushed, that have held pencils and long after felt emboldened by the graphic rhymes of stuff and body. They are well moisturised, merrily veined, always warm. They couldn't possibly service all these people, whatever their needs.

The world being so proud and lonely, and no longer pretending that I am new to the experience of being here, the rooms in this building offer fire escapes at each of the compass points. And piles of rope, flat nails and slivered planks. They are heaped all over. Discarded by some lawless landlord who cares neither for access nor incrimination. They too are evidence of an altered body. A new possibility of collaboration. These materials that allow for an accident. They certainly don't point clearly to either slaughter or decorum. Maybe the history of adultery here is long-standing, a roping and nailing of flailing body parts. A screwing. A hammering. But there is little softness to settle into. No headboard, no sheets, no mattress. Not even a rug or much wool going spare. The silent people can attest to this. And the beams anyway are too low and narrow to sling a noose and dangle effectively so I think about the invitation of idle stacking or military restraint practice. I am often reminded that ropes and household furniture are just two of the tools used in Western-style bondage. Like handwriting formed in the dark, you only need to imagine it to know it's there – no matter how misshapen – this possibility for a body.

The question then: should I remove my shoes? My scarf before an inevitable decapitation, or keep it on, tight about the neck? And in case I am never to resurface, should I pen a note to this month, to my mother, to the milkman?

Do you remember what I looked like the last day you saw me? Do you remember the quality of air and the wind glimpsed in the speed of children running, in the cascade of things off roofs, the near wallop that the wind made as it busted through the grass, tickling leaves all over like one part of the world's natural sensation was quite carrying away with another and we human bodies would have nothing more to do with it? Do you remember how small and terribly gentle my head felt when I pressed it tight to your chest, how thin my hair was against the thick pink fleece of your nightie?

One belt hole tighter than when I arrived, I order a taxi and it comes, inching along the road. Nobody emerges or follows; just a bluish bird who bursts to happy heights and watches me leave. The sky is fallen out, sky grey, sky mutton-clouded: inedible. I open the taxi door.

How are you? I say, reattaching to spoken words with automatic shame.

Just coming from church, he replies, *so full of the Holy Spirit.*

How nice, I say, *How nice*. The continuous black mark of disturbance runs through me.

Trying to stop smoking, I am, knocking my name about prayers. Sometimes I even wake in the night for a cigarette, he says.

I light it, breathe and drag together, right on the edge of the bed and wait for the same spirit to touch my hair. Sometimes the curtains. A ripple. It's a big waiting game, this rumpus we call living.

As if to confirm the addiction, I smell his breath. Sour, not the reek of benediction. I imagine smoke weaving with spirit in a complex knot of mingled faiths. He is a big man, with short legs.

The crushed chrome of his car is distinguished, like the good weave on his suit which leaks the quiet holiness of a raspberry garden. Lines of wool run over and over. I think they could do the speaking for me. I am clammed. My hands soiled. It feels like the end of a day.

A red parrot hangs from the rear-view mirror, its eyes too big for its feathers. It swings as we drive. Should I call my own guilt *Parrot* I wonder? It too is full of problems and happily throws my own words back at me, repeats them hollow-vowelled until they become real and exotic.

My head is one part dread and one part cheer. Rubber head, dislocated. My crotch burns, feels thick and heavy. I didn't insist on torn pockets. Attempting to soothe myself and focus, I think back to the little I can remember of the oldest surviving Buddhist manuscripts, twenty-seven of them, written in script on curling birch bark. Where I have seen them, I don't remember. Gautama Buddha – *The Buddha* – is said to have developed transcendent abilities, no need for sleep, sustenance, medicine or bathing. There he was, an eternal baby, always with his legs crossed and knees so flexible he conceived of a painless birth without need for intercourse. Without fucking and knees croaking at all turns. My head sticks against the taxi seat.

If *The Buddha* had a seat beside me, settled together in our taxi ride, I have no doubt he would forsake the chair and simply levitate on cushioning conceit, on his skin-deep eminence. I'm certain I wouldn't have liked him. I feel chastised and ugly. I'm certain he could tell me things of those people and their places, their consumption of spirit, their task of planting roots in the world. I'm certain he might have answered this man's prayers. I'm certain too that the winter clouds above the car won't stay put on his account or mine.

MESSRS. EXTERNAL & CRUMBLY

Cellophane

When he doesn't drink a little he will crumble. These are the claims of his body. His name itches at him. Dot is long gone. Flora Dorothy. Lily Patrice. Rubbed out. All his neighbourhood has is its garages to console the lawns, keep everything neat and square and careful white; no image of the sullen suds beneath. The city sewer passes under his home and he winces at the sugary pretence of it, propriety drawn over like a curtain. Sometimes he walks to the lumberyard to buy his wood and thinks you can read sex everywhere. Always ablaze. In the air between the grass blades and ratios of heat or hunger pouring from kitchen windows. He sees it in the dog's code, on the ends of its teeth dripping. *Ethan Ethan Ethan Ethan.*

The sky in his garden drapes down over the shed, knowing how perhaps it was complicit in the hiding, in being the dark accomplice of night. Has he lost his mind? Words come so sparingly now. The hard English of shit, so too the soft squirt of metaphor. He just hammers his nails and pours his glue down over smoked fillets of timber. Makes little nods to his clients as he arranges the nutmeg sweetness into neat flat lines. Always wood. Hard.

Herringbone, tongues and grooves – all the gaps and grouting for dream to occur, the occasional grinding of bones on floors, the changes in depths of breath and exhalation to prove that he is not just tangled desire trapped between some fence and the sun, that he is not just glue laid down on a site of careful lateral flatness, that he is a living being with hope and composure. But he holds the language close inside him, a narrow cone widening out a deep hole to be penetrated. Maybe that is how it happened. To Ethan. That inside bundle which burned like a private fluorescent advertisement. One that turned to lies on nocturnal occasions and suddenly there is a man standing at his door with a blue-yellow hat urging him to buy a spade and he takes two and invites him in for some water.

PATRICE

The Age of Obsession

The King of France chose the lily for his garden because it was a plant with deep roots; it still clings to slopes. His shade of narrative marking was pale and bright, sunshine critical. The lily dropped its bags and spun out across the scenery. Its foamy petals drank up the seasons and waited for the time they'd be mown down and covered with a drinking fountain or some offices. The lily dug deep and waited to find its identity.

Immoderate points of people are all linked and held in the structures we leave behind. In the trees that rise up in complicated cities. In arms that shift to praise their leaves, the formal gestures of greeting that make us brave and a little beautiful. Like the lily, I too have learned about waiting, a passionate sniffing about on all fours, to unearth the great conquests of human evolution. To spark the flames beneath our maladies. To make them boil. Archaeology is required. If people feel oppressed when they are forced to exist in an undifferentiated mass, then erupting the bones and spoons of our ancestors, those mashed down in mud, is one way to find new voices. To find new speech that might whisper tentatively at first, whimper as mist or rain sinks their words, these new people and their history of not being dead.

Desperate seekers of figuration, I can confirm that thumping about in soil is an aggravation of something, something not quite evil, but rearranging!

Even putting out food for the birds is an extension of waiting, a positive waiting if you like, where the arc of the arm scattering crumbs intersects with the arc of bird flight and suddenly you feel that history after all might still carry on.

In a museum whose name is unpronounceable to me, there is a photograph of many holes dug in a field and filled with linen. Held in tightly by the tiny square-format edges, men and women of all ages surround these holes. Muddy tubers, too.

I look at the people like a plane over fields with my own aerial voiceover. I can peer into the cabinet, up over the image, and see *hello hello* that these figures have climbed through grass and are dew-stained. The fabric of their trousers is dark in spots, their footprints together thin lines spanning out.

The photograph is frozen so the little arms and legs of the crowd are fixed in their earthbound gestures, but they seem hushed regardless, their faces not wet one bit with tears or storm, but worried nonetheless. Worried as though all the dug-out soil might refill if they, the people-minders, were to stray too far away. They look like they are in exile guarding these humps of earth, one knee of every person equivalent to a hole in the ground. A sum of parts, joints, watery women and sparse hair. Of all things I have seen before, it looks like a clock. Time built from mothers and sons with their linen and their loam.

The museum catalogues the Age of Obsession. It documents the history of possession, the crags of family, the seeded infinity of people and their actions. The museum explains the origins of camping, the evidential sleeping bags and triangulated plastics with their dark recreational secrets. The museum documents the all but inevitable murders between families and their arpeggios of tent strings. I know a modern somebody who's slept with the father, and the son, next the holy ghost, and that family wants to bury her bastard corpse quicker than you can say *ascension* so I think yes, perhaps these people camped around their holes are performing something similar. Perhaps they will retreat to the recesses later and share coffee and cake, forlorn for their actions, a little shady in mourning, but relieved to have buried the ones who wrapped indecency around them. I think this image captures the space of positive silence, like the space of positive waiting.

On the way out of the museum, I read about the women who dipped their legs wet in the morning, walking through fields of wheat so the husks would stick and clothe them. The women who painted arks for their children and polished scarce silvers to trade for land. I read about the men, wrapped tightly in felt, who lay in the sun with eggs packed close in their knee bends and arm pits, harnessing warmth to bake the eggs slow for a late outdoor lunch. I read about the children, too, naked but for strips of unsoftened blue hide, cabbage dyed, that with all their pinching and touching would be supple come the Sabbath.

The photographs are pinned all over like a great Atlas, a flexible rhythmic shell; they breathe but are stuck, struck out and shrugged off. My nose tingles whilst looking at them. A feeling like a sound, somewhere between the aloof delicacy of a snake cracking out of old skin and the gorgeous fractional blind spot when staring at the sun to squeeze out a sneeze. A migraine of excitement. The museum has thousands of pictures of people and parcels smothered with violent dots, so many numbers joined in great athletic exercise. I see a pair of children's trousers hoisted up a flagpole: it looks sad but the legs still wave in the breeze.

In looking at all this *information* I distractedly wipe circles of dust away from the eyes of unnamed figures. 'DO NOT TOUCH', the labels say, so I wipe more fervently, deliberate circular motions in a stab at completeness. Looking at these people might be like hugging zombies, old bodies newly sodden, newly loved by fingers and my own salivary wetness on their static cheeks.

The images are all shot in oppressive sunshine.

I can't quite envisage the undead surviving under this sun. Everything looks rich and ideal. But then again more than 90 per cent of people walking around in an ordinary neighbourhood are unhealthy. This being judged by simple biological criteria. It being fact that most people's organs are blighted by sludge and childhood psychosis. Blighted by depravity and moral decay. Swimming and dancing or vegetable gardens and still water are knitted into our systems at the periphery of importance, more like special socks or cashmere mittens than the grey dull pants scooted onto bottoms day after day.

An ugly complexion is little but a marker of shame for your own body, your own baby, your own basic biology. The museum labels say little on those subjects. How about a word on density, I think, on us being all too full, too fat to fit?

At the entrance I hold a banister to descend the stairs. Brass reflects. It is a reverse bidding of goodbye, this cupping of my hand against warm metal, a finger-down wave, wiping grease across my palms. It attracts my mouth. I think if I followed my lips along this rail I'd find myself filled with hidden foods, the flecks and flakes of real passing human. I assume wheat and beef or dairy; I assume vegetable matter and mineral trace. I assume blood and nails. A full spectrum of dietary preferences. The well-attended museum is a packed vessel for culinary perversions. For pigs and their pork.

At home there is bed. Another perversion. My pillow is creamy ricotta. My blanket little gem with aioli. My skeleton its own slip sole licked clean and offered out to the cat.

Full of face

In the morning there is tea and television. Donald Duck in the mass murderer episode tramps about on stage, firing round after round of machine gun fire into a talent show audience. I watch him rub his shoes in a pause, an absent-minded gesture of busy distraction, plucking the end of a lace and teasing out the bow. A body undone in seconds. His tail wiggles as he marches back and forth. The gunfire continues, not with the sound of bullets or bleeding, but flowerpots smashing, as though the case of a brain were one of ceramic. His face with its quivering beak seems poised to deliver anecdote, filling the screen with white and yellow until an animated hook jerks from offstage to drag him away. The sailor suit rips to unanimous applause. All that colour flatness feels good and clean, not like me at home with the fuzzy outline of my own body, waiting for my own backstage hook, my machine gun, the choreographed spots of my own stage light. In Donald Duck even the dead and the murdered have volume, just like the dust engrained on a museum banister. It's simply a matter of tuning in to the right frequency.

And that is what I believe about anthropology. My own biography is short: I was born and I continue.

At dinner my friends approach me with a moral honesty. They describe jelly stomachs and elephant thighs in the abstract until I catch their spiky words like stones. Like flints aimed. It doesn't take an adjectival genius. They talk about pity as though it is a molecule to be steamed with asparagus. My innards hurt. All those words doing what they will, what they must. I'm no longer hungry and resign to swim in the mornings.

The barrier broken by swimming is a kind of penetration of a black hole: the gravitational field is so intense nothing could possibly escape until you jump in and burst through it. Let something out. Let a cool trickle reach right inside to open you up.

Warm bodies in cold water are liquid in a funny innocence of hot and cold mingling. I pee in the pool, exercising my right as an elaborate example of plumbing, my existence as conditional parts whose physical reality is proven by elbows and U-bends. Head submerged, breath enormous. Sinking, floating with water in my face, the water becoming my face. And I know this must be similar to the composition of love, an exercise in modal logic, a Sierpinski gasket infinitely subdivided, overlapped, expanded into smaller and smaller triangles of length and feeling.

I exit the pool thinking of jelly and elephants. Not ashamed, neither comfortable. That walk like a dripping swine across mottled tiles, sucking in one way, bumps pushed out the other, a swell of charitable eyes cast down, looking like black pudding or old tripe. The body demographic and how I might bite the ass of all of it. I flush red with coldness, not blue, colours run in a mixed wash, nothing to be proud of, watching naked figures in the shower and hoping one day a boiler repair man might fix and insulate a broken heart with the same perfunctory quickness he employs with the heating system.

The lady serving tea on my train back to the house tells me how the gentleman behind us is using his phone plug to hold it upright. She says *gentleman* not guy or man or boy and is so excited her eyes look two ways. I want to ask if she believes in astrology. Instead I celebrate my own small freedoms of expansion, wiggling my fingers against the seat upholstery and making a soft pattering that brings my breath fast and jerky. The shadow of the man's hat tips through the gap in the seats, bouncing lines of reflected movement against the glass window. We are rhythmic partners and I feel all at once local and desirable as the trees bend fast away from us. Arborescent models and me at a highly functional centre. The train has given me its public approval. It's the trigonometry of desire.

We fly past a church so I elaborate on some sins:

Dear Father, it's been a long time since my last confession. My pool membership card, which far from swaddling ideas of inclusion of pastoral care, rather reminds me that I am little more than the dull air buffering one database name from another. I do not try hard. I am a digitised rung, a point of contact through dark water set on an infinite route to swift and bloodless replacement. Deliver me and replace me. Towel me dry between the toes, Amen, Amen.

There are events that cast shadows. There are bodies that cast shadows, and someone thumps the headrest, manoeuvring their departure. I feel my damp, pool-knot hair, the water stain spreading through the gym bag. I am opposed to the sudden sharpness in this feeling of wetness. All the composite materials of my situation are witness, are marked by the delicate condition of my disadvantage: I am wet in a situation of dryness. Like other unfortunate quarrels with the laws of material information it feels good for a minute, then painful. The perversity is over-bright and under-sophisticated. A problem of consistency and territorial assemblage. Like how the Internet tells us to use rice when we drop our phones in the toilet. I wonder if that same super absorbency could un-wound or reposition fluid excess in drowning souls. The duffel bag drips. If only it were possible to learn to divide your accidents and solutions more specifically, with as much individual clarity as every mini-grained ellipse of that rice.

MESSRS.
EXTERNAL & MELANCHOLY

Birthday

Two weeks ago she bought a sweet white loaf from the Mexican store on the corner. Anxious and bothered in packaging of orange and blue. The loaf was already cushioned by a little dumpling of air, by yeast and steady heat. One of those loaves so heaped with sugar it could already be fifty years old, baked up with floury moths and pubic hair. She soaked the whole thing in that tiny hotel sink, water rising in an abrupt change of climate, our Patrice retying the bag newly soggy, doubling the plastic with a black trash bag and pushing the living lump under her bed. Green and black mould is beginning to bristle like lichen against the condensation. We think of it as a birthday cake, a transformative thick icing into which one day she might stuff candles as we all sing and inhale the thousands of microscopic particles into our private respiratory systems, them also growing, expanding, proliferating at terrifying speed with impeccable atomic ferocity. If our teeth fall out we will stick them in too, like icing to be swallowed with a wish.

She has wished for many things. On some of those days she wishes only for total quiet. Most often she wishes for men and their senseless saliva up and down her legs, vainly performing some kind of symbolic task like touching her buttons, licking her fingers and counting the seconds until some spit or other dries in the air. Her erotic inventions have endless criticism. They fill gaps in the present. On these occasions she leaves her room thinking bold ideas but as soon as her feet cross the threshold, the word *dream* becomes technical and means very little.

It is like killing a fly and once the buzz has gone all remaining frequencies feel like a conscious experiment for stillness that leaves you wanting nothing more than three dozen flies or at very least the preoccupation of a dripping tap.

ETHAN

A pair so famous

I need to send a letter. One that once forged will reattach a bit of substance. A letter that I hope will swipe out this personally cultivated moral leprosy, as in those rufescent bits busted by the wayside, to realign my dignities in relation to all.

Let's call this situation something like wringing fat from a sausage, squeezing out liquid until only the most elemental matter remains; sinewy skin to the sausage and only an outline of movement left of me. The outline of that movement being a thin but newly hardened hope that the honesty of a letter will puncture the certain deathliness hanging over. The idea, even, that fresh ink on a page might slough off a few of the infinite infections I've gathered, don't ask me why, so close about.

And as my mouth is fixed, like an oak, like a face whose yellow sail decided long ago not to flap for every wind, my hand with its proximate fluidity for writing may just consider itself more flamboyant. However shallow and commonplace it might be, a few written words committed to paper shall keep me 1. Puzzled and 2. Busy.

I think my letter might unfurl something aberrant and unclean. The lives of my successive sins. A letter that upon finishing will require the imagining of bathing in clear water, or swimming deep whilst rain passes high above. The pleasant satisfaction of swimming, with its very perfect construct of water as a liquid coolness to shimmer through, useful as a tonic to hose off any icky or rotten feelings. Or at least provide a shiver which after the heat of five million digital messages and their corresponding URLs all crashing their hyper-linked manes against each other, all sending image after image of food and girls and lonesome hard-wood furniture into my less than virtuous frame, a shiver would certainly service testimony of a good conscience with regard to natural pleasure. With regard to water.

Lord I am looking for one virtue and finding not even a vague swarm of it. Not even one blonde-headed experience of nice light and a happy angle. Instead of eating lunch, this necessity of confession is one I must comply with.

It was always about prodding and pushing with us, or un-prodding or re-pushing the great landscape of earth into a colour that most complemented our particular pantsuit for that day. Digging for our own particular shade of indulgence. Dressing to suit ourselves and each other. Our dribbles of sound in the kitchen were perfectly tuned to match the particular hues of our depression, our prostitution, our blissful arrogance. Happy throbbings.

For breakfast there was sad avocado on multi-grain. Or some crumbly cake soured by our own protest, a juice with all the colour and optimism of pesticide. And then pregnancy like quick fast sand suddenly swallowing us up. We looked like a couple laughing at the solemnity of ourselves.

I thought mostly about myself. That general fog. Eating fruit and there I would be carving out the theory of loneliness in the stone of a peach. It sits there buried, I'd think, in solitude, alone. Little dark pit cold and singular, a oneness of itself. And then I would wag my finger at the fruit flies and change my mind, thinking no, this is not loneliness, because that stone is cushioned by its own delicate wall, the delicate *wail* of ripeness that surrounds it. Its happy perfumed flesh makes it full, round and delectable. The solitude, then, is not so lonely. I'd twist the ring on my finger like a terrible cartoon and jerk my hand down to slap the table, leaving it there until it numbed and fell into my lap.

The trench that falls between lethargy and enthusiasm can be a deep one to cross and I couldn't remember your body without mapping someone else's face on top. My truly teenage fantasies were couched in clumsy bastard tufts. I pondered tacky epithets and squinted less and less at marital derangement because it was glowing in plain sight: *What is a palm tree but a nice haircut? What is a hedge but a horse to pet? What is health but death in coaching?*

I couldn't stand the idea of borders. Of territory. The act of just standing up at the ironing board to map flatness onto my shirts in the compression of one's natural exuberance signalled immediate horror. It signalled the cotton-faded weariness of coupling.

I would have preferred anyone else then. I did prefer something else. Anything to make me feel less under the thumb, the tongue, less a colourful fool in some odd enshrining of the family unit.

That my frequent ogling of other body parts, parts not belonging to you, would set me all in a quiver, would elicit a contemptuous roughness from you. A response told through an urge to smoke alone outdoors, with the door slammed tightly behind. The odd and early lament of putting up defences way before it got dark. Slamming the door being equivalent to a slap in the face or a hard, pain-intentioned whack. We couldn't tell the difference between traffic and sobbing.

After the curtains had closed, then came the frying pan and the handbag – what would the genealogists say? Buffering with one, banging with the other. With function often relocated through rage, through sadness, to the physical chastising of a spouse. Our family tree was withering. We walloped and cowered in corners, imbued articles of our daily routine with sexuality. Underpants were removed, but never obligingly.

Well what is a body anyway, when framed in words? A dough trough? A collapsing figure for poking and kneading? For baking, for burning, for pulling apart like a hot-pocketed roll?

I have begun to believe in garbage. That the melanin in our skin has eyes. It sees everything. The body is always eager to enact its own improvised terrorism on our primordial romances, the ones we seek to hide, if only to remind us that contemporary life is often out to fuck you. Every step ill on the path of modern practices, between modern do's and modern don'ts, and there goes your body gleefully witnessing it all, hurtling along with its hand up to sell you out at the worst possible moment. Truth only adds to the vertigo of these moments.

By keeping our clothes firmly on, by exposing as little flesh as possible, could we drop off into another tense? Into a past tense where what I did hasn't happened yet quite simply because there was nothing exposed to see it.

Skin learns trace imprints, cold and pressure. It unfortunately learns pleasure and heat too and like a superficial fungus infection, once you go there there's really no way back.

I need to pick at a pudding whilst I do it. Write this letter. But to what end? To apologise? One or other of us was always dissembling with marital love. Right now I'd spell it wrong anyway, write *martial* love and be ushered swiftly with a head kick or body punch where it'd hurt for days. Because however keen you may be to receive them, my words will not be fresh from the band-aid box of loving brilliance.

How should I slant it? My writing. With something sweet and elegant, not bagged and tagged straight from the store? By wrapping up swarming commentary in a tight bodice with pink ribbons gushing over the sides? The more I press and squeeze and stuff trying to keep a neat package, the more it all fails prescription, losing meaning in a frothed-over tangle of minute grains, solemn words slipping into cunning phrases that dilute, expand, say nothing. Don't they say reason has many shapes?

I should congratulate myself on the wide progressive leaps I am making manipulating concepts. Just touching the paper makes me feel better. I should refresh my coffee, although I am yet to find the right cosmic plane for this assemblage. I hate geography. Perhaps the classic lover's lament of packing my note in a bottle and tossing it far on the ocean's table would offer a painless delivery. Something spit-soaked and bold, a filmic navigation of your address or longitudinal position to cast me as intense and romantic. More likely there I'd be, stumbling drunk to the shore, falling on the bottle, tearing a vein, beating the sand. Or throwing the wrong misspelled apology. Casting out my note to the wrong wronged. And being hopelessly far and unable to get near the bottle again, setting about drinking the seawater to make a dry passage for recovery, exhausting the possible definitions of sorry and unambiguously choking on salt. Unambiguously falling down not dead but dead fucking sorry. A martyrdom by note.

I'm trying to keep it positive, practically scrawling out *Office of Friendship* on this letter here. Ready for my public approbation. Me the dumb peasant uninformed of ethical laws, paying out heavy compensation for my infidelity. Damned in lieu of judicial formality to tramp around cold and naked for the rest of my days. Dumped whimpering on a ring road. How seductive the silence seems.

Especially as apologies seem always so endless, unhealthy in the certain route of futility they take. They turn on themselves and linger. Like the last photograph ever taken on a certain day which captures someone or other sucked in as unwitting as a fly sealed into amber. That's the problem with a letter, with an apology. You refuse to believe it at first until it falls somewhere on your mat, is read aloud and becomes fact. Becomes the truth.

A godless herding

I recall many years ago encountering a dead sheep on the beach, its abdomen puffed with the hardness of death. I dispatched a wish towards its belly for the maggots within to explode in a geyser of rot from its navel. I wanted a return of sorts. I was watching in the very verby sense of it – not *watched* – I was *watching* in motion for some signal of horror, for the impossible thickness of malaise to mobilise and spring onto me like the great sucking goop of a rancid goblin. I wanted to smear it over myself, to lose myself. I was as greedy and debased as a pigeon.

I recognise now the crispness of memory. How images once seen can rarely be unseen. How they slot in between other powers of recollection and can be summoned in an instant for a newly insistent debut.

This is the power of truth. How we colour it. How the approximate details of subjective imagery suddenly become fact. There is the brain stubborn and blockheaded, operating within the construct of a trick. I never saw sheep maggots, yet I remember how they moved. My invented imagery is a proxy for how it all really happened. Memories rustle up their own pleasure labyrinth, their own hierarchy, first cosy in warm dry arms, next slippery multipliers remembering what happened and what didn't with equal clarity.

What is memory really but a reissuing of history via simple triggers? Notes left under the welcome mat like marital communication primers: through-the-mail leaflets with step-by-step details for the preservation of soft-core ashen secrets and libidinal shrieks.

And once you'd seen me in bed with not you, well, there was no way back.

The short of it is that your hair amounted to violence. My lips amounted to violence. We enacted violence.

It's always simple scenarios that invite most speculation. Even here at the kitchen table as I try to write, it reeks of mushrooms, damp and a little fishy, yet still erotic. Quick as a flash I am seeking to humble and lower my mind. There are always simple images. You with your coffee mug like a machine gun, your slippers like camouflage, like greenery, good and natural. And simple triggers.

I've learned to pre-empt volatility. To relegate it to scenic detail. To dull it. I'm currently grappling with an alcoholic indulgence in the alcove of the fridge, squeezing out the cork whilst stalks of old chervil stuck to the bottle peel off and down onto the floor. There are water scars down there from when we forget to defrost, cobwebs where the split siphon of the fridge leaks a slow pool, all of it folklore. Unsightly stains bleeding into the other. It's an ugly floor so I never cared. There is more ghastly matter down there with the floor, it just a cheap coffin lid propped up over the ground to support our movements from room to room. Our mutual shadows like columns, also propping up.

We'd grouted the kitchen tiles on together, exercising great caution with our patience and the light on well into the night a general invitation to insects we hadn't expected to see indoors. I'd thought how much paste we'd wasted, how much of that particularly fluid concrete had fudged the floor, our clothes, and rubbled in miniature boulders that would have looked better under the hedgerow. Our rubber floats and wet sponges were quite newly electric in the naked light, so hotly illuminated against evening that they seemed heavy with allegory. Our own forensic architecture.

I felt then the boil of panic stir under my muddled shirt. Even with the guides of factory-instilled straightness, even with square tiles and their perfectly adequate dosage of regularity, we'd tilted way off course. By the time we were finished, the kitchen had been given a new slant with the horizon just dropping off and sinking behind the cupboards. The sink was blocked and I hated the newly tiled wall, freshly acoustic like a graph awaiting the plotting of our personally despicable peaks and troughs.

From outside we must have looked painted shut. Painted into our particular scene just waiting for this moment. Waiting for the dowels to warp and stick the windows tight, for the tiles to fall off the wall and hurt us in a soft, poor, failing kind of way. The long drawn-out ache of security rusting and slowing, falling out beneath its frame.

I remember too when the newspaper brought images of the first prisoners of desire. I'd been thinking so much of desire, how it leaps at one's throat at a bound and sticks there, so the propensity to mirror my own life in the observation of others was ripe.

A *raging contagion*, the press called it. All the homos and the godless plopping off the Earth with nothing left to even scratch an itch. Weren't we all godless homos? And I saw them both in the real and in the pictures, all the people convening in gyms and saunas with Bible covers wrapped around their pornography and freshly washed shirts angled towards redemption. And so quickly the *them* turned on itself and I thought of me as well, fumbling through sheets and always thinking elsewhere. Often loving elsewhere.

And again in newspapers the piously inflamed were there clutching a little too hard to their children outside the gyms and the saunas, hoping for a massacre to compile more corpses but horrified, and secretly aroused too, that the people inside just couldn't help themselves from fucking in great groups. Fucking together in hoards and pairs, riding bareback and barefoot over one another in fantastically squelching heaps of pleasure. The newspapers were so busy with hatred, chastising them for thinking they were tidy or sexy using the same cloth over and over. All of these things, once vices, now certainly being virtues in my book. Or customs even. And I loved it all.

The ones full of God could quite frankly go home. Could get lost as the insiders were doing, glorious in the beautiful aching motions of all of their bodies together occluding any taste of fear or shame.

It was so confused and inconsistent. My longings raged and burned on red. And as if in negative linear correlation, the more I secretly indulged, the more pallid my contribution to a common level of honesty became. But all the pleasure was contextual, too. I felt guilty, but not enough to issue myself with any pointers for corrective behaviour.

It reminded me of when things were good. When the bed frame shook and all the screws were literally flung out to slam into the wall. And all the screws were figuratively flung out to slam into the wall, like the time we both came so hard, so mathematically weighty with togetherness, that the boards of the bed just sighed and broke in two.

I wasn't accustomed to so many inclement feelings outside it. Outside of us and our baggage of commitments. Our weather. I was not so good at sucking it up, at stuffing some very loose emotional wadding between the models of human justice and what, desire? Medicine? I wasn't so upright.

Rather my cardinal directions remained sparse and continue in this current moment to be slipping off, heading downwards beyond the equatorial heat otherwise known as hell. Perhaps I should draw flames at the bottom of this note, bundle in a teary picture of myself and tie it to a brick easily en route through your window? Quite some letter. A shattering accomplishment.

But then again who is mapping the hell that I'm about to whirl off into? On what scale is it rated how much damage and pain will come to my body? Who is the 'I' writing these pages? Which bit of what part of me can be held responsible for the content, for the execution? Will there be footnotes or some tacked-on appendage to clarify what I really mean? Is it possible to write in the third person?

I know my *doing it* sounded like something – it sounded like a lot – but what did the seeing sound like? Was it something like pausing time and hearing the waxy thickness around it settling or being pulled out so that only a painful throbbing of heat remained? The sound of sound itself being heard in the moment of seeing something you didn't want to see? A lifting the lid and scorching off anything ordinarily termed *basic*?

We had spoken about the distance being near as a covert way of describing how our mutually exclusive desires were very much within reach. It was a competitive display of chatter. And then suddenly there was I, alone, the one extravagant and frivolous component in all this.

Sometimes the throb of traffic fills the air so deeply my table stirs in response. Things were always shaking. I was contending with horrendous blood pressure and breath that smelt like nail polish remover. With a chemically synthetic personhood. You called me nutty and by that you meant *see a therapist* and what I saw instead were just massive piles of rubble in both directions.

This new concern of mine, this letter, seems academic to a fault. My elbows hurt now, so long they've dug into the table as I rest my head. I stick a biro in my mouth. It's disgustingly sticky. You'd think I'd have a bigger drawer for all these secretions. All my writing utensils piled into my #1DRAWER, my *favourite* drawer, with contents including tweezers and matches but not precluding shame on opening when seeing also the shreds of one's own mortal vanity. Names and numbers and the dark repressive emptiness of a space splattered with talcum powder or Vaseline. My hands are shaking properly now. Certainly no good for a letter tonight.

I can't even describe what the mystical basis for your authority might be. The sway you hold me in. Something like the way the waves whiten over the sea as they rise up and over the gusts of a mounting gale. That sure and certain firmness and god forbid anything in its tumbling watery way.

It seems impossible that I will ever commit words to paper. I see my insistence on the strength of a truce weakening with every day I sit motionless and solo. How mischievous is it that conscience should come up and ruin the most pleasurable parts of my day. I can hear the reality of this thickening in my voice. Perhaps it is a sob, a proof rolled over. If it's shame or amazement I can no longer tell. Instead I'll just email over a picture with a few scrappy lines that seem just about enough in value or depth, like the most humble of all cards in a pack:

> *Dear X,*
> *These are kitchen rags drying, with a chorus of accompanying Agapanthus from the garden. Funny they are also called Lily of the Nile and my door opens right onto the stinking brown canal.*

Old soup

I loved green. Always loved green. For the full twenty-four months of my sixth and seventh years on Earth I wore nothing but that shade: shoes, trousers, underwear. I loved it because it aligned my limbs with grass stems. I'd pick up a pencil and feel as though the arachnoid must of old sheds, the petals and stalks of all plants, were authored by my own quiet left hand. The green of that time gave my small head its own secret well of life.

Flowers now are a conjuring trick of reproach. With their perception of loss they hold the most pain and wilt with accordance. Theirs is a grand pretence that mirrors my own neck's droop.

The things that sit before me are silent with waiting. I know I cannot get up and sing or write because the words will not come. My voice derives attributes from masonry, from the aggravating roughness of lime. A crude pebbled song may choke me quite up forever, a little voice stuck down in a deathly hole. So I'm sitting here shirtless plucking at my chest, pulling those simple hairs as though they might trigger an answer to that fundamental question: *What holds me together?*

This structural danger is all over. Everything is damply bloated. Food around me sweated in shape and smell. There are plants in a plastic sack and anemones in the basin, neither of which I have delivered to you as intended.

My eyes wander. Nothing to jolt or rattle, to chew or thread. There is little in the house to set distraction afoot. Boring things are what keep the cupboards quiet. Things evacuated of their mortal fleshiness and withered out to abrasive dust. Things like Melba toast and French herbs. Food that tastes like its historical analogue. Doubt shelters well in silence. No eggs even.

Perhaps I feel that to lose you completely would be to have my heart ripped out. A smashing up of common metaphors and me slow on my path like a simple snail feeling for gaps to avoid accident. I'll crawl into my shell and sleep.

The unfortunate truth is that my pulse continues when my eyes are closed. Organs pound out their needs. My stomach, my brains, my great heaving heart still boiling away as though simmering in a dull vat of vegetables en route to becoming soup. All that breastwork, the songs and flowers, all the flustered nights, they're mulched up and put back inside me in a colour that looks just like sickness. These clocks that insist on revolution, that tick to point at incidentals. The system continues, backwards and forwards, into empty air.

I need a pharmacist to consult regarding issues of doubt. All this hurry but too late. Half roasted. Taken away. Not pitied. I think it would hurt so much. What should I do? Like maybe hurt forever. Just fold up as a shadow and disappear in the crease of another pair of legs. That is an answer not a question. And just as quietly as you hear the grass growing, then too you would hear my heart slowly splitting along its seams and falling away.

But it doesn't stop me from wanting other people. There being something about fucking the person you love that brings out a more sensitised version of your own self-loathing. A fictional edifice from which to stare down whilst two filament bodies tightrope between horror and pleasure, sacrifice and orgasm. Is this a new feeling? Or just another technical relationship to translation?

So now what? Am I to cultivate some sorrow of tears and send them upstream to your door like a little river of explanation? Wrap myself one last time in your effulgence of hair and soundlessly glide away? So many questions for my mouth to formulate. And me endlessly talking from the past-present instead of thinking about anything that might ever surface in the future. I would snip off my shadow to avoid all this.

Dearest,
I say this with the edge of my teeth over my lower lip, which is perhaps why it sounds forced. I blame the foggy air for my scrawl. I wanted to say that the narrow space that lay between us in the bed has widened. I'm glad we didn't embroider the cloth above or paint the headboard. The bedroom makes no sense. My neck no longer feels so long or delicate.

Or in the kitchen. There are departures. Just now I turned to face the counter and there sat the pepper mill, the mayonnaise, Greek yoghurt and cinnamon, all of it unmoving. My eyes were rosy but everything else white. All the plastic curves and cylindrical waists overlapped: never was one thing visible without appearing joined to another. That visual space could exist like that, flattened in a single retinal plane, horrified me. If things once they touched in space could never be separated again, I felt surely a black hole might soon deposit itself on the white wall and quite suck me in.

But nothing moves with the weather. It all remains negative, watching me. I feel wet on my elbow. This rhythmic sequence quite horribly shakes up coordinates. Condiments. Truth and untruth piled together like a hybrid of my life.

It strikes me that this is an affair of ideology. An affair. Some ideology. That there is a new insistent me ready to not be alone. I am over-fevered this month. I suddenly sense I should break away from the arrangement, go outside or run a bath.

Oats

Cheap cheap cheap. That's how my bathroom sounds. A quiet hammering of indignities, all those cabinets stuffed with thick tides of Nivea cream, shaving cream, a foamy surf of things you just want to feel in your mouth. Pink Pepto-Bismol heavy in its bottle. Makes me think about laying a blanket over a corpse and walking away. A veil over the top so as not to see the face waxed in its marrow.

My own bastard face. I wish it would rearrange itself overnight so committedly to a direction of difference that any groggy morning gaze would throw the condition of naming things with certainty quite out of the question. Something to hurl the whole project of consistency built into human nature into an incongruous blackness. A big zero. Nil. Those red, well-bitten lips – are they body, machine or object? Quite who does that absurd haircut and a face the colour of mould belong to? The inventor of the mirror poisoned the human heart.

And if my only face might change, then what of the lousy reliability of all the other bits around me? I often think these thoughts, with the cold bathroom floor painful against bare soles, the mirror strip-light fretting, and me an urgent integer in between. The acquiring of exotic new facts takes only a minor circumstance of discomfort. Checking cuticles for a small but persistent gathering of toxic fluorescents, a little grime that's settled and become part of me.

I am a live-in male bound by the margins of a low and grey sky of my own making. I should step speedy to the grocery, get some organic oats or bran, feel like I am pursuing living habits for leisure rather than the lacklustre bagginess of the present. But then like most people I loathe the supermarket with a compliance of hatred equal to if not greater than the turmoil of brushing my own teeth. All the aisles, the lighting, the figures straining against their waistbands as they reach beyond emotional paleness to place some molasses-type heavies into a cart. Smelling like greasy potatoes and rust. Ice cream vendors and clicking lottery wheels. All these unspoken and very basic rules, the very bread and breath of it all. These are a set of fears that require survivalist Tupperware and stores of supplies bought far in advance.

MESSRS. EXTERNAL & STILL

Milky way

Oh lethargy! When at five o'clock the sun tires and ceases to be functional, then come the lights and their local switch, connecting everything to an impossibly huge grid of global electricity. The grid we drag ourselves over and remember. Lights on, lights off, there is no way to escape space.

This is the time for walking, we believe. Or at least sitting out in the air with the common language of nature. By canal or river, with its water combed into straight lines. Not mirror gazing into a paunchy wasteland.

We are quite adept at stepping into the street and vanishing. Imitate me, say the Elm or the Sycamore, and our fat chicory legs stand still and sturdy, new bodies of milk and curd, fretting over chocolate wrappers and dead leaves at our feet.

We watch from the canal by his house, Ethan's. We look up at the house and name the door. The neighbours will name their windows and the curtains they pull over them. There is terminology for the shrubs and seasonal sowing patterns of the garden. Summer and winter, heat and water. It is the threshold parts that remain without a name. The bits between windows and doors and ivy. They are known but not called out, not greeted. With these grammatical certainties the house is full of rhymes. On one side the theory for building and living, on the other side the language for building and living.

We sit for some time with a sense of grievance. We are grieved. Unmoored. In need of a rope. We could untie a barge and take our pick of slow new diversions, but we are Messrs. after all, purveyors of calm. We sit still on a bench, on an idea like an egg. We sit on our hands so as not to touch others, or ourselves, and watch the water pass, only reflection, only breath. This ancient weir busy rinsing cans and condoms, bathing the sawn-off shotgun that nestles waist deep in rotted soils. We see it. We feel the volume of all this detail in our bones. How the flatness of so many different perspectives intersects and creates a shape to step into. Unhappy pebbles, tossed, juggled, measured in the palm.

Our man needs a shower. We must sniff suggestively. The libidinal jelly of *jouissance*! Perhaps he feels the pinch of pleasure still on his skin. The swell of attraction burns in the blood and can't be shrugged off in the bath. One part hallucination, two parts pain and rage. It cannot be contained. It fascinates. It destroys.

How still we can sit on our hands by this brown and dirty water. Wind huffs its enormousness. Other things move and mould around us:

a sodden baguette, a rat, half a pizza drizzled with weeds. All so soft and slow on the surface. The sloppy waters of the heart. The choppy waters of the groin. The stomach who sways and announces.

We are raisins dried up in winter sun. We hope, like you, to be eaten soon.

ETHAN

This Tudor trifle

My neighbours insist. They don't keep any great column of air between us. They breach the boundary lines of my property, paying little heed to the built hierarchy arranged to present an aspect of comfort to each of our privacies. They insist.

The discovery of starching fabric seems to have come to them late. My neighbours and their giddy fondness for laundry. It imparts a stiffness to the small shirts on their line as hard and headless as a minor execution. The children who wear these shirts run on with their long trousers and pleated crotches. They tear up my lawn with trucks and plastic. They lick their lips as they watch my house and dribble feebly into each other's hair. They are not nice boys, with names like Satan and Herod – their parents either misinformed or miscalculating of the world's innate tilt towards evil.

The parents insist on halfway blinds. That is to say the bottom half of their window is covered with lace like a tender pillow for the dead: neck upwards is all you see floating about the ground floor. The mother's face is as pale-soft as bread and written all over in slapstick shorthand by eyebrow pencils and lipstick. She is a kindergarten make-over. She looks like a stamp above the curtain's scallop. Like John the Baptist, all head, no body.

As my house shelters me and I watch these boys, at my desk with my pens and paraphernalia, I feel far away and anonymous. I have all the ingredients to justify my lunatic ideas, to myself and to others. I have my stamps to send my lucidity and logic out into the world. My feet are connected to the floorboards, them to the flagstones; my bent legs continue over the chair seat and mask the similarity of posture between a crouching man and a silent man. Between a dead man and sleeping man.

In this moment, my postal stamps are another kind of decapitation. Their subjects are so grim and dusty in inks of currency-green and blue. Who knows at what episode of focus or translation their heads might have been frozen. Where do the torsos reside whilst their heads are suspended in a pickled tint? There is no landscape. And why never mint stamps or coins depicting men ambling away from horses and waiting to be shot in a ditch, or children throwing coats over themselves to keep their eyes away from hungry birds? There are never capsized cargo ships submerged and paralysing in their flatness, or boys and girls weeping whilst their parents look on and pray for the sacrifice of an alternative neighbour or cousin. It is only ever lonely heads, singular and imminent.

I am offended by the indifference of these playing children, as though I am the foreigner lodged savagely in their midst.

P.S.

The cat of my insisting neighbours was called Peter Schlemihl. They named him for another Peter Schlemihl, who sold his shadow to the devil in exchange for a bottomless wallet, for a sack of bright Fortunas. He snipped it clean off with one free hand.

This cat plagues me. Always the sly postscript of my evenings, literal PS, slinking home with solid brain and twitching scalp, a wink before diving through the flap. My own indoor face watching, frothy and illuminated. This cat has reverent eyelids, frilled ferns and a little pink tongue a violent nut of colour poked occasionally out, tasting the wind for an occupation to stain his leisure. He hunts with an automatic nature I am jealous of, licking his fur in the crawl space by my bins and leaving gathered clumps of fuzz I mistook for rats. We were shadow people rustling on top of one another in the dark, ebbing into mutual focus and quick dissolve.

I would watch with binoculars and note the patterns he made on the ground, in the frost when the wind was rotten with ice. I wished the sugared snow would tease the blood out of his body. I wished to act like a lad dropping stuff off the highway bridge: a smash of apricot, a stone kicked out, a falling puss.

Pictures of him and his feline breath appeared all over telegraph poles. Pictures of him on poles with telephone numbers stapled all over like a mad votive totem. Pictures suspended, xeroxed sheets with their poverty of black and white. The disappearance was edifying.

The boys halted their trespasses into my garden, leaving only a red cart into which to pile my longings. I felt like a savage, wrung out, but secretly pleased with my pathetic concept. The mother neighbour cried *witch* and *sorcerer* and I wished I could concede, wished that duet of words was truly made for me, scooping hounds and horses from the air with my hands whipped only slightly open. If only to remind them that all of us are always just one scratch away from freaks and suburban horror.

Peter Schlemihl never came round again. Lying on his back beneath the waterway underpass. His shadow fell fast, a spinning black coin dropped from my hands through lampless air. He landed near bull rushes on the banks with suds on their stems. He landed chopped and askew. On his back, legs out, hair mingling with the brown of those rusty log seeds like microphones loud on stage. He landed lying on his back, no shadow. Lying on his back with his face to the sky, Peter Schlemihl's fear near killed him. The impact saw to that, to a newness as uniform as cloth. In the reflected glow of snow light, away from the bins, out of the gardens and all their insistence, the colours for a moment were hard-edged as though recently dipped in water.

PATRICE

Darkling

My magazine shows a picture of somebody eating an olive, somebody assigned the duty of tasting. I begrudge the sensation of pleasure this man is experiencing, so follow my divine envy towards the petrol station for a jar of my own.

I must check my oil too, must stick-dip into my engine's belly with the same spirit of contemplation I saw on the face of that man eating his olive. It is a peculiar thing to do, this gesture of entering that draws clear parallel between our two dark holes, my car's black petrol throat and my own mouth, dark with old wine.

I begrudge the sensation of purpose that other people around me are experiencing filling their cars with petrol. I seek to improve the situation and make it my own. I squat behind the car and the woman leaving with flowers under her arm makes a wide berth, her arc an impeccable mirror of my piss as it curves towards the central drain. I white glob a little spit to the floor. Snowing. I'll buy some crisps too, feel their angular crunch, all these people looking at me like I'm filling a hearse not a station wagon. Driving is just the theory of inverse degrees of actually getting anywhere.

You really can never tell who might follow you in fog, so I hate it when the weather is too coherent. I harbour an almost industrial distrust for bright clean action. If I saw a stranger dying in the street, nose and mouth all broken, I don't know if I would rush to his side or run wide steps away. Even from my car, being outdoors, straddling lilies in ponds and taxis on streets, make me anxious. As in one lone human garrotted by pony hair and daffodils.

Outside I feel the acuteness of being a body, with trees and their far flinging upwards arms to prop up the clouds and considering the weight of the world miraculous that a caucus of crows, those poor pagan spooks, can tumble above with such patterned grace.

Outside I think *tell me everything!* Every tiny detail from the colour of the sand down to the direction of the last stick laid in the nest of the proudest seagull. And how many times it flew in and out, the upthrust, the squall of feathers and number of parasites under its wing. Tell me, did a cygnet's beak – twitching, ducking – plunge beneath you? A barge? Was there a bridge?

MESSRS. EXTERNAL & SLEEPY

Coffee all coffee

She slept in her car, our dearest ducky. Scrawled across her forehead, sweet recumbent woman, are little hairs from a fringe that write a perfectly innocent alphabet of her character. Everything is spaced out across the face. Others call it expression.

She dreamt of chairs placed alone and chairs gathered in pools of light to reinforce the character of their positions, local lamps, some wood, some wicker. She dreamt of the soft pink colour of low-fire clay and wondered how to perfect the feeling of a connection with the earth, with her surroundings, how a person might bypass the mechanical wash-easy paths of asphalt for something altogether more soft and soothing. There were cracks and mosses, an outdoor room with a terraced slope where erosion and rainwater moved quite freely and for once touched earth in all the right places.

PATRICE

Hortulan Greenth

I am stiff. Landscaped into the shape of my passenger seat. The trees today serve their purpose, the bark of one just pierced by my headlamp, an especially nice fruit tree, hanging its branches over me like a benevolent umbrella. We need trees.

I have an urge for it, my own garden, where I have long expected to come across something unpalatable. Lest it seem to my neighbours that I am strange or unwell, I fix myself when digging with a physical posture proximate to the vertical infallibility of my spade. Although eager to resist stereotypes of a single person dwelling alone, I am frustrated with the quality of the soil. But I do not slump. This is fertile territory for speculation. Too much clay, too much water: everything a bog.

Sometimes fatal sparrows dead with poisonous fruit from the Elderberry and English Ivy thump down silent in the soil. I pile their winged bodies into bags. They say the shadow is a reservoir of human character, a hinged well of shade impossible to chart. The folded edges hold hundreds of planes we cannot see all at once. There is little sunshine here so dandelions disperse their seed too late. My garden is a mound. Often its brightest moment is right before the neighbours extinguish the light in their simple window hot against the night.

I hate nature for how people behave in it. Out of it. All that deference and superiority. When I am tangled in shrubbery my boots feel so large they stomp out all the vagaries of a life lived outdoors. Nature deserves more.

The world has its blossoms and cicadas in their sickly clash of cordiality. Then flowers and shrubs, ponds raucous with their fountain splashes, their rumpled marbles. Even the Koi – barbing, finning, bathing – exhibit little resistance to the happy garden scene. Even the Koi! With their big buttery heads busy seeding new theories of freedom inexplicably founded in reflections of sky or cloud in the water; theories inexplicable to anybody who hasn't swum down there themselves and understood something about primary loss. Even the Koi, for all their Aprils or Januarys passed under-fin and seasons sprung by, would hesitate to break a morning dew with scornful words *against* the garden. Even the Koi, happy with their large size and ornamental ponds. Even when newly divested of their mothers or cousins and observing them laid out thick and pink on trout platters one evening's fish course would hesitate in telling you that the gardeners got it wrong. That the homeowners got it wrong. Even the sides of Haddock from the streams or transoms of Eel from the ponds purse their fish lips in agreement, happy gills gasping agreement with the general evolutionary turns of nature, its people and its places. Even the parsley, its crinkum-crankum greens newly forested with scrolls of mandarin glaze, would cause little dispute about the righteous pleasantness of the garden.

My neighbourhood comrades are merry gardeners, arcadian dilettantes with their hierarchy of espresso and wild grape tea. You hear the water rushing this way and that, so quick are they to lower themselves into bath suds fragrant with the smell of the current season. I've seen so much import-export that one day I'm certain the blooms will gather up their buxom petals, their practical upward mobility growing shorter, as the horizontality of our anxious sunset grows smaller and more mean. Only a little orange dot rigged over everything for a few moments more before the coloured earth droughts and burns up, charcoaling its weaves, the stalks, all propagating ingenuity parched and gone as the planet sighs and drops down towards clinical poisoning.

I feel a drama coming on if I place a bouquet on my table. My name binds me like a victim to the natural world, but Nature never figured itself suitable to run in our pipes, to caress itself to green congeal in vases. I myself am a gelatinous garden-maker, a clipper of roses, a calibrator of new widths of green and depths of beige alike. I huff and puff the garden. I slay with an archaic devotional activity that often arrives in the form of plastic purples from the garden centre: herbals over-watered, under-sunned and thrown out some weeks later, when, like the effects of poor diet, the flowerbeds look like cavities and the rot being only half disguised by bark-border filler needs treatment, needs grave remedy, needs quite frankly pulling out.

That's when the imperceptible violence of shadow really settles in. When out of the window there is no neat green square, but rather a damaged ditch rigid with lampposts and their omnipotent vanishing points. This is when I bolt the front door and struggle a little with the latch. When I am certain some fraction of error is working against my fluency. Against my house.

MESSRS.
EXTERNAL & FALLING

Ducks, electric

The bar is always too warm. Grease-wrapped, soused. Ethan's mouth too is inhospitable. The tomatoes in his garden have been trampled, the chickens stolen. It will take much more than a busted hedge. He has a craving for salt, for sweat, for great oceanic feelings. Liquor will do it, the lovely liquid vitamin. Eddy the barman is a drunk. He looks like Halloween with his hand gone and the stump waxed and hard like a dry sock. Eddy uses the negative space around it like a hallucination, he beckons drinks out of it and Ethan imagines seeing it spouting with permanent blood. Soaking his face with the hot iron stink. They say a pickup ripped it clean off whilst he siphoned petrol out with a hose. He says his name isn't really Eddy. *Divorce in absentia*, thinks Ethan. If not from your heart then the fingers that clutch around it. The confusion of love and torture overwhelms him. The peanuts have nothing to say about it, the suds foam their yeasty vectors up over the glass. Always up.

Ethan handled a pistol once and felt how irrelevant true or false was in the pursuit of knowledge. He had felt so alive. He had felt his temples pulse in his crotch. In this chattering bar of heads and hats he could place his hands around the throat of the man on the stool next to him. He could knock himself out with violence. He could drink until he vomited and lie dead like a mouse on the floor. Someone might pick him up or kick him in the mouth for men are never a site of calm. And if he had to move forward or backward through this time or another he would always be looking the other way.

Outside where the earth is exhausted, he lies face down and scoops dirt into his mouth. The little pebbles rattle his teeth and thicken a chalky foam against the alcohol's sweetness. It feels like dessert although even his tongue is sore and swollen. This is not a perplexing habit of falling, he chose this position, how the horizon outruns its lines, outraces even its own flatness. The air and the noise move over him and he feels them like a quilt, wonders which one is heavier. He spits, flips onto his back and pulls his thumbs into the loops of his trousers. We know that position. He wants to fuck or cry. Back arched off the ground, the pink-green light of the bar falls against his shirt. The colours are abnormal, gassy and pastel. He fires his waist fiercely towards the stars. His plaid shirt is full of lines directing the pebbles that trickle through his hair. The dust, the moaning fields. And him under his breath: *I am no better or worse than the rubber on these car tyres. One small continuum growing slowly thinner, burning to naught, always unfurling myself, despite all these atoms.*

A duck waddles somewhere close to his head. It seems unreasonable, impossible. One wild migratory thing with its flat feet and green neck glittering. A quacking solemn joke. It is so wrong it's electric. Nights are a cul-de-sac that you enter with a squeeze. He wants to trail his hand through the spilt car oils on the paving, raise possibility in this fallow evening, force his slickened fingers against the brown pucker of his asshole, get up and shake hands with the other men still inside in the bar.

Unlike Ethan, we are not drunk. But the effect of wine is on our cheeks, its goblin glow about our necks, smoke wrapped then thinning around us. How we cling to everything, our own traces on car seats, across soap and its drifting suds, hair or spit and shit a smearing alliteration, obsessively unstoppable. We see all those picked fingers as a clear surrogate for fixation, busy hands only a minute away from a cigarette propped in the mouth. Oral, anal. Sex as a function of geography. Outside here, where the night is black, sweat is ozone. Something sharp and chemical. Something to poison with. And the bar lights so bright against it. It is no semantic coincidence that the word for colour is rooted also in drug, remedy, talisman, cosmetic, intoxicant. Flushed. Coloured. Poisoned. Maybe dust never settles, only clears briefly from the last failure.

MESSRS.
EXTERNAL & HOMELY

1,094 bones

What to say of the narrative of an enlightened house? We're not sure we can tell. We can no more recognise Venus without Cupid than look at all these houses stuffed with sofas and chairs and point out people from the bodily innuendos. We've dug ourselves deep into upholstery. The grimy bubbles of the home are bursting all over with their catalogue of monsters – the fat men and their balloons or the drooping mistresses hung up out of sight near the raincoats. Dare we confess what frightful and unspeakable things we can discover in these nooks and crannies? Who says homemade lemon pies make the house a home? Not us.

We don't doubt what we have discovered. It begins with the outdoor absurdities. From pavement to garden to front door, with doorbells or knockers and language so grey. The town is unfriendly, of course, just a dusty resettlement of the city. And nobody likes company so fences separate the dust of neighbours into inch-wide tracts with poison in every corner. Or rubble, finely arranged. Pets and garbage add their ballast. Canines like martyrs with their endless woofing. Those awful lone caravans and their stickers advertising superior children.

Then downstairs, that restless womb! Downstairs is heart and stomach. The bacon buzzing in its own fat, or some men's mettle made in the meats of ruddy cattle. How many licks to a loaf? How much butter, how much curd? What about a soft utensil for some peaceful oats? You could say it was quite a gorgeous landscape, this downstairs, with dinner nudged along, crusted cabbage, and flies. Everyone loves a still-life: yes, this gorgeous landscape, we must eat with it, we must paint it sometime.

Let's sit down here for a moment, cross-legged in front of the home. Their old home. Ethan and Patrice. Does life hurt less as we speak of it, look at it, gather it in a whiff of air from those inside who come and go with their wearied faces? It does not.

Houses are weapons with their windows tilted to watch the world; houses are packages never fully unwrapped. Houses are skins and paper with their old plaster and eczema wallpapers. Dusty houses, dusty blocks, dusty barns all over.

This is not even to mention the children! Those longings to be whole, to put a ribbon on *family life*, so out they pop, the rubbery foundlings, like snakes from the absurd hollows of the broken home! There are 1,094 bones to the modern family; that's the parents and their brood: one blubbering babelet streaked afresh with mammalian love, floppy bones unfused and with seven bricks per square foot for the average family home, add 8,176 baked blocks to compete with the bodies.

It's hard work this busy hazy city. All these many billion thinking houses with their mathematical shadows: fat round kitchen explosions, lines of laundry with their nibbled clothes. There are ordered groups, ordered fields and common shapes. History. Even old Archimedes loved his screw pump so much that two spheres and a cylinder mark his tomb: there's always one shape or another on the horizon.

Did you ever stop to think about the long steaming train panting into its sheltered station? We did. Arriving with a great rolling hiss, a sigh, or a cloud of moist white smoke. We're no doctors, no shrinks, but we're telling you that our sex is in the details of it all. This is a loving interpretation.

Just look at the bedrooms! Real Adam and Eves camera shy with their high-value kidneys and excellent sperm count. Talking excitedly about love triangles. Everywhere bodies crinkled in and out of nuptials, with metallic lies and a common sensation of barbarism.

Does our conversation have any relationship to reality? It does. The great laws of air and fluid, of substance and spooks, spill over the eaves that hold lives together like sinews of peace. It's sharp and masochistic here. We don't need to reminisce about the expensive trousers.

The bathroom scene is bottled water. The toilet is a poem satirising a minor incident!

All houses have knives and wedges, workers driving wagons, babies in baskets rush-fresh and diapered, simple eyes, names in print, mechanics, sailors, toughened beautiful women, odours and bodies and breath: so many lines to wrap around the planet.

And then there is the basement – the sweet-rot cellar. Next to the house we know you think of us as small and extinguishable as a maggot. We are! All the volatiles are here to set us on our way, the wine and firewood. Lesser torments have marked our weary hours. There are so many toppled objects. So many bitten-off nails pounded to dust, crescents waxing and waning.

See the house is like communication and once you've departed on the great bold liner of language it's hard to turn back without imagining the damage, the old grand phrases newly wrecked, torn up in pieces or washed adrift like polystyrene on a cheap blue sea.

Look how we sound! *We love it!* Like the fall of a hammer! The snap of a bone! *We're out of hand!* Like the old wisteria that grows its ampersand in cracks around the window. We sound like an index that equates your weight with a piece of real estate and hollers it out for all to know. We stick a sign in the soil out front and offer your secrets for sale.

But think about it: people deploy bricks and mortar. They stir their minds out of dust, then slam doors with discontent, sit with conversations they hang up at night to reuse in the morning. The house is made from the ashes, a bonfire waiting to happen. The house is a big body, a macro mass. The house, *don't groan*, is a form heavy with its own blundering embarrassment. People rub down their floors and think about moving.

PATRICE

Margarine

I don't think of moving, but I do sit at the window because people are by nature phototropic: they move towards light. When you are at the window, on the inside, it's possible to look like pastry, like you have eaten nothing but chalk for a decade in pursuing a pre-digital insistence on looking like the china, also in your window. You can sit for hours, for days, and then some new dawn emerges with the turnover of sun and there you are groping about unwashed in the low-level dim of another accidental afternoon. This is the kind of time that stinks or people say *what a loathsome spectacle*, and I wave freely with baked-on eyeliner and curtains pieced together with scotch tape.

The window is a screen. A little hatch opened out to chart the slow syrup of days slipping by. Pictures rearrange. I sit here and move as though I am only one muscle, one single organism through which both time and image pass. All that getting up and down to the toilet or freezer is only a shaking up of the hourglass's gravel.

I could do the same faster online via those websites which move with their blinks and clicks and no sooner have I pulled an inadequately padded chair with poor lumbar support and broken castors up to the table, than time and cash have puddled around the ankles and I've already bought thirty things arriving all uniform in their splendid cardboard before day has even broken.

There are select factions of society – like me with my slippers drawn up and dusty – whose dailies, whose grocery gatherings, codeine syrups, clever books, cars, sins, wives and salutations are all procured via the window screen. I am amongst those who scan online scenarios as big and punishing as the biggest bluest river. It is the creation of an inner sadism, enjoying one's own pain as if it were quite perfectly somebody else's. It reinforces my status as a totally average citizen. All that unspecified watching and waiting frays the nerves and sets in a chilled conviction that perhaps nothing is worth hanging on to for long.

My screen eddies reassurance, making certain my recreational ingestion of *stuff* is so extraordinarily and carefully curated before my blinking eyes that it is both freakish and beautiful. The colours are enhanced and violent. It's possible that I can sit there with my new low-chemical deodorant and smell the scent of eminence, of cardamom, and experience a new impossibility in the distinction of things around me: the clunk of rain, the splat of rain, its tinkle, drip, wash, its roar – I can make no outline of difference. The room and all about it becomes a general incongruous blackness.

People who've generally exhausted a capacity for love or patience are ambivalent to scrambled bandwidth, and the promise of stillness and some clipped gasps of satisfaction provided at a minimum line-rental fee of a few pennies per minute through a smelting of miraculous cosmic plastic is increasingly the path to choose for those whose palate for general social engagement is shrinking.

I do in fact exhibit high-level exhaustion. My capacity for speech and explanation has withered. I have endless boxes of household mix, household clutter. They no longer dispatch ingratiating terms or kind words in my vicinity so I design to get rid of them.

Outside the self-storage service centre, there on the telephone box is the corrupting stink of selling. Three things are pummelled towards head level: telephone service, free Wi-Fi for broadband customers, 99p hot chicken wings.

At least 85 per cent of the available space is given over to the impossibly greased contours of the chicken's batter. Its crusted flanks are so outlandishly big and bronzed that the bird could comfortably seat a family of four, all sports gear and shopping. In my white blouse and flowery skirt I am the perfect vessel for assault. A pitcher into which to pour optical wonderment. I feel the sensory triage as my mouth waters and I imagine the hot and tasty bits, some wings or nuggets or other unspecified hunks of basted bird whose juices I might burst against my face. There are small lights banked above it, baby halogens under which the chicken no doubt glows as bright and good as any stoic corporate hero. During the day in merciless sunshine it smells like wet paint where bits of flies and pigeon feathers are trapped in the glaze. I feel historical and wary knowing this psychic planted image will wiggle with a targeted energy later.

Because of course no image is meaningless, no collage just a quirky mélange of texture and form. It carries capital value, capital buck. Even the superficial skins on advertising are one way or another paid for by everyone and if you don't buy the product right there on the spot, your mothers or fathers or children fall over themselves to make the transaction later and where are you then but culpably implicated? It's a conspiracy of magic.

Bowl and box (storage)

The doors were open and my standards low.
The walls indigo blue with painted eyes and snails.
Four purple exits and *ho, workers, we'll be watching!*

People with dull skin or bad nails or both were eating doughnuts with sugar crusted onto their faces. There was jam on their desks. They'd really gone out and drenched their souls on curves. Between twenty different box sizes and twenty different room sizes and twenty different tape colours they were busy alright, these prehistoric lumps, orbiting the gassy skin of my outer space.

They wore great swathes of fabric to hide sex and sin: bodies half covered with dust sheets. Actually there was dirt up to their necks and everybody slapping to keep the collars down. It was a miracle they could work at all, looking like they had tumbled blindly into urinals or custodian sinks and found run-off not water.

They were blue and yellow patches, shorts and shirts, everyone keeping time with the cosmos, checking the sky for a signal. Except you couldn't really see the sky proper, the trodden blue kind of sky all trotted out with the marks of morning. These were unruly walls built from looped music, with call-waiting and its lines and their rhythms shaking foundations. This was a perforated world shadowed with sienna. A storm of words and printed somethings meaning nothing to me, meaning I would buy it all, meaning everything.

There was no clock but a clearly visible sign that hovered perfect in graphic terms. A twenty-four-hour neon scuffed up with white paint that hand-revised the original four to a three, to a new twenty-three-hour accessibility. Margins of latitude, I thought. And all of it written out in a big wave of colour like a summer proof, rolling over red to yellow light to blue. Skin the colour of just-about living. That stoic neon. Discharge tubes and noble gasses. Pudgy glass hot-melted to a welded frame. A parody of conjoined hope and menace. Like the apothecarial snake around its heavy mortar.

And what did they do with that lousy sixty minutes off anyway? That hour spared. Time being something that we all troop around together in a circle, I wondered if in this instance it had sufficient propulsion. To move forward I mean. Everyone rustling around one after the other, the one in front holding the next's tail, plodding measured steps, and all spreading the same canker as they went. It was comforting though, to think that whatever they were selling would be available to me at almost any hour, if I ever chose to sleep or not.

The symbols recalled an astonishing capacity for anxiety: a mountain of bubble wrap, some cobwebs, so much paper. Something like nostalgia or death in the sound of a mosquito. And that mosquito with every minute beat of its wings broadcasting a kind of philosophy to the unresolved intellectual problems of the desk people. An impart of wisdom to treat their solid and semi-solid ideas the same way we treat sewage.

The depressed brain is a tapeworm with its lousy skill set of image rescue and recovery. Refracting ideas back across other ideas, it swallows authors and their hands, their keys and directions.

This storage centre blots it with silica gel moisture-absorber. Wraps it in paper and beds it in a box. The plan is one of architectural unease: everything is temporary, yet obsession attends it all.

I simply stood there with my list of boxes, their room origins and their sizes. Kitchen, bedroom, bathroom. I could have been processing life in a devoutly muscled way – like, believing in this service of self-improvement like I believe in religion. The apparatus of reality doesn't sugar-coat, but speaks plainly of desire and despair, dumping it all out on the floor. See everything exists in relation to the ground, true. But what of the personality's black hole? Or civilisation's red one, where the smith's anvil we've all been fashioned from is just floating around in some impossible undefined space? I seemed to be watching a primordial swell. Trapped in a whirlpool of endless potato salad re-runs.

Here, you, they seemed to say, *we offer some rapid eye movement from another lifetime away*: some sadness punched out into noodle boxes; whole rows of houses who shimmy to any rhythm; your very own personal effects fermenting so long and hard they explode on our storage facility walls. There are scalps and bio-hazardous material. Trauma, damage, residue. All of it packed up in polite white sachets, in economy boxes, in unicorn boxes, green moulded environment boxes, black casket burn-after-reading boxes, all of them distributed by couriers whose bad days are about to get worse. Everything is mostly grey-brown, some lemony paint and lifetime bonus contracts.

I wondered if every town was the same town, just in different colours. Or jam-packed with theatrical empathy ready to pump out for excited psychotherapists. This one anyway was feverish with faces. With sunshine flogged out of them and rainwater sopping from mouths down to soggy shoes and swollen white clam feet.

The employees seemed packed with joy as they wrote down assessment criteria – likes and dislikes – for all the people they spoke to on the telephones. Out with riddles or some woolly mythological mission. Their fidelity and constancy to the company was remarkable. Truly unbeatable:

Would you be A. happy in a hole or B. flustered by the irregularity? Would you steal from a gift shop or buy aprons for all the family? We'll throw in some gleeful plastic bits, branded of course. One month free, some sponges and all the foam chips you can use.

It was the echo of something specific. A raving language. Just syllables of sound strung together with spit. No more tender than a stone pillow. No more sweet than a brown baked pot of honey. No more salty than a spunk rag flung in my face. So much blonde hair and entitlement when really their ethics stank like a stagnant pond.

One yellow man is pronouncing too many vowels to hear properly:

Did you see the blue mouth? The tight mouth? The mouth so disinterested in forming the right shapes to deliver our company policy? That's right, our company policy: the freaking Christmas and holidays policy – we get your problems solved, your problems stored and order placed by Christmas and the holidays or you get your money back. The world might have its diaphanous policies, its other policies, but right here ma'am we're as legible as your everyday classic bold font type. Your bold font type and peppermint paper, all right here today.

There are instructions and anecdotes for the callers: how to store the pooped-out four-year-old condom that in the many days of its hibernation has grown legs and a sure facial resemblance; how to repurpose the crutches thrown down with eyelids upturned to God; all the packing methods based on family love and herbal practitioners with many ribbons or natural-fibre certificates to their names. The storage people have options on the call centre switchboard: replacement, reattachment, reassignment. That last one something about part-exchange. The handbook proposes some temporary solutions. The handbook that neatly adjusts itself annually to the complexities of modern life: the nuclear deal, mostly cardboard and bananas for the babies; the homosexual bi-monthly, with free re-issue storage keys, flat-pack options and corrugation; the deals for the elderly, the lonely; for the singles and their vast caves of emptiness, their vats of obscure poison and ovaries on ice.

The phones don't stop shaking. There's sober advice, then secular advice, then sacred advice. Different payment terms for the tanned Europeans and the rest with poor credit history. *Forget it*, I hear them say.

They're asking questions about climate control and padlock preference. All of it interrupted by plain barrier or blue barrier borders, with barcodes and manufacturer contact details in tiny serif font.

I heard so many traces of desire for pleasure mixed with plausible geometric arguments. As though it was so simple. The employees sat still and held the phones to say everything is symmetrical and not: that these are our parlances of war and escalation and war is always balanced when you're on the winning side. Shouldn't I know this from Chess, where the board is so quickly marked by the advantages of who-goes-first? Shouldn't I know this from marriage and the dictionary where some people keep letters from lovers, ex-lovers, under S for sociopath?

That's what you wanted isn't it? Is it? To set your family life on fire?

I really must insist on some quality control.
Oh just abdicate yourself. Abolish your good self, go on.

I'm not really *speaking* to any of them, sitting on my boxes raging, bound like a cheap detective to trail the sick and jot notes from afar. It's all in the head they say. This tinted population, anthropologically certified. Meaning they're all real people. Me too. And my life's clutter, my squeaking heart and dirty shoes.

But this place is surely a poor location for memory. Why condemn the junk of yourself to the poor emotional release of some reused boxes whose context at best centres on the deployment of unfulfilled potential, legions of dust and lunchtime jerk-offs in the shadows?

Can I get some help over here? I was under the impression that the genetic code had nothing to do with language. Must we always use the medium of language? In fact quite precisely pure sensation doesn't exist anymore.

Is it absurd? I hear them whisper.

I love it, they reply.

Pray for me, I say.

Must your hot itch

When you are a person who believes they are the nose of a joke – the butt, the armpit, the plain explicit asshole – when you are a figure untethered, you cling to the patterns of other people and are stunned by the collisions. It helps if the experiences are written down, plastered onto the walls like a ruddy fresco of figures and faces. If not, you forget and without these illustrations to remind you of the borders of real life, you'll be buried in the constriction of a heart that feels more like a deep narrow hole than anything designed to feel.

Sometimes I carry on weary old conversations in unreal parlours and sitting rooms. I look at my scrapings of stuff on shelves or stuff in boxes or beaten down to fluff on carpets and they don't fill me with any happy measure of comfort. All the items of distraction bring on delay, whilst tired and lonely there I go again, plodding along the beauty belt of each day.

Who needs a heart or a hand to hold it? There are so many organs you can technically live without – kidney, spleen, colon, stomach, appendix. Some people die. Sure they do. But parts of the lungs and heart can be hacked out and you'll still do fine. You belong then to a certain new world, one that moves closer to the curious immobility of death and is reckless and happier because of it.

When once I worked, one summer, and picked apples in orchards, there was a wispy old man who had virtually no blood left in him. His body was a shopping bag of bits, no fidelity of constancy with regard to organs. Not like those blue and yellow storage employees. But a shoddy body put together by surgeons, nuts and balls and a hemispherical bottom.

These experiences of other people make you attendant to your own self. To look at a man unwell reminds me that everyone is merely waiting, expectant and neatly dressed until the hot contortions of loving bring about feeling too huge to ignore. The imagination infects and cannot be explained by any of the common laws of things we know. I realise I want more. I have given things away. Look at the crushed paste of my skin, this sad pale face. Hasn't it acquired lucidity. Why always so negative?

When I returned through the front door without my boxes, admittedly to a broader range of spatial options and a deeper mistrust of my own emotional listening skills, the house was full of the sound of fucking. The upstairs characters: bodies bursting through themselves, out onto the floor, connecting roughly with the carpet, only a little dampened by its fibrous muffle, the atoms of their forms, all the chemical factions and motes of being in the room – I could hear them moving together. The sounds moved together. I felt caught in a knot of construction and repair, between people and building, between the idea that problem and solution are bound in the same mutual sequence. I felt rage and sorrow. Perhaps I had an understanding that the word for 'house' might equally be *lost* or *love* or *particle*.

There was little to hurl or poke up at the ceiling. I upended a plant, cracking its cheap plastic pot against the wall. I held the short dry sticks of its old stems and pounded the carpet with the same rhythm. I hadn't eaten all day. That great crunchy chicken came back to me. My stomach rolled. I wondered morosely if I could I solve the ethical problem of food simply by suggesting the vacuum of loneliness and voyeuristic listening was big enough to fill you up forever. The expanse of hunger and its ungraspable edges of emptiness being just another kind of inflation.

There I was in this crude vacant room, dashing back and forth from one dull corner to another like a ridiculous mouse, as though I was tethered to a little string swung enthusiastically back and forth by the couple upstairs. I felt reactionary. I felt like an erotic example of kinetic energy, held in by the noise above, like a pebble in a thickening eddy.

This listening to others was like having a companion's evening out. My very own movie night built from imagining the shapes of my neighbours busy fornicating in front of me. Their pleasure as my pleasure in an ironic demonstration to even plain-minded folk that my life, *hello life*, was about to shuffle off towards a big nutritional zero. A small body with adult feeling; my rhythms of exchange and the early evening smudged with that feeling. I only had to sit on the floor to be part of something larger than myself. Anyone could come padding down here with bare feet later in the night to claim me. I didn't even have to step aside any cardboard boxes to let the outside enter.

Somebody whistled and a door slammed. A flush. When the croaking voices upstairs sneaked back, I just knew it would get steamy.

MESSRS. EXTERNAL & WEARY

Rainbows

The social and erotic influence of sleeping in such proximate conditions to one's neighbours, of feeling the juggernaut snores of labour, the lengths of desire, the squashy pricks of pleasure or pain gasped by men and women being fucked out and away from themselves, that experience takes you through the fundamentals of rage: the white livid heat of hatred, its purity; the yellow-brown of evil, of the wish for fever and silence and torn skin on those you cannot see; the green fog of misery and all its clammy vapours; the blue of tolerance, ignorance, loathing; the pale drawn-out violet of acceptance that this boxed-in precarity is now quite simply your life with all its timidity, its frozen possibility, its frothy sweetness so fake you might as well be carved out of soap, glistening then gone, and suddenly your lessons from school flood back and no diagrammatic purity can make the rainbow seem like anything other than a fraudulent piece of shit because its spectrum gives you no scope for edit or causal adjustment, for nothing but fear and misery, and finally there is that rock-bottom colour of nothingness, of shame and sin, of a need to be held or touched for just one second and that feeling is so far away, so implausible, that colour quite simply cannot be fathomed. Colour has moved away. Life is a black-and-white dimensionality: breath in, breath out. Pupils dilate. That is the whole sordid barrel of humanness. Its ugliness, its smallness, its holes and hollows. We have it all. And we have packaged it into cubicles with dusty carpets even dustier against the satanic sheen on these duvet coverlets. The rights and dignities of the criminal, the feudal bonds of family, the libidinous spontaneity of the bourgeoisies, the defecating mortals, the couples, the triplets of children and their mouldy mothers infested with life in all its flimsy sordidness. Quite certainly some people adjusted themselves long ago to dying an unusual death.

ETHAN

An occult alphabet

Once you wrote out *THE EIGHT THEOLOGIES* using an upside-down calculator. It was in encouragement of a locus of assembled paths; it was a breakthrough for us. We laughed, feeling sly and mathematical, at our crude attempt at belief, at making the *us* of you and me feel holy, with our legs twined together, grasshoppers at the breakfast table. I always felt something pressing against me, rising up, so replied to you quickly with *BOOZE*, then *BEES*, then *LIES*, clearly marking our relationship's shift from weak to strong. Strong as in naked, switched quick with the lights: on our clothes went, then off again.

Before you left and I generally wondered if it would always be so hard just to continue breathing, I had thought about making a sign to say your pussy tasted of sleepy greenery, advertising our cylinder of private – *scratch that* – public exaltations. But people are conditioned to find this dirty; it is by definition of no use.

So much terrible leisure we created for each other. You had high morals and me a low-cut top so we threw a mattress on the floor and left it there because we couldn't keep our hands off each other. And there it was: the apotheosis of our decorating career quite plainly those fine white walls and floors dabbed with clothing.

By absolute necessity we unstitched all the clothes in taking them off. Plain, lapped and abutted: picked them to scraps or ripped in French seams with raw edges. But we were still neat and lean: bodies like flowers unburdened by flesh.

I had first seen you in the supermarket, savouring your image as I yanked milk from walls of cartons banked in those enormous fridges. I tripped over my own tongue pronouncing simple kilos and cuts of fish. Just to get a word in. The afternoon we spoke, I crossed the street to get somewhere less soaked with light, less hot and vocal. My clothes were out of fashion and I was wearing two pairs of trousers, the legs thickened in a roll at the bottom. Other bodies swelled on past me, some stronger chins, baggier eyes, a few faces made up like radishes, ready to plant or eat or bloom. And I marched into you with your mobile phone held out like a gun and your body like a telephone pole. You were anyway moving ahead of the flag, ahead of people and packs, ahead of light, of communication. Or, in the wrong place at the wrong time, perhaps.

All the others, that woman a millionaire, that man a dentist, those mad kids, little breasted, draped on the stairs howling. All of them and I couldn't get you off my eyelids, a condition of recklessness: how obliging life is sometimes.

From your bed, the sky was so devoted. It hung evenly above us all. Evening wiped it, not entirely out, but towards a darker, more masking gauze. They say the earlier you get up, the fresher you feel. You said the older you get, the easier you'll wake. Not me. My emotional self was left clinging to a sleeping rock, poked at, laughed at until it was eventually prized free and flushed out into the woken world.

My own needs were too round, they rolled about; your fingernails were too square. Together our figures were an analogue of time spent. One hand holding the sand, the other letting it slip right through: on the left side, a pile, on the right, nothing. Biased scales. It all looked just like life.

We spent nights licking each other, or burning incense and using our fingers to draw pictures of weapons on our foreheads. The slapping of our lips was so wet the sound effects were all foley. We became master engineers. It wasn't a normal night view. Sometimes we lasted through till morning and woke with boredom and rage hammering to get us out of bed.

Day came in the shape of an unclothed miracle, a blue-green avalanche, a planet Earth. We watched television and tried to find ourselves on seen-from-space programmes designed to make us feel small. And at night there was us asleep with these planets in both eyes; with the sun in one, the moon, waning, in the other, us poised to tip over into permanent silence.

I sometimes woke up in a different part of the brain, eyes jerky with unknowing. There was a toy skeleton kept on a hook by the door, something you won, a little key-ring. It bobbed fiercely every time we came or went and I'd feel reassured in my condition of structural rearrangement, that the embrace of abandoned space could be countered with a *Thank God: see, we share a shape.* And then you'd speak from the pillow and I loved it: how broad your voice sounded, full of information on tax models and big tits. Your interests kept me from humiliation. Thank God for words. Thank God for dust, our communal remainder. How much softer could the dust get? How much more useful? More diverse? More, *dusty*?

Sometimes I wondered if this life were just a prototype for the next and all the fumbled moves, the paid rents, the dressing indifferent to reason, were just steps made towards building a delicate structure yet to be inhabited. A testing of what allowances might be made for difference. Something like a syntactical form of mitosis, with each article of speech, each pulling of the bathroom plug, each lunch and breakfast in bed, all of it only a comma in the great future run-on unfolding.

So I look back at that immeasurable net we created, with things passing in and out; our windows perfect aquariums. Night plants quaking on the sill. I don't regret it. And now the world again is a needle, a barometer stuck straight up. And what flexible furniture I have here, what shivers of terror.

Farmyard pH

The newspaper this morning says the world is full of good news. Great News! *Big News*, it says. News that makes my dry brain feel a little less tethered to itself. News that makes me feel better and worse about being alive today. It always makes a sour sense:

An elderly man dropped dead from heatstroke and his head was quickly devoured by his dog; a young grocer was mauled by bulls whose intestinal system was gutted by their horns; a woman was murdered with a pitchfork by her wife; a sixteen-year-old who, after throwing her newborn into a fast-flowing river, jumped in herself with a sack of stones around her neck; the outdated car-making machinery in a Mississippi factory tore the thigh and collarbone clean off one of the company's longest serving employees; a choir of forty teenage boys, all stabbed to death, supposedly to preserve their honour; a whole province exploded into a shrieking chasm by the extrajudicial bombing of overseas administrations.

I seem to find myself here over and again: an unhealthy shoulder slouch, back against the window. Gargling with the news and so many international people losing bits of themselves. All the publishers of the papers ensure that everybody is richer, more complex, more full, half dead because of it. Somebody half dead everywhere. *Made sure of.* Gone off across the sea leaving a wake of profanities and a heroic photograph.

It all reminds me that revolution is slow but technology accelerates. It reminds me that I don't feel naturally. That we're all basic people internally chopped up with ten perspectives and a short scenario of difference. Like blind people who can see. It reminds me that it is the newspapers who gush with the kinds of crookedly curving facts that permit me to look straight ahead, with alternating hells, breath and patience.

I catch glimpses of ankles and knees as they hurry past and I think: is my own body still so essential? Is there so much difference in the doing of feeling and the feeling of feeling? It is true that it is quite something to feel the invigoration of a singular and imminent personality, but with behaviour and feeling stored in the skin at surface level, it is equally nice to feel unencumbered, quite unidentified by any walk or stride. The newspaper spreads out across my thighs and slips crumpled to the floor.

I'll sit a little longer, conscious now that in thinking about walking, my feet will be conspicuous. Like a visitor in a new town, looking both ways when they are crossing a big road, like they are shaking their heads in confusion. Left, then right, then left again.

My breath hits the window as I look out, hands in my armpits. A slice of breath, a slice of breathing just like the quarter hour on the clock, fifteen minutes of respiration and you can cut the breaths into pieces as well, with their tick and their tock. I am a warm machine who smiles openly with large teeth. I am a fucking human being.

Time today is making itself known. All the little cars have moved off the road for a funeral parade which passes by with its sorrows spread out black on black against the tarmac. The sun is as bloodless as the corpse, fish limp, no rays to shed and the coffin, tight-wrapped at the head of the herd, leading its way to church with tears and soon soil. I can feel the heated silence of all the brothers wrinkled in their wreathes, dark hair and neat suits and everybody making stabs at private agony with their collective thoughts on suicide and premature loss. I watch only partially obscured through the curtains, barely moving, feeling my sleeves tight about my wrists and the steady pulse of blood through the sheared skin on my finger.

Perhaps I am alert today more than usual. I notice how the same leaves roll over the same puddle. And a cat in its dark shine, new visitor, stops to lap and look. What's in the air for us today kitty cat? It doesn't matter, there is no matter to air, only organisms clinging to every surface that care little what we eat or in which direction we travel. There will always be someone somewhere passing by.

The day has barely started but what are the statistics for this evening? Television and a pie with American territory. A pie with dark meat, perhaps, something to do with unmatched emotion.

Animals can help. To give you a sense of scale. The ones short of breath, sort of despondent and therefore loveable. The snakes, the rabbits, the ants, the sheep, none of them pets or vermin. When the formation of local centres with all their gongs of scandal and newspaper garbage pound too heavy, the countryside offers its relief, its positive outdoor space. Consider it a pastoral tonic.

After my fretful days with the newspapers and so much misbehaviour from the neighbours, after all the deaths, the births, the marriages, I sensed the crossbones practically strewn across me. That is, I felt devoured, unwell, rumpled. And with the use of drugs and creams and pharmaceutical sprays having no effect other than prolonging the fat sizzle of my anger, I decided: I will hop the night train for pastures greener.

The goat I encountered was grey. I encountered him with sadness, with a certain geological curiosity, wondering in my clean trousers how skin could grow such a crust. Out back of a shed, with the rats and mice and carrion crow.

The goat was happy, I thought. There on the floor, scrabbling amidst beetles and earth, sucking calcium bars and sculpting his own pillar of salt. Warm air hugged the ceiling. A lick today, a few more tomorrow for the rest of his life and all the ample solvency was there – straw, sugar, water – to judge pleasure distinctly attendant.

I was jealous in a way. The goat a graceful cod, trafficked in his own happy language. King of his own garden, attended only by the ills of goat variety: bloating, cystitis, foot rot and pox; or a chewing on everything around until lymphatic problems or abscesses wiped him out. The sensitivity of the modern man is synthetic, I decided.

I sat on a bank to eat, wagging my own tail as I unwrapped a tin-foiled lunch of bread rolls spanked with sauce. Some boiled sausage. Cheese, mostly Cheddar. Birds around cheeped their sweet dumb song, flew down to nibble near my feet. Beholders of pine and pride. The good smell of nature filled me. The gorgeous slushy sound of it, *delicious*, was a froth on my ear, my lips.

What had I been expecting to witness alone in an unmarked field? Had I hoped to catch onto the half-hidden parts of my metropolitan self and midway between a gentle breeze or some wild flowers go about the futile pretension of explaining my place in the world? It smacked of nostalgia, of déjà vu, yet I seemed there without explicit point or purpose, without even a raincoat to keep me dry when the laughter sky opened up its mirth against me. Outdoors there are few built structures to back against. But was I afraid of rain, of a little water? I was never afraid of thunder or rough headlands, but rather social drinkers and garden parties, of those who heard all I said and remembered.

MESSRS. EXTERNAL & GRASSY

Spirit levels

We have noticed that all the real estate hoardings around this city have names like medieval warlords. Or Anglo-Saxon tribes. Bloated businesses marshalling their warriors not back and forth across battlegrounds, but up and down scaffolding like neon-clad mites. Instead of illuminated texts they just flog up coloured hoarding offering asset management and new growth.

The art of construction has been claimed to be the only true art, an art currently deployed by the mathematics of machines since the human spirit is currently too clammed for acts of such deviant delicacy.

Nobody builds well anymore. There are no ruins in bluish stone. There are few innovative young things who knock boxes of matches to the floor, noting their curiously patterned post-tumble intersections, and without striking fire just following the spark of simple exuberance and earnest goodwill there and then devise new timber-frame joints for beautiful houses full of light and uncannily still like a mysterious but elegant forest. People don't do that. The ravishing inferno of ideas has, well, died back a little.

Instead our surface pathologies are layered over:

crazed love slaves and adulterated best friends are almost visible but carefully not quite behind PVC windows, cardboard and glass. Who even takes off a shirt without the curtains tightly pressed together? Nobody wants to blind or interrupt the train and car passengers with their mostly flabby and startlingly white flesh.

And behind it all there are people everywhere, busy shucking incidents like shucking corn because the propositions are too difficult to understand and it's easier to clean a surface than down in the cracks. Lay down flat something hard to process and stick something else on top, that's one method. If you can't see it, it's not really there. Forget the tautological death drive to tidy your home, let alone your mind. So *screw you all* we say, and watch as the grass continues to grow pleasantly over it.

What we mean to say is that we bury in plain sight.

Ethan didn't know what he'd do with the spades. You must clear a room before laying a floor. He is a floor man. The dust is supposed to settle, the furniture shift aside, but it is not work for spades. He has his hammer, his measure, his glue. He has powdery shadows that move with him as he works through the light. The two spades lean against the wall by the yard, giddy uprights and the space between their handles a blur, a hole in which he sees the great rough nakedness of maleness. It feels like the most private part of him, the alibi of gravity simply holding everything up whilst the memory of a rough tongue in his mouth all but breaks him open. Is there reassurance that the world of desire might not be recast from words, but made of language in the first place? All that thirst and ambush. The violence of aphorism teases him: nothing is broken, and yet.

The woman next door is new. She pushes her breasts through the fence towards him, threading weeds against the paisley of her smock. It seems she is the only one who hasn't heard. It seems he is happy in the disguise of beginnings. She is no more a lover than a loaf of bread. She looks like a greedy horse all shiny flanks and he laughs to imagine feeding her a carrot. A fine head of broccoli pressed between her lips. We can be cruel. But we see them both wondering about the other. Ethan mostly if she can draw any sense of immodesty from his house, smell an event in his character, an absence or recklessness. It requires a paralysing excess of focus just to say hello. It fuels an animal part of him. He pisses on a sheet of bubble wrap before the door just to hear to the quick continuous slap of liquid. The excess of sound awakens something. Not a welcome mat anymore.

PATRICE

Divining the dog

I had thought the rights and mysteries of two legs might be explained to me by heralding four into the house.

The first dog died.

I scanned the sea for months for what never returned. Marching out a daily widow's walk: high trees, brown canals, thoughts of a certain lighthouse. Uprights and horizontals. I lay on a dark bed waiting for the sun's abandonment, but knowing that dogs don't like the moon, there were never any howls, or panting. Crouched waiting by the open door, I longed to smell that dog's steamed breath, his incense stink. I willed the return like one wills the rain in drought.

Instead I improvised. I stacked a perfect wad of coins into a four-legged pile. Some herbs for furs, dried out like marijuana in foil and scotch tape. I promoted myself after naming everything correctly and remembering all the right contours of personality with their character shapes and translations. Dog: Hello Dog. World: Hello World. I wrapped and poked everything together in happy semblance of the real thing, like they do in nice restaurants when foil and swan merge characteristics in encouragement to enjoy your meal with a static and taxonomically bad-tempered avian. A bad little birdy.

The friendly postman with mail, with friendly mail, would arrive clanking the letterbox, bumping the door. Notices from the bank piled their heft on the mat and I felt both brave and grim enough to push the whole pet thing out of mind, to kick the constituent parts to the back of my wardrobe. I judged my external displays of melancholy inartful; I was not an artist.

When the second dog died I gave up improvisation. My coins anyway were spent and I had little disposable *matter*, just a tin of raw tobacco and my almost-country walls with their lichen making faces and haircuts, so many shapes in the wallpaper. I had little surplus, only the sea and my slim sliver fingers. My dogs, my lost dogs.

I know I know I know it's all generally speaking and I didn't actually go for walks, so I sat as I might have done before, looking at the scenery of mud and lifestyle fragments. *What kind of man will you make?* I whispered into air. *Can you flit from side to side without stopping? Make five cups of tea with few leaves? For now you are silently crafted in this perfect grotto.*

We only know shadows are purple because the Impressionists insisted. They made paintings that reinvented what was right in front of them. I tried to join the dots between my present self and future self in a more productive manner. I ironed and rolled gymnastically on the bed. I tried to stretch out time with realistic suction, to fill my own days with better light and importance, with an image of sunlight in mind. I wanted intimacy, not its decline.

I made a home for woodlice inside a Bic lighter. Eggs refused to crack for me in shapes other than the geometric outlines of their provenance: the country boundary lines of Kent, of Wales and the Scottish Highlands. I was tormented by detail. By questions of providence and arrival. By banality. What to make of all those polysemic marks, black on white, meaning nothing to anyone?

There were not enough visitors in my lunar desert. My miserable apartment. My falling down house. My own emanating vibrations were not strong enough to turf up even a small rivulet of town dwellers. My lunch friends piled out excuses about dealing with snails and ant infestations. The carpenter and the sister-in-law or the niece who's chairman of the committee were sometimes around, but not really. The plumber. The bin men. Even the decapitated neighbours kept away. I broke things only to lure people round to fix them. My hands grew dirty in incandescent light.

But the sea was ever there. Geographically: from the canal to the river to the sea. The bridge to the train and the trio of vanishing cows down the lane by the little house. Even those cows and their calves disappeared, possibly something to do with continental customers begging for pink veal. The restaurants in town filled with tourists on their knees for a gob load of Ponzu Angus. For the widespread acclaim of our local Beef Shorthorn. It wasn't confirmed by any of the tabloids. But the milk would be good, I thought. The milk.

And the canal and the caves strung with rope and kelp pods: they were always there. And inside I had my building newly crafted like a den wrapped in light, with my shed of thin metal a pastel blue tint and a rhyme for the waves and ships, even. I built bits into my house like a still-life, with all rooms separate buildings: I lived the experience of an orange, a water jug and a fish head. Me and the smell of old dogs, and the new boys and sometimes girls.

Weekends slumped by. The postman stopped knocking his secret knock and the hazy shadow of his hand grew quicker in the mail slot. Sometimes naked or in my clothes I spent hours in the bath, losing track of the congruence between thinking and feeling, hot and cold. Occasionally I would wrest an insipid sponge from between my legs and lift it to trickle over my contemporary head.

Most people's reference to water is general. Wet. Cold. Blue. Most people's reference to snow is general. Just snow. White. Cold. Covering. Many people think the same of their bodies: quick limbs, hot, unhealthy. I didn't make an effort with mine.

I've learnt to find the positives in the negatives. Modern violence. Ha! Isn't it just so modern to refuse the meaning in action? It's true: I simply refuse to limit my personal definition of what it means to feel love. Instead I authorise hope, becoming well-practiced in the art of excavation. Got busy hands, will do! Burning off summer mould and sweat; burning candles burning gas.

You see I no longer have use for real horror because my own skull is steamed. I have my own perfect stew-like dribble of ideas and oak trees, all of them crusted over with fungal fruiting structures, with honey-coloured mushrooms and their caps slimy after rain. That is what a modern brain looks like: lesions and boulders with toothpicks jabbed in the sides. This is modern life lived as a lost dog or one beetle fighting another for its ball of dung.

Nothing escapes the conditions of matter. The world has an obsession with taking up space by having volume. Not even the fish escape it. Not even memory escapes it. All the time past scenarios gather themselves together in reunion. Gathering seasonally like bacterial leaf scorch. Like Gypsy moths and spittlebugs ferrying shoestring rhizomorphs to bark and roots. In mid- to late summer leaves are wavy, reddish green along the margins, then white with foam. The brain is happy, sedate. The brain is soaked in ozone. It doesn't need to think. Then come the Oxytetracycline injections from a professional arborist and eventually the tree dies. It's chopped to pieces and handymen mulch the stumps. The brain switches to silent and we think about turning off the lights.

MESSRS.
EXTERNAL & ANIMAL

Café calling

A dog walks into a café. It is late afternoon, something like June or August, and the sunlight coils snugly over everything it touches. Sugar looks like value. The waiter bounces between tables asking who owns the dog. Nobody owns the dog. We are the dog. A colloquial equation of fur and legs and heat that sticks us together in a form to be stroked. We might bark excessively or buckle our legs to sneak a sausage dangling from fingers. Our heart is torn. Between sentiment and satisfaction. Because nobody owns us and we are the dog. We whimper and walk outside.

PATRICE

Time

The fourth dimension of time. I would trade anything to have been there in the beginning, with the stoics and their wild grey hair, their eminent noses and strong chins assigning the numbers and atoms to everything. Their logic was a neat envelope, never general, never far from an empirical outcome. Never something like desire, all hot and runny. I would have jabbed irritably at the air with blunt instruments and burning sage. I might have spoken fervently as I folded and unfolded my arms and pointed up and down, forcing a move towards a classification of time more plastic, not flattened by continuum but meaning something specific to all of us.

I do often have it on my hands, time, a touching off of seconds on skin. I've made toast and other arrangements. The crumbs are testament. Used one or several loaves to overthrow ontology. I've spread jam relentless and bored and not the slightest bit hungry. In the kitchen, the bathroom, every corner of my home, there is time weeping forever on my thighs. Yeah, time thickens: time fat at my face and towards my ungodly waist.

All that kicking around in slippers and soon enough the flusters and disoriented squeaks yield something productive. Especially on carpets with no-longer thick pile, a little condensated with damp, my carpets with their specks of dust and chaotic crystals of other house garbage, whose newly high-moisture dendrites also squeak, like snow squeaks when you step out on it afresh, those carpets don't just silently compress: they give back. When you observe things at nanoscale and are compelled on slouch-shuffle operations across the house to a frequent and possibly deliberate stubbing of the toe – in these conditions the possibilities for ground-level discovery are very large indeed.

In a book filled with graph paper I have found a page full of red lined heart drawings. It was under the carpet, the book, and their arcs – the hearts – are a perfect smoothness, not rough like a compressed extraction, but sweeping and precise. The book tells me they are cardioids, mathematical curves that produce heart shapes. I cannot think where it came from but I wonder if there is something in this discovery. All these baroque semi-circumferences exude a kind of unspoken yet compelling rationality. They take the abstraction out of feeling. It is possible, I think, to poke and squeeze a polyester cushion such that it too resembles a lovely heart and the terms and existence of this heart can be parametrically and with little fuss defined with algebraic function. The hearts of maths: you could put them on a mouse pad. Just more rolls around an identical circle, like the world and its maps and blood all caught in my throat's pulse.

I am, then, the newly merry creator of a less pessimistic system. I can throb gay good cheer. It only takes a little flexibility. Me sitting here, toes, abdomen, follicles – beginning, middle, end – all undergoing change.

MESSRS. EXTERNAL & WOODY

Glue

Today he is working a floor in a large house and something four legged approaches to sniff his crotch. It won't let him go. The glue, curing. He doesn't mean to get aroused. And suddenly he needs it so badly he locks himself in the bathroom and masturbates. He studies his own imprints on the window where he wipes himself away, imagining the refractions like assessing distance, as though through touching his own face on the glass he could measure the infinite. Turning the handle he smells his own salty scent rise off his fingers and panics. This is legislation appearing, the terrible twang of his own paranoia, how his face alone must be covered in signs. A bottle by the basin says *thick original bleach* and he almost takes a capful in his mouth just to feel simple, eroded. His t-shirt is pale blue and how his body must sing out of it, wild and twisted.

Packing his tools away, the flutter-pattern of the wood grain steadies his heart. He feels like he is witness to a gruesome scene and yet the room is clean, new floored, wrapped around by the quick music from somebody's room upstairs. Even the song now could be a nail in his jaw, whining up and down.

Outside it is so hot. Every minute some new bird swoops across the sun, bees sliding down the air, dry bodied, unable to escape the weather. The fabric of his clothing indexes his body to the house and we see thoughts seeping from his skin: *I could stand inside a freezer and never open the door again*. All the wild elaborations of nature are soiled and slow.

He must remember to wear shoes stronger than sneakers for this crossing and re-crossing of his city. His steps are short, closer to gardens, pinching here and there a piece of leaf and crumpling it to dust between his fingers, hands against beige, against canvas. Those greens would become exhausted in the air anyway. If his pockets were organising information, they do it quietly. Maybe cold hands in warm weather mean something. He is heading home. As he waits for the train he watches a mouse get electrified on the live wire and it feels good.

PATRICE

Cherries, newly

Having not for nearly a week, I dressed and tried to eat with composure, me with friends and our intimacy gradients flushed with colour because of our closeness. But the shortest route from our parked cars to the kitchens had proved long, and finding everything then shut up, closed with curtains down, the feeling of loss hung huge. Our empty bellies rang out, pierced the air before us. Some girls adjusted their belts and stared sadly at bins which spilled bananas or potato rind. Time had withered leaving our pedestrian precinct rolled over with weeds.

Being hungry, we weren't sure how to deal with the hierarchies of open space. We were near the forest, on its edge, and keen to lean in and say goodbye to our disappointment at the town's commitment to our appetites, we felt urged to walk through trees and try our luck on the other side.

Perhaps there will be ancient inns, I thought, those of low walls and trellised walks or teenager's private entrances. All those terms of use and privacy that make a general positive experience of space. We could all see a vein of smoke some distance ahead and with our eyes thus charmed in the imagining of rolls hot from an oven, charmed by the possible crack of scorched yeast bursting through crusts like bark splitting in cool air, thus charmed with our pupils hugely dilated, our saliva was thick and our feet were willing.

Whatever we found, we were hungry, and knowing that smart girls love each other we felt ok about the psychological transition from street to soil.

I knew that in the forest there were certain rules of foot. Certain changes of surface or level. Like leaving your house via the front door and feeling the transitional sound of carpet-becoming-concrete ripple right through the sole of your shoe, through the muscles of the leg and into the memory centres held for *pavement*.

In the forest the wings of light thinned down by the trees are different to the light that carves volume between the houses in town. The slipped discs of sunshine feel obscene. They feel obtrusive. The light says something new to animals, to grave-sites and holy ground. Chirps and cries that sound rogue and rouged in the bright AMs shrink volume in the PMs, dying softly in bushes of heather.

My friends and I were prepared. We knew green areas before had accommodated bonfires and carnivals. We knew the city too needed its dreams, its premiums, and so we set out walking, our feet patting rhythms of restoration and repair. Our hands that did the dirty work receded.

Knowing that all city humans are tethered to ritual, I was prepared to feel a certain sharp separation from self when the loop of local roads ran out. That snuffing-out of central highways with their black velvet wrapping and shaking would lower our diction to darkness. Were we the first human landmark? Our skin, our soft cells and compositions exposed to new air, might scorch. I expected face-sore feral folk. Figures who'd clap hammers on our heads if we stepped out of line or sprayed city lumens too freely about.

I was used to this game. My empty days had primed me and I could feel my fat pouch of stomach ripening, could practically taste the steaming bowls of clam and roasted birds I saw inside the hypothetical me on the other side of the wood. I hoped for cosy berries in flabby tides of cream. The soft smell of new strained cheese. There would be a house cluster or a row house or a cabin house, some public house all warm with food to welcome us. There had to be.

We had left our cars long behind. If we'd had horses or dogs they would have trembled. Or fallen down dead right there and then, wicked shrubs spiked on the ground to cool.

The forest had other plans for us. Its solution for our hunger was to widen it. The woods whispered to us. The wind fed sound and matter through our faces, down our ears, our arms, our legs. Our organs flinched. We walked our bodies out of the sensation of walking. We became greater than ourselves individually, sparked by a new kind of core that took our *human*, that took our very personal *alive* and made it something other. In a roundabout way, we were completely lost.

Waking muddy on the road, varnished by ice and maybe rain, my brain was a steaming clump. The night would have come and gone and I could read nothing of its beautiful arc. I knew little more of the health of the planet, the monochrome dimness of the polis, the regions, the communes, the law of Earth's people. Deciphering space is not a horizontal motion when you are lost and wedged upright in a muddy hole. My friends lay scattered around. Some moaned and hugged their knees. I still saw smoke and our shoe marks running out intense spheres of exchange. What a sight we were. Tissues and dead phones on the floor.

French bun, plaited wraith, burnt anchor twist, cemetery, colonnade, victim, dairy pony, red robin, high bob – you can usually tell what century you're in from the haircut. My own hair fell around me uselessly. I remembered the shape of my face before I remembered my name. My postcode before my birthday. I remembered the birds who watched over the garden before I could even grasp the gender or age of my own children. My children? Were there children? I felt rotten, uncomfortable. Pale enough to make terminal all woodland animals.

MESSRS. EXTERNAL & HEAVING

Dust

She has found herself once more. On every tile are things arranged. In a vase, a twig. Patrice is skilled in the frequency of fractions, the hydraulics of motion and nature. She is neither plump nor pained but searing with the clarity of a dolomite.

Her big problem is getting all the dust off the floor, out of the joints and crevices. She's damp-mopped thirteen times today and still dust; used the ShopVac, mopped again: dust.

Look at the slim stalks of her ankle, washing herself softer, more lean. It's like she's churning over butter with that body of hers, dreaming of all the French kisses still to be made, here or abroad. She has been here for many years. The dust never leaves.

Time can be so ill mannered! Those passing minutes that twist the nerves. Those pudgy mornings that scare the fox out of its hole. The bracing from brasserie to boulangerie: bake the bread, balance the books, bathe the baby. We are here and we are gone: as shooting stars erupt and lightning forks its charges; as sunsets crescendo their most absurd crimsons; as envelopes are licked, cigarettes lit; as grey boulders slip from muddy hills and dusty logs of ebony splinter and burst into flame;

as everything is, always and forever, somebody somewhere is punishing with refusals.

Ethan is watching through the trees like a big male child. Like a man who started wearing cardigans to dim the visibility of his garrulous urges. He can see quite clearly by the way she wields a mop that she's really leapt the barriers of audacity.

Patrice is taking the cobwebs down; she's talking to them. Perhaps she knows we're watching. What she's doing there with the duster, her soft accord, the pearly string that beats against her breast – she is fitted with elastic! Her arms, those legs – an all-over caress! That little apron – what's it covering up?

In the garden, the flowers are full. The greenhouse stocked and heaving. The night-blooming cacti, for just one night, bloom en masse together. Their flowers are white, sometimes ringed with pink or custard yellow. Like ideas sprung at the moment of orgasm, it is a moment impossible to revisit – they are there and then they are gone. Unlike dust which is here forever.

Ethan has thrown off his hat. He is crouched and rolling, enclosing moving motions, humble spit, bushes creasing, spirits cursing, cracks squirting, legs trembling.

Patrice empties her mop bucket over the steps, dislodging some chips and mud. Slender whirlpool. A portion of sky is reflected back, a spreading turnabout of ups and downs and orientation. She feels close to the fluid Earth and its oceans. She loves water. In times at the beach she carries her milky way of thinking with pride: she throws her head through the waves and screams *I love you* into the salty howl. She's addressing herself, determined, casting out a net through that basin of blues.

They have seen policemen together. They have consulted the law and paid for its lines. They have discussed relationship scenarios using words with vowels so long they stretch out beyond the circumstance of their understanding. They are hypothetical. They are rotten cods. Their cheeks are wet and ripe as cherries.

These people will die and recourse to water eventually. And what is a body anyway but many barrels of grass and algae and organs? All stacked and puffy: tubby pillows with sallow hairs.

We Messrs. think differently about death. Of the philosophical space that flanks our before and after in asymmetry. Could we have lived earlier, longer, better? Some people die from cerebral bleeding or lice infestations. Others are knocked down by Great Danes, by laundry trucks or wind. Some prolong life with warm loaves or the bitter and pithy sanctions of their own will. Some are buried in forests, near houses. And some will be bludgeoned so finely to death that even their own wives and daughters gasp at the grave.

The wind now is a chorus, some notes, the key. The house is neat with its hedges, no loose brick or stone to rain down on anyone. There is a flag wrapped around a pole on the porch: a navy dark sky splattered with fireworks hangs above a harlequin tablecloth, red and white. The diamonds point north to south, merging on the horizon, left and right, with two triangles of green. Green, we presume to be grass. On the picnic cloth is a wicker basket and a baked pie with one slice missing; both the pie and basket are filled with the same flat monochrome ochre. The deep deep colour of fury it seems is burnt brown or brown-yellow, not red as we had assumed.

ETHAN

Specific antibodies

My trousers are ripped and my knees scratched. I feel a few inches less adult. The glue under my nails feels hard and sore, my head awry and drifting. I have drunk too much. I can smell myself and I am hard with pity. I call for arms. I call for troopers and the European academy. I call for gravity and sage winds. I call upon the boiling sorceress Nobody Home Tonight. I call for my darling contemporary daughters. The shape of my body in these bushes is one I can only describe as pulled from dark scenery. Even the leaves seem languorous. Bone and marrow of the past collected in the same figure. My twisted hands are tied.

MESSRS.
EXTERNAL & SULTRY

In a fool's coat

A steaming mulch of timescales, of temporals – what do you call them? Modes? Lobes? Fictions? One moment there's him running down the stairs, coat flying, pores breaching, and the next he's hurtling back up again, round the banisters with such exacting eloquence you'd think he was tracing a snail's shell.

But *timescale*! Is this where we're at? This not knowing your ass from your ears, your coming from your going, downright silly with psychiatric scripts or rotten with sickness so phonetically complicated it requires several hyphenated breaths and pause for salivary replenishment. *That* kind of time confusion?

We told the wife so much.

Patrice, Ethan needs his sleep. A sleeping board not a drawing board, we said, and *look at yourself, vice versa,* we said, at which point we figured we'd reached an interstice for the evening, flushed as we all were after pushing mushrooms up and down the sides of plates, attempting camouflage but eventually just letting them soup in the middle, brown and conspicuous. And wine. The spice of much wine. Sodden with wine. Our faces were flustered from the boil of glucose, a new plateau at the gut meaning our own buttons were inclined at any moment to untether from their holes. And because opposites attract as they do, we leaned all of us towards the wall, it cold and calming against our tremulously heavy heat.

He'd run up and down all night, Ethan, sometimes jumping down with near hymnal imploring. Even against the racket and the semi-solemn threat of suicide nobody was blind to the rising sight of his wife's tits behind her top, the foul gems of her nipples miraculously appointed escort to the seams of her t-shirt. The otherwise chaste and involuntary seams of her t-shirt. How *couldn't* we notice, what with our horror of the unspecific being so root-tied to topography, to bumps – the whys and wheres of how they made their fall.

Some time after the pudding became background, we noted a prohibitive silence. A silence that in its vaulted thickness can only forecast something ruinous and unwelcome, and moving into the hall we fully expected to see Ethan, crumpled, neck all loop-di-loop in a perfect hyperbole of death. Instead we found the door flung open, rain sweating out a puddle into his abandoned shoes, trousers, underwear. His yellow rain jacket was gone from the hook. Two absences a doubling suggestion of lonely *and* queer.

What could we think but *socks in a shade of puce*! Them lapping at the floor, at the sweet *café au lait* of his pants like small scraps suddenly as big in volume as a whale. Who'd have thought that a pair of trousers so crudely empty of their warming form, so crumpled as an empty human shell, could look quite so horribly crucified. Crucified down and dirty on the floor. A figure in the swim of life and now this little bit of it not moving at all. There's a problem to get sorted we thought. And Patrice's sleeves bloomed and we hovered, our palms slapping their whacks into pockets, casually mashing our cuticles, nervous apologies ready to get started.

A twig flapped down through the front door, a mocking finger in the darkness. His absence and the lack of stair thumping was now as foolish as a deserted esplanade. All of it stupid and glorious. The heavens were no place to start: our eyes rolled and we saw our own selves watching.

From the doorway she screeched, squirting out breaths and cries scented strawberry and sherbet by dessert, deserted. And him, how funny, the deserter. The rain smelled like fennel and the night moon, squashed in its perch, hung crooked, a pleased smile over it all.

Oh Christ in a rowboat, Christ on a barge, Christ in the examining room, Jesus Christ, gargled Patrice.

We admit now that perhaps it was terrible to find her switch from natural conversation to unpolished curses moderately, no, implicitly arousing. That seeing her lift the withered brake off and away from her usual heron's poise, the peevish rescindment of her former state of linguistic honour, was quite as effective to us in the impulse department as baring her breasts. And we do not jest, for hazards of this streak, of this adulterous fire, often turn livid on the spot. Right then and there any one of us may have wanted to rip off her skirt and expose those miraculous white legs to the outdoor breeze.

PATRICE

Table of excluded dishes

What was I thinking inviting that man back into the house? An agreement between enemies. Thinking that food might be a ladder, that plates on the table might protect the house from harm?

I sat there stewed on wine and rage, pushing around on my pink cushions and feeling their zips pulse through my silk. Ethan did not sit. He thundered intent on ransack. He shook the ceiling. I sat clammed, fast understanding zip function as being linked to secret decision, as in to release, as in to urinate. I should have pissed all over him. That lousy beetle. His matted head. Instead he pissed on me. For all the words that could have fallen from my mouth, more fell from him. He set a fire and without waiting for the small hours, ran away into the night.

ETHAN

A kneaded clod

In English language the place outside the home is the outdoors. Out-of-the-door, to extend the definition laterally, and you can whisper goodbye to explicit symbolism, to the sensitive functions of entrance and exit.

Formally the outdoors is often an awful mess: symmetry in nature is vanquished. Unless you are wandering a maze manicured by a gardener of rigorous mathematical exactitude, a gardener who likes his bald head held and fondled by flowers and grasses alone, unless you walk a maze enhanced in beauty and geometry by generous light from the natural sun and the amorphous glow of many excellent greens together, unless you are walking *there*, then the general road, the pavement, the country lane or dirt track will be, no doubt, an unambiguously hazardous trial.

The outdoors is electric with propaganda. Great boulders appear delicious like lacquered hamburgers. Just sitting waiting, deciduous trees watch on, barely rumpled. There are whitish bushes in the sky and patches of lawn on which your croissant body feels newly puffed and folded. See, all this explicit persuasion to look around, means sometimes your eyes roam quite free of the brain. Quite detached and dreamy. And at night when the deep navy boils light to only a thin and disappearing line to run towards, then accidents, well, accidents happen.

Monster

The woman drove the road. Hideous, hideous how she did it. She wound down the window and screamed, *I DON'T GIVE A FLYING PHEASANT WHERE YOU'RE GOING GETYOURHAIRYPINEAPPLEOUT-OFMYRISE. MY EYES! MOVE IT!*

Hey there hairpin, I thought, I'm en route to dispassion too, are we really every second less alive that it's come to this? She screamed again and placed it out on the air. I mean, Christ, it just hung there, foul as a mood. That was the quality of her mood, insulting, making a nice model for general indecency. I partook in the horror, in the convenience of shorthand, raising my middle finger with an empirical experience of hatred.

Our humours were disarrayed. Bodies browsed and deserted, bodies packed with untold depths of poisoning from road and moon. So thin we all get. So hungry: *ain't life a breeze when the wind sighs for home!*

Her eyes looked dark in the extreme. Sodden black with anger and disgrace and her great comical bottom at the steering wheel. I raged at her with my own optical fire, burning boreholes, two upon two. Everything slowed down.

It was like how I'd stared into the too-warm lager only several nights past and only half noticed how it had ringed out my very present spokes of fury in beer suds along the tabletop. How spontaneous bursts of juice had escaped from the glass in the same way that acid escapes from the skin when peeling an orange. Rings upon rings and always liquids escaping whether you called for them or not.

I had left wearing little but a vest and my chilly sense of being a single citizen in the republic I currently thought of as *myself*. A republic that was loose woven and held no *you* within it.

There had been corrections and offences and we had re-established ourselves: we had agreed to meet, to try and put the busy bumps and dents if not behind us, then at least to the side for the time being. We tried to redefine space.

The hours that night had darkened off fast and when you greeted me, you greeted like velvet, crushingly professional and maintained. I wondered if you were happy, squeezed into those impossibly hideous shoes. And your tightly buttoned clothes all but screaming pheromonal psychopath. Marking en route a traffic-jammed heap of corpses on the pavement.

I listened like a good worm to your speech.

Made myself sure to misappropriate the sentiment. For you, I made myself a granular personality – the kind that without even really trying might drain away through the little rectangular slit on a plastic coffee lid.

And I knew as soon as you slipped to the bathroom and the traffic light outside flashed red reflections into my drink that I could put my lips to the same part of the glass where yours had been and see the greasy protein trace, faint like a moment's old fossil against the table cloth. And from then on my pints would never more be amber but a boiling red, a boiling red cock with its end practically glowing like a flashlight in the air. This was the heavy shriek of destiny and I knew it, beer drenched peanuts and all.

Because information and light often signal on similar wavelengths, especially in candlelight or traffic light when the romantic manifestation of signs flickers much slower and more carefully. These are the rules of reaction. And being a good follower, I looked at you to commit your shadow to memory. Awash in the hot red light and I wished to wither you like cut grass but alas you were here to stay.

So out on that morning pavement by the road I was easily drifting. A slender sky and eyes already fogged. With my head deep inside you and me looking everywhere but ahead: seeing and feeling everything, but also not really.

And then down on the floor, the pavement, hard down on the great whorl of brown tar. Tears or some other wet dripping from me like a little box of broken milk. Baked warm and hot in my own blood but comforted from afar by flowers who seemed to call out my name, kind as the oldest friends. And my poor head now a colour so ill-defined as to be white, as to be a kind of cartoon smothered with violent dots; a caved in new kind of purple flushed silly and blind.

It's funny that we use the word *artefact* as a platonic bridge between the literal archaeology of our ancestry and the more intangible filth at the edges of human manufacture because there I was, as implacable as dust on the lens. All those usually vacuum-packed body parts suddenly opened out, frantic in their millions as new dust. The scaffolding of my form powered direct to OFF by a weight heavier than my own. That fucking woman with her car mowing me down to hijack my physical self, just then so totally unaware of how it was supposed to work.

And before my lights went totally out I prayed: I had dissolved the taste of you and now again it rose with an acid bite to flood my tongue and gums with a miserable bile. Some solemn psalm:

For Jupiter's sake! For the daughter, the music, the prince, our headboard!

Maybe I mumbled.

Perhaps I sought to calm myself with an inventory of all the wooden things in my house: walnut writing desk, tulipwood penholder, sandalwood oil, books. As though the sensation of wood and its upright strength might impart something timeless and solid to me.

I was floored with all lights off.

One worthless junket ass and some speeding crumpled metal growing smaller as it ploughed through perspective away from its crime.

And there lay a soon-to-be-famous minstrel: me.

Somebody called for a dog, another for an ambulance, as scattered jerks overrode my limbs. What a pain in the liver, all that shaking out of alignment, liquid everywhere with an impressive crudeness of volume. Always liquids escaping, I've long known it.

The sky was so dark and wide. Minutes before I had seen what looked like a cardboard house on a balcony. Or a woman on a balcony, or some crates for milk upturned and covered with cardboard that also looked like a woman, there on that balcony. I'd felt the keen stare of an onlooker.

I lay still, flat like the cardboard, marked by a condition I now so clearly understand as material distress, visibly soft and waning with old rainwater. Everything, then, sad and *yes we depart*, soggy and vulnerable, blue and bluer as my bare wrists and ankles.

And so now I am here, in this bed and these sheets, crunchy with hygiene. And I peer out from a body that only days ago had been mine with all its plurality of shakes and direction.

The medical tendency is one that falls quietly, guiltily, beyond the patient's capacity. The system being a judge you could say, or a test to reveal the extent of one's own vision. *How to die well, how to live well*: they should hang it on the walls of hospitals. Empty reasoning really, when you consider how many lumps are scooped and spatula'd onto bunks, how many previous happy forms are reduced in only moments to livid bundles of not much at all.

I imagined myself quite the coarse vision: hands fixed and dead, broken off from my arms and articulated to suggest certain verbal subtleties. A posture of muted vanity and real weakness. I must have looked like I'd been boned bit by bit back together by a stonemason. Or a pork butcher in hobnail boots who'd been out and tramped across my fringe.

I see lasagne and plastic cups rolling by and I groan. You'd think the whole place would hear my generous heart pounding out. The compulsive and tyrannical scent of hot buns and scorched meat fat is nothing next to the quantity of food I would gobble down were things not stuck in my throat. They don't even offer a straw to my lips.

Next door is often a radio. I hear news and scandal. Memory swells and the medics puzzle over fluid levels at my veins. My crotch where I leak on every side. Who knew we were so full of cracks, such crazy glazing.

I hear the melodic beats of broadcasting. I hear of some principles of agriculture, some blemished women, blemished men and familiar boys. There is joke time, therapy network hour, and a questioning of the profitability of zinc supplements in brain cancer. There is global news, human affairs and the defending of some opinions. Am I missing goddammit the *perfection* in this situation?

And wishful visitors – there were fewer of them gathered here as the days lengthened, the aisle waning with use. And noise – well, it drifted off out to corners with the dust. Always a penny rolled off somewhere. Molehills for cleaning attention, grit and grain.

Those who stayed looked outside to the clumped grass and the neatly square resolve of light from our always-lit predicament. I had never before noticed so profoundly the difference between indoor hair and outdoor hair. How separated by the walls of a building there are ringlets of living hair sandwiched on both sides. Hair in nature is flicked about by wind and sneezes, making original beautiful moves that nobody scripts. Indoors, moulded into one's sick bed or guided by a heaving stomach, hair just simply *is*. It's parked in one place in that dreadful way it curls on the ill and straightens again on the deceased, as if pointing out that the elastic nature of keratin is no longer applicable to the afterlife.

I had for so long taken for granted the equal pleasures of sun or smoke and the dark tedium of night. I who might be slammed tight in a box any day now. They say that the blood of the sick dries up inside them. I was iodine all over, infection-orange and tangerine with my dreams of patterned paint straight from tins. The light in here: so bitter the way everything disappears behind it.

Oh that ghastly bull of a driver with her jersey leggings and melted chocolate scorched into the rolls of her pussy flab. I would somehow ensure that her descent and the slope down which she rolled would be neither gentle nor pricked with too few thorns.

It's easy to think like this when the pallet on which you lie is something like your own private Raft of the Medusa. To feel like that painting where most everybody died and those who survived practiced cannibalism and other hideous deeds. It's easy easy easy to rely on my most singular natural resource currently at hand: hatred. The stink of hospital blues turning yellow.

I remember again how prudent and good it is to make a list in times of contingency, so in solitude I hurtle without motion through common accumulations: American dinner sets, Worcester salad dishes, Canadian toilet sets, men's heavy pyjamas, gent's laundered shirts, patented union suits, French cambric drawers, handsome corset covers. So much modesty. Maps should be made of these things, if only to provide a sense of immediate orientation.

Perhaps I will be horizontal here for many unbidden days, a year in my private mind spent thinking about grilled cheese sandwiches or farm benches in polished woods. Jackdaws and rain. Things of velvety taste and touch, of drip and flight and warp.

If I could be more electric or savvy or mobile I might have sat and told you all: *Thank you for the nougat and the lovely (sad) books carefully wrapped with pretty stickers which I will enjoy crying over but also for the beautiful tulips which opened overnight and are lovely.*

My sad parents: I see them too acting a part, example humans wheeled in to crouch by my bedside in a gruesome litmus of emotion. Parents can always be counted on to manage the soggy outward temperature of one's personal demeanour. To sweeten the food for their children and teach us not to vomit at the sight of greens. How not to puke in the flowerbeds but wipe our mouths and carry on by. How to fear sex but go furtively at it in sleeping corridors.

Father and Mother, my closest progenitors. The Units. Solemn. Now sitting hooked preciously together. They look like nesting and courtship. Their speech warms the atoms closest to their lips and I am pleased to feel contact of some sort. *Is that vase a gift?* he asks. The organisation of their care is innate. My mother with her runniest of egg mayo and its dribbles down her chin; my father picking at pastrami on rye, a classic upright man straight down to the leathered soles on his feet.

Natural sweets

I dream of sleeping inside a hollowed-out white loaf with lots of same self, same sex, heartless passion and headless chase. A soft loaf with a huge loading bay for service vehicles to spirit away the dangerous crudeness of my limbs, these hands, my feet. The professionals ought to be able to examine me. Discern whether I am a newly glowing cherub with no morals out of line.

Dearest,
You don't want to hear the lament of my dreams. The tendency to list grey events unfolding in even greyer landscapes is a bore. Sure you'll hear of patterns of blood. Or blunt beheadings. You're

always keen for gore. Perhaps the notion is that lodged down in the folded creases of my duvet I've confused the word hatchet with wood complicating my culpability for trees and this paper and my ever-fogging ability to write things down as they happen.

Restlessly yours, E

MESSRS.
EXTERNAL & SUNNY

Open sky situation

It seems now clear to us that when the city smells of the sea rather than petrol and hotdogs it is because we are surrounded by sex and death. We are making maps to chart the progress:

A white dog next to a tree laden with white blossom sits in tepid light, crystalline.

A doctor skims his eyes over recent test results and reads a palm tree in the numbers.

At the grocery, aubergines in bags printed with their purple doubles produce texts for the unwritten world and its capacity for speech.

The nurse who practiced her own taciturn version of tenderness waves goodbye from behind plastic.

The psychiatrist, stiffer than protocol, explains how he wants to say something, that vernacular models and patterns of certainty might twist towards a new rude plasticity. That things might get fruity, blurred, emulsified, but it's all on file.

Humans have thirty-two teeth and twelve molars. The outpatient offers a mouth newly slimlined, lightweight, gapped. He walks on a curve, metal-pinned, repaired, eyes straight ahead. The life of the asphalt receives him, this figure who sees new shops with their un-bought buns twinkling in rows, fat icing and Santa waists puffed with cream.

That body kept his hands in pockets, fumbling the brass of keys and their heads like small cold potatoes. That body looked ahead to old women tapping out the stones. That body smelled men and children crossing over tramlines, wetting new paths on the paves. That body blew out a plume of smoke from his lips, a shock of violet air amid the features of a face, a train of smoke that with all its fresh atomic curiosity might have spelled out words: *Hello, I'm Ethan, how do you do?*

There is feeling then in everything. Every hairline crack is a great chasm to explore. To wound when fallen into.

PATRICE

Little mushroom

There is a teenager who sits at the bus stop outside my window every evening. I'm certain he's older. He is tanned, hair blooming on his bottom lip. As he sits at the bus stop, back and belly folded into thighs, his profile is so slender you can see almost entirely through him. Secret actions couldn't be concealed if he tried, his body more a sack of knots than a singularly angled wedge.

I think he is an allegorical figure, testimony to my period of transition. Maybe he smells like all night coffee or piss or granular egg. Perhaps there is bacteria in his colon, I cannot tell through the window but he signals unwittingly from the dusk like a balm for the seedy and dispossessed. The whole mass of his form throbs for attention. He's a page torn from a medical volume, illustrating the prolificacy of germs in an urban scene. A reek of chain-smoking and glycerine. I'm certain he could turn a profit with those good looks.

If I blow my own breath onto the window, the laws of perspective allow me to draw scattered arrows all over. I can draw a heart in the fog, shooting expressions in his direction that envelope him completely. It gives me a strange uncertain power. A kind of persuasive interruption.

Some other men are there too, busy out on the ramp getting low down drunk as a goose. I spoke to one once, hoping to catch the eye of that boy, but they all just sat there like sagging wood, ripe young bellies gone bad. One shouted: *What were you hoping for old crow? Giraffes drinking from a bloody fountain?* They laughed their big laughs but I was sure something flowed from the boy as I passed, a rivulet from a summit, a scent of coniferous forest.

I portray and refashion my own clunky desire to suit the hours. Right now he seems more like a little boat blown away. A light thing with his soft cap and rough socks.

He frequently just sits, sometimes with both hands down his trousers as air frosted by weather is warmed in bursts by traffic. I can sense the hot stream of information entering his body. Insistent banality pours inside. I wonder if a boulder was pushed down on him by friends and family, too. I wonder should I rescue him.

I think perhaps we might cry together and go to sleep. Or fuck in the garden with the lights off. Tear open the rambunctious hole of anal sex, toss him tartly off and watch as his invisibilities mix with soil and the twitching of my neighbour's curtains.

I mean I shouldn't, of course I shouldn't, but when the air inside your head is offensively polluted, things happen quickly. Caligula in his madness appointed his own horse to the Senate of Rome so why not go off breaking the routine and divisional barriers between girl and boy?

He's there now. I lay my head on the table listening to the amplified tremors of sound, flicking and stroking the wood. I imagine this is the noise his heart makes as it tumbles liquid through that small living chest. How I'd fold it carefully into my arms, happy as his form disappeared inside the warmth of my own frame. *Boy, young man, body of desire like body of water all fluid and rushing in*. In this way I try to keep living in the world. Perhaps he'd bring lovely orthodox candles over – thanks ever so – and my own emotional landscape, well, I'd leave that to be narrated by the firm hard voices of my neighbours.

ETHAN

Maltworm

My newly released self deserved more than a bumper pack of firm toothbrushes. I was re-emergent, not lost, but surging. So I went away. A holiday. The heat was impossible, huge. My skin fried crunchy under the alkaline sun.

Wives, accidents, women and children – they had bubbled me over with un-nutritional fluff. Taking off my clothes, the jolly scars that ran in vivid fluorescent patches, not so skin-like at all, reminded me that I was not immune to category. I was punctuated all over. My limbs were the mobile plane for these derelict lines. They radiated the strange pang of an inorganic sexuality.

Let's say my relationship to concrete formalism at that point was pretty slack-jawed. Lying in the sun, with my scant skin and scanter clothing, I was a sad sack of boiling cells sandwiched in their millions beneath two scrapes of dizzying blue. I was a curl on the sand. I played with it, piling it, re-piling it, gathering it into a heap around me. Seaweed in my hair or banana skin under my nails, I slept on that beach for hours, deprived happily of myself and furnished instead with the sea and its florid carpet of shells.

Returning tanned in part – tanned on parts – I made my first commitment to really indelible naming: a wiry tattoo above the crease on my left forearm. Whimpering with my arm stuck to leatherette, the pen scratched me bloody. It stung hot as pepper for days. I felt like a loser king. I felt smart.

My black lined helix would be a new order of space, I decided. A different kind of DNA. Something that whilst I balanced my cup, my plate or cigarette in one hand, I could make wriggle with the other hand, watching as the hidden life of the skin, the rolling, shearing, staggering tilt of my own inner chemistry was given an avatar on the outside. Perhaps I would fall in love with my own sensuality! What petty fraudulence!

When the skin stopped peeling I felt myself pedantically sanitised by science. Those tight backbone curls. It made me feel ripe with mystery. Together our nucleic acids boiled with infinite options, major and minor grooves.

I felt visible and I'm not talking about the eyes of God. I'd drawn *attention*.

Shone a light as they say. And I loved to imagine it, this spotlit centre of me: a torchlight on my insides, that place where no glow, no candlelight however elemental, could ever shine.

The toxicology report came in positive. I clearly hadn't realised I had consumed quite so much nutmeg. Or wine. Or Nyquil. Or barbiturates. Or rage, really, but didn't they always say take those bastard feelings and urge them into light, flood them with gospel song and illuminated script? *Well.* I had swallowed down all that lager. Fizz turning everything stale as you in that red pub turned again and again to leave for the bathroom.

Things were settled in moments. Routine papers, fees and all the standard etceteras were waved and blinked about. Fiscal inflections led us to cash piles of strange equivalence: we did our legal bit.

Having been launched towards an interrogative mood, I loitered in the chambers to learn more of the law and its lofty leanings. There were weepers' veils and others emboldened by their crime. I stepped through open courts, mostly seeing parents turn white as policemen, their babies guilty grey and yellow eyed.

I lowered myself onto the mahogany rungs of an open trial. A heavy metal court case: *Aluminium shouldn't turn magnetic so when the residue chips of an industrial milling machine were refused by a scrapper a metal analysis certificate should have been demanded. If only to determine that the load in issue was not a bad batch with the metal factory workers getting dinged because of it.*

All the little shining men this way, all the little shining men that way. The place was full of heads and collars. Their warehouse rats could have smelled it out, the verdict. The question was whether or not the scrappers, those piss gophers, should have gone away to pound sand, retreating with jackets drawn up to their ears in shame. Men plagued by a bad time – you could see them wheezing – always done in by lungs and by coal.

The jury was shown a similar case, an example of corrupted magnets dipped in oil inevitably picking up all manner of materials – plastic, sawdust, aluminium, copper, hair, *dust*. Oats and obligations. Hissing through teeth and, plainly wanting to stick a knife in it, *quiet down*, says the judge to a whole gallery of eager spectators.

And I knew from the TV and other cases where they'd tried to shrug off the words and their consequences that if you fling an epithet hard enough, you'll see it is more than just a putative ensemble of sticky atoms. All that metal: a Doomsday texture. A parley.

Science describes how neodymium magnets can create enough reverse electromotive force to drag a piece of aluminium along, imparting a reverse current, developing polarity and transforming the aluminium itself into a magnet. These are Eddy currents. The room is death on legs. People are humming. *Warm it all up, shake it all out*. Legs crossing and postures sliding down the wall. Science describes currents looped together in new electrical charges that oppose the magnetic field which created them. All the faces look like switchy squares somewhere between thick and approving. Science describes carbide end mills that can impart a magnetic charge, enough effervescence to bounce right off you. This only stops when the motion is stopped: we are told this because there is a logic to metal, to mills and charges; a logic for atoms and filibustering. It's a science thing. Get yourself a decent rare-earth magnet – boom – attraction. A man with a diagram thumps his chest and people at the front shuffle their papers.

I hypothetically weigh myself and throw the scales into a pot. Weigh in with the metal case. I am dozing, taking advantage of free heat. Is my wife having an affair? Not sure if she still loves me: these are obstacles so big I cannot see. Swallowing saliva, dripping some, mouth no longer a definite article, sleepy. My life path just tiny stitching on global denim; my body a massive haemorrhage. So sad. *Small titanium chips might stick, but only once before their charge drops*. I presume a ghostly glue is holding all this shit together, cruising round the perimeter of a ditch. Cruising hard with tongue out. Blokes heard it said that they were suffering molestation. Fancying a holiday or a nice cup of tea. I hope I hadn't spoken in my sleep.

Before this trial they say some moneyed person had tried to put a halt to legal proceedings and make amends with flowers that were already blossomed but all the employees, outrageous in their overalls and hamburger sneakers, were out sick. The boss was a freaking bugmaniac bidding on beetles and lots from Peru; no interest in metal or figures or constituent parts, pieces. Stone bones, steel parts. Always paying them off, or not paying them at all.

One testimonial writ out, handwritten, described steel holdings close to the dying vats by the railway where it stinks of the dead and boiled pigs even though they claim to make plastic or lunch boxes. A heap of jawbones and five quid a day. £5 not so much to keep the mouths shut, to keep the leaky holes from leaking down at the pub. Even the beer is dark and bad.

I've lost the thread of it. My needle head is heavy with half sleep. And that's the nut of it: if you miss your connection, you don't know if you've been or gone. It's hard to put two and two together through broken teeth. What the judge says. Something about image or trust, a metaphor used: something about selling frozen garden peas, how they tumble from their pods on luminous freezer packaging, all bright and clean, then batter with disappointment on the plate, with a shade of green so passionately sad as to be grey. I'm stuck between voices, carried away through the heat and the sweat. There are layers of betrayal in everything.

Low-background steel and trinity tests – the heads eventually tell it all. Can't use that junk in space-related engineering: dead man's iron, pig iron, earthbound stuff. *Samarium cobalt, alnico, ceramic and ferrite magnets*. It isn't supernatural science.

I think perhaps it's not about the metal, the false colours and readings, or the scrappers, or any domestic tablecloths. Handcuffs, fisticuffs. None of it. But something more humble about memories of open squares, of a visible world strewn with happy people and broad daylight. An expert suggests they should bring in a Geiger counter to rule out the emissions of ionising radiation, to rule out lofty words insensitively contorted just to pay rent and buy the food.

A clever one with a big head steps up. Works in the factory, reads all the way through lunch. Everybody listens hard now, as though he might squat and burst into flames. The jury isn't keen; clench your teeth and get on with it, I say. Lots of red-haired people involved. Lots of historical fire about their heads. A six-person jury with their constitutional hair.

The courtroom artist has made some fantastically bold sketches in a colour, which captures the curiosity of the crowd, these groaning Romans, with some bold and sticky futures. The kids have marzipan mice; some of them want to stand up in the front row and talk like the trial. Some of them a little slanted from pre-atomic lead and birth control. They stand up like impish men and women, acting the part holding hands.

About the bang at the time: a noise familiar and curdling. Outside the courthouse two cars ploughed into each other like an organic oval collapsing at its tips. A crack of antlers. We heard it during one of the sessions. Legal aides rushed to the window armed with duties and over-sweated polyester.

One body inside had no luck, had all the versatility of strawberry scooped out from a soggy block of ice cream, brain cold and abdicated. Bags of smoke and orange flames. I thought, oh, it's a pleasant colour.

Now the two metal frames rest crumpled. The black diagram of their shadows overlaps my past with the dark fuzz of this present. Two sleeping kittens. A metallic Alps. Nobody laughed, rather nodded their heads with a moral soundlessness.

You're never sure who's special till they are gone, all scrap metal now, and some tired man will say *was it you who took away my wife?*

People don't tend to think much of scrap metal, but I've learnt how it's well connected in common law, statutory powers and geological movement. It's part of architectural consequence, part of our cultivated pollution.

It took time after all that noise but they called a mistrial. Something about procedural conduct – all the written numbers and written letters packed up in a box with heavy heads needing new jobs. Heavy boxes. I think the perspective changed.

On the day of the funeral, I heard they sent seeds spilling into the wind. And just to be sure carried with them a polystyrene head with brown wig, ready to trim the fringe to suit so her body would not rise to heaven with a cold crown.

Cardinal directions

After everything it would be nice to be on the depositing end of some empirical guidance. Alas I left it all behind. I left my books, my papers, my things behind. I left my sex behind. I left my love, the great distinction of it, darkly communicated, that two is company not crowd.

And now in solitude I'm practicing the January method of birth control, when there is no shared sex to be had at the beginning of the year, which is fine anyway because it's mostly too cold to take clothes off and exhibit members or hollows to the elements and watch them die crudely in the inhabitable structures weather creates at this time of year. Although would anyone make complaints at my wandering male gist?

All this change, this corruption and I've been thinking a lot about my head. And how the world, too, is just one big round head hosting us with our billions of unique passions, us blushing apes, with bodies ready to plug in mouths or ears to whatever sockets avail themselves free of charge.

I am also beginning to think my palms are infected. The speckled skin maps out. I see the future and the past unfolding within them: the physics of everyday things, all accident and skid-mark forensics. What now?

I know I must be very sick. Like the Invisible Man who is sick too, and crazy, by the way, despite his protestations. Death begins as the beggar we all are, are all complicit in being. The neat box of my body walks around with germs flapping, culturing until there is a cough to hear or some purple-ish ankles. I'll say it again, I should get some air.

Is there a garden I should visit?

Are there birds in a little red coat?

Some quick colours to soak my eyes in before the weekend?

And dabbling ducks – I love ducks – with their underwater boots and yellow flaps bashing rushes to push out water rings that stick in our eyes. Like liquid software, mapping us all in stealth.

Well, I love ducks, I said it already. We have DNA in common. I love DNA. I love ducks and chickens, mice, apes, dogs and humans.

MESSRS.
EXTERNAL & COUNTING

To grasp a fish

It is said that our eyeballs record the last thing we see before we die. That there is a biological pigment locked tight in the back of the retina whose proteins bleach in light and recover in the dark, leaving some images outlined like drawings in a colouring book. Maps, of a sort.

We look down on these awful people and their endless capacity for enhancement. Sometimes we're so far above the world, it's like an electric train set, rigid in its respect of hygiene and good behaviour. There's slow music on every loudspeaker, it's sick really. We see the roosters beckoning the morning with their wicked crows. We see sheep flocking. Sheep too being just careless and colloquial terms for our own insomnia, for how we shepherd in the clouds around us at night like a careful map of cosiness.

And we worry. Of course we do. There are no instructions to live by. No handbook found on special shelves in the elevators of freehold owners. There is little but the wind to guide our hapless folk. Sometimes even our own miraculous wit fails us and we need a rest from demand, from the supply of calibration. We think *get a real job* and what happens then? We pause for a minute as the world rains its fluorescent ash down on us. We sit motionless for a time, perched upon a point of rocks, fishing lines merry between our knees and suddenly there is the bright spanking future. It jumps up and takes our bait and we are happy. We think even in this maze of grimy back gardens and freakish bimbos there is a pale forehead worth wiping down.

Yes, we need tea. At least we understand *that* mortal necessity. How it helps to realise one has survived the gentle death of awakening and it's ok to put shoes on. We Messrs. do believe in magic.

ETHAN

No fixed address

I like to draw things and pretend they are charts issued by ordnance surveyors. Each time I map directions for a stranger, I close my eyes and there is a halo of white light around everything. I like the company. It's a whispered circuitry.

And I am still thinking about my head.

My own head. Yes I've been thinking a lot about my head. How I dread the day I become worn out, that last day, when I gorge myself on beer and frankfurters plastered with mustard and suddenly pop, out will go my eyeballs, too fatigued to take the ambush. And all the images and memories and tears will just slide off and gather in suds on my cheeks. Like the weak flies that crawl down the mottled plastic of my glasses, inside the lens *get the fuck outta here*.

I imagine my wife calling, making a map of her as well:

Do you picture my face when you talk to me? On the phone I mean.

Of course, I would say, not listening, seeing not the soft peach of her cheeks, but the pucker of a disembodied asshole surrounded by a silvery wig of hair. Mapping the features with an intensity of purpose and recollection.

Yes I am constantly mapping as I sit on my sill

with great landscapes out of the window. Or as I lie on the floor. And there is the doorbell with its shrill ducts straight into the marrow of my mind.

What were you expecting?

Did you expect a woman?

Did you expect a gun?

Somebody delivering a parcel or taking your recycling away?

The small noise of lips in thin air?

All of the above?

MESSRS. EXTERNAL & YELLOW

Two flowers

How his face had been at the door. The blue-yellow hat. Like a billboard so purposely presenting itself. Ethan answering and opening with his sleeves rolled up, a little damp from plumbing, the rolling work of tightening and soldering. *I'm selling spades*, the man says. If there is a story, it must be recounted for. Time sped up or slowed down, Ethan doesn't recall anymore. And us, we don't care to question.

How either of them had known was not part of the sanity of inquiry. Not in the bedroom or kitchen or living room: none of the places that snap you back to the reality of care, to the rearrangement of any relationship to the machine of the home. But out back in the yard, that feels neither familiar nor awful, simply local, so more rough.

He was always upright in the moment. He was flaming red of muscle, the abstraction of one yellow coat thumping against the wall, rolled sleeves slipping sadly down. There was a dog, of course, panting. Stutters and curves of touch, his whole body so tightened in knots right then unwrapped, boiling. He had thought of groceries and their bags splitting, pouring away. He had seen the grey octopus tentacles, the rubbered fish eyes foul and reflective. He had seen his name, *Ethan*, and hers, *Patrice*, strung out thinly, puffed from a cigarette with no graphic clarity. He had closed his eyes to more touch and the redaction of anything he had known before. The wet shock of something new and electric. There was the boundary of bone and skin all broken open, the magnetic field of hide-and-seek as he pushed himself into zeros and then his wife standing in the doorway. Right there. One small witness to that comedy of modern relationships buckling to unspoken tragedy. Still and simple, standing in the place where information intersects itself. He would never be able to explain the dislocation, that sense of missing transport, of something lost in the mash of senses firing and all he had heard was the phrase *move on Earth*. Clear in his ears as though the new philosophy of this desire was impossibly cool and calm and collected. Her hands with two flowers for the table that same purple-grey as the beads around her neck. The earth would soak up his spills and maybe something lovely would grow. And she would put the vase on the table. And he would never touch her again. And she would always be turning away, climbing the worn wooden stairs, all of it snapping back to the stifling lozenge of weather so hard to swallow.

PATRICE

Busy (future perfect, feminine)

In my left hand is my breast with the miraculous nipple – pink, luminous, celestial – in my right is a bottle with one glug remaining. If the neighbours looked through the window they'd whisper amongst themselves, *there she is again, in the kitchen, polishing melons and touching her privates*. First a climax of pleasure and then the recurring autumn muck and a steaming heap from the family: wash your hands, comb your hair, fill your bank account.

My own figure, as far as I can tell, is a proxy image of the future, a scale of tipping fortunes. In one hand that gorgeous nipple, the other busy with wine.

Not often do people see my pert breasts that one generally assumes to be meaningless but actually catalogue every syllable said. I've long believed that an extravagance of feeling is healthy like a high concentration of vitamins or minerals so I've plotted my current adult life in accordance.

There was a time when cycling to work at the florist even the trees could sense my purpose. Trees so close to my fingers, grazing bark and limes with their tips. They always moved their leaves for me and I wouldn't mind the sun out shining light on everything, every movement of my life.

I love your work and you have a beautiful face, a quite beautiful face, my customers would say. Their words were so eager, with qualities to burn at just the right spot in the belly. I liked feeling hot like those flames, bright as though under some ancient examination candle, scorched to a crisp all over. Surely they'd do better to save their flames. My waist with its junior flex being difficult to pin down and illuminate anyway, amidst all the flowers and an Earth I generally considered as garish as a fruit bowl. The Earth as an aubergine, an apple core, a banana, and me a tortoise slow in its shell.

The florist owner with his careful arms, a little stiff and lightly muscled but tight like a sign painter. He was all day arranging and coaxing the wind to push out the sun and deliver us to dusk when the flowers would come back into the shop and we'd go home. So polite all the blood had left his face, as though the blush or bloom of living might offend me. All our stems cut off so short and straight.

They closed down anyway – the florist – something about business turning a corner and falling down, not through a hole, but straight out of the bottom of the world. Like our planet had been flat all along and somebody had pierced an opening just florist-shaped enough to squeeze through. That was the end of that.

And now I'm out of a job, out of a pair: am I a bad barleycorn? I've got no more sophisticated afternoons made up between stems of rose and narcissus. No face, practically, just a crunchy penguin toy with eyes and wings glued on. No legs but garden pines from Vermont all the way up. No feet or arms, come to think of it, but a delicate set of dangling moccasins, deerskin stitched and hotly embroidered x's and o's. I am this now, more or less. A set of random qualifiers, some adjectives and dirty clothes all over. Talk about me any which way and here's a metaphor for free: I am a bloated football kicked way outside the box.

I haven't washed for a while, not because I'm lost to hygiene but because I long to rekindle that dizzy florist must, the honeyed sweet pea and fresh-cut rot. I want to bed down the far-sprinkled seeds that have caught in my folds and are newly sprouting stems around my ears. How noble, how Roman despite it all. You see I dare not dive into the bath for a swim and under the surface find all those countless worlds of me and you and everyone ever swilling around in warm light blue. Or find that heartbeat again, another waterway, filled with a few cubic leagues of hellos and how-do-you-dos.

I know the neighbours think I've lost it. *The neighbours*. Dogs still bark in this neighbourhood of mine. Cats, and all the men and women, seizure where they stand. Stupid grimacing neighbourhood dogs who run around with gristle in their mouths or children if the season's right. Fleas fucking dogs, dogs fucking cats and me not fucking anyone at all, or, not anymore, anyway. Oatmeal dogs. Rubble-eyed dogs newly smacking and licking. Like the boy who smashed his head on the pavement and broke it clean in two so his coral brain – a stained tennis ball – bounced out of its shell and packed off rolling down the street. The dogs got hold of that one all right.

I devote my time now to what I like to call an indifferent mystic state. *Don't think of time*, say the civilians in ancient libraries. Don't think of it rosy or with retrospection for it will then pass too fast or too slow. Neither the beginning nor the end is a place to linger. I am here in the now, the now of me, and I know just enough of what will come and what will go to pass the time without thinking about it at all. I am my servant and my master, in between Time One and Time Two as though a page awaiting print – rolled flat between a cylinder and a die. The present, the past and who knows where.

I read things in the entrails of animals. I read things in bones and stones, in smears in the sink, in roosters pecking at grain in lucky days and not so lucky ones. I go out in daylight for milk with grass stains on my shins, not from sliding or rolling with farmers and seamen, or farmers and girls and semen, but from kneeling to kiss the sky. And when the neighbours say something rude under their breath, which they always do, I hit them with a quiet truth.

I know some people imagine themselves to be fortune-tellers. Some people with their cut knuckles believe the glitter stuck in their scabs was delivered by spooks of the most heavenly kind. I sound things out in light winds with a spot of hoodoo and root work, with Tarot cards and palmistry. I'm trying to vent the great wall of my frustrations towards something soft and cosmically multi-sided. I'm trying to make some furniture outside my head that might make for prudent storage.

Since the florist, my salted fingers shall be of the earth. Inside the earth. I'll take my losses and plant them with seed. I will never be a person as neat and corrected as a well-taken photograph. Never part of gangs who walk together, who change direction together. Never a welcomed neighbour nor a puritan who sat so long on well-oiled furniture that her back hardened straight into modernity.

I am knee deep in ideas dragged from behind and pushed to the front. From the weather, from the road, from dust. My instructions are not sullen or frivolous but sound to me something like this:

Today you are a reeking poet. You are a slender pantomime with odd gymnastic limbs. Imagine love outside yourself as a single almond blown from a tree. Watch it fall to the ground. Feel the soft thud as it bumps to the earth, rolls, lands away from the roots, but don't cry. Don't laugh either: it's a category that's complicated. Watch it. Watch it in seasons: watch it rot like pork, stink like a turnip-white abscess, then dry – bone dry – and crumble like pumice. Do this with more almonds. Imagine their place on the soil alongside other plotted marks: a Kleenex snowflake, small stones, a gummy worm, a dead frog.

I won't come out and say that if you breathe hard enough all the goddamn secrets of silence in the air will reveal themselves to you. But I do know, grinding my jaw with dedication, that if you tie all those lines together – the almonds, the Kleenex, the married this way and that – and hang them out, it's just so damn easy to spot the universe's perpetual flow. Taken as a cluster, these marks are the mathematics of making a life. Every minute gathering of facts, bodily cramps and cadence; every splay of the fingers; every alabaster fringe jostled in the light; each tiptoed stretch and milk from the fridge; every pungent slandering word, sharpened nosebleed and erasure of rubber from your sneakers; even every burst of hell from the neighbours and their bastard kids who want to go to this school but it's full and they demand it so they force some others to leave.

I look to weather to lay out the facts and when the sky bodes happy winds that favour drying I'm busy in the kitchen churning out zeros and ones, packing them neatly up in paces back and forth. And boxes, always more boxes. Or rinsing stains left from the grass on my knees. Or rearranging the flowers in the peach tub I took from the florist and won't return. Only a lunatic could wield a pattern pretty enough to extract sense but no law can prevent me trying.

Before I lost the job, I invited the neighbours over – a small act of defiance – to consider the Viburnum wilting on my stoop. My handwritten party note had suggested that we might give it water and ask, in shades of hopeful green, for more leaves to spring open. I'd suggested a game of football to galvanise the wives or gin for the mopers with their ragged plimsolls and fluky dreams. But nobody came: they all had their own BBQs to attend, eating French fries in sun hats so haughty you'd think all the world was theirs: all the rivers and plains and a sea of mayonnaise.

And now my unemployment benefits are not so beneficial, really, at all. Because sometimes things can happen casually, like how I'm employed on a temporary salary to commit suicide every day; employed to cut flowers; employed to translate hints about the neighbours' cats and all your lost socks; employed to issue garden centre tokens; employed to rank the world's greatest philosophers on a stupid contingent scale, or that's what you think. It's all a distraction. And distraction simply doesn't pay.

I know of the constant rummaging behind my back, the spit-soaked whispers: *What kind of sicko paints a house black? Over the white and leaves bricks in mourning forever after because no one, especially her, will be bothered to paint it back again? What a cuckoo, a weirdo, a clown.*

There's a wisp of truth in it, yes, I admit. And against black isn't it easier and more gleeful to see me walking around like a living diagram of dissatisfaction? The only thing left is an unbroken neck and a stream of awkward ticks and I'm saving those for later.

I suppose we all need stable forms of insult and eradication. Countless notes in the mail. Letters sent or never sent at all. Notes of chivalry and encouragement from all the dull senators and sons of senators with their peaches and their impeachments. Neighbours and their issues.

When asked to comment on my situation publicly I tend to plead the fifth, the effeminate, a creative resistance. If neighbours knock at my door with one admonishment or another, with leaflets or cake, *hardly*, I tell them I'm busy building a conceptual home for conceptual opinions;

a place with threads of Ash and more almonds, two sprays of rosemary, lynxes and lizards. Things not parsed in common definition.

I tell them I know my position at the florist's suggested an egalitarian stance towards all flowers, but please take those hundreds of hideous orchids off your goddamn windowsills.

You can see I need a simple barometer to hold my new thoughts in continuum. Something friendly and Quaker like Amish toys and cross-stitch; a sniff of heather and some curly willow to keep it calm. Me and a cat, me and a kitchen, me and a rolling pin slowly rolling back and forth forever.

But between us, I dream of replacing all the crap in my hall with more swaggering ideas, scooping chips of eggshell and toast aside in favour of hemlock and hart's tongue on tables laid. Fancy gestures, I know, but a little glamour, with animals stretched out over pewter dishes on benches waxed to a shine: that never hurt anyone. In these moments of clarity and desire I can read the clouds like a Rorschach. I can take advantage of the rocket and spinach in all simple salads crusted over with their scuds of pharmaceutical dirt: a legal high. I can even lie myself down on the kitchen counter and open my massive legs to massive hands to receive it all if I want to. I call it *looking to the future*.

Christ I'm feeling a headache come on just thinking about it, really. A migraine in copper pennies. My headaches that take colour, every living colour, and toggle saturation so quickly back and forth in intensity that all you can see is white. There are eyelashes stuck to practically everything from all the shaking.

I long to return to the florist. To see the quince and pear blossom and peonies all coloured so vigorously. To be busied by the tasks of reclaiming nature with my beautiful face. As it is, I don't care so much now about the names of trees or flowers, even birds anymore. This older me who is furtively busy with aqueous lotion, who is furtively awash in aqueous lotion. A nice pink smelling cream, which wraps my skin.

Today it is not even Halloween and I've dressed up for you, for all of you, as myself. *Ta dah! What massive legs*, they all say, as I drop my flowers and run back to the kitchen with blustery eyes. I know they call me a witch with elephant legs in that garden choked with busted grass blades. *Well don't run on my fucking grass then!*

I'm not sure of my master plan today, but I can certainly tell you tomorrow. Sooner or later it will dissolve off my tongue. I'm busy today. Busy searching the Internet for pictures of myself or others like me: people naked against decent pink sunsets in their tight pink skin. Pink as that drink for indigestion, that insane gorgeous pink that no light can possibly damage.

I'm white teeth in pink through the dark and busy busy busy. I'm a fistful of oyster shells on a bed of ice, soon just islands in a melted sea. I'm stuck in a brown dress packed for lunch, sweating in sunlight onto the papery sides. I'm not even photosynthesising for anyone, how embarrassing, how cruel. There are no daisy chains to keep me company: all the flowers are long dried to dust.

Instead there's urine or wine un-flushed in my toilet bowl – *if it's yellow let it mellow!* There are spiders in the cutlery drawer but damn right I'm sophisticated enough to keep horn spoons for eggs alongside silver spoons for ice cream. The sick smell of baby breath and granny breath is heavy, but *remember*, no thinking about the very beginning or the end. Maybe it's time to stick it out in the middle with a spot of cleaning and a fistful of ibuprofen flung down the throat.

Maybe my straddling tilt has tilted too far, for my shame at this point is covered with a thin something, barely contained and looking like it is about to blow off. Leave me grumbling on about this modern cumulative incoherence. One never built on a canon of minorities, of outcasts, of shells, on twitchy wasters like me. Get me out of this kitchen. Away from the new cat on the doorstep, which I suddenly feel sick and sweet for because its face looks a little like my mother as a baby. And wow *Jesus* look how it only takes a nasty bit of anthropomorphic familiarity to back you right up and slow down.

No good blood there, children; Catherine, Felix, Matilda, Joseph, Megan, Charlotte, Matthew: wise to watch from afar; darling are you listening? That's the neighbours speaking to their kids huddled up in their garage. I can see beyond the curtains that they're watching so I wave to them but they don't wave back.

All of that.

That is the bubbling froth of unluckiness. Like falling down on your bicycle when all your friends are watching and hurting yourself too much to laugh it off convincingly.

Don't cry! Don't cry! Don't cry! Why are you crying?!

They say.

And to top off the shame and collude with the pain, your new trousers are dusty and ripped at the hem where they caught in the gears.

ETHAN

Boon (future perfect, masculine)

Newly in my new yard, adjacent to my expertly patinated home (rusted), I have formulated a structure which provides a sense of solidity as chemically in between states as my own commitment to personhood. It is a state I have come to enjoy sitting under, disappearing beneath.

Strung with tensile integrity cells amongst a web of slender tendons there is a complex network of pipes. Water is pumped in from the pond. The water is filtered, passed across a welt of natural fur for snapping out the animal tar, the oak leaves, the dirty ossicles. The water is fine-misted, dissolved, excreted by a dense lick of high-pressure nozzles. A smart weather system correlates with the furniture of my smart weather head, reading the shifting climatic conditions of temperature, humidity, wind speed and direction. Much is high pressure, much high-grade heavy steel. Discrete jets with their tiny apertures. Water is forced at a pressure of 80 bars – not weenie but whopping – onto finer needle-points. Water is dropletted, atomised, innumerable. These tiny drops, 4 microns, 6 microns, 10 microns in diameter, project in their thousands across space, are suspended within air. They are indignant. They scatter and nest in adhesive blobs on leaves.

Their arc is curved. They follow the curvature of my spine, the stalks of my grasses, the lines of the flowerbeds, these droplets that hold me in. Their suspension saturates the wind with moisture and creates the effect of mist – my own glorious personal humidity cloud I privately call *the blur*.

The blur effect provides escape from pragmatics. From the hammer of my body and the blunt of my brain. It fuzzes out drawbacks. The blur effect creates a tender bloom of moisture that instead of holding up a mirror to nature, stomping on my vitals and reflecting objective crappiness, rather allows me to sit still and content like a pillar in a cloud. I don't need to be hampered at a desk rapidly cutting squares from newspapers, underlining the bleak pulpits of advertisement made, or reviewing the state of my cuticles, my nails and the speed at which each finger enters my mouth for chewing. Inside the blur I quietly channel calm in the cool soft wetness of non-specificity.

Outside the blur, it's true, I wilfully embody some of the gravest effects of medicine. The general scraps of obstetric distress pulled together in adult life towards a category of definition they call *man*. Terminology can be declarative. The blur, that too could also be commonly termed *garden sprinkler*. And when I am wet from dashing through it, often in the morning when the sky hasn't turned and few can see me sopping in my towel, the drops on my forehead are beaded with an energy I attribute to revelation and repurpose.

Although allergy can trouble: I am allergic to my own spit if I feel like it. Or my own blood. Allergic to its boiling ferric swell that might dissolve everything if I feel like it. Auto-immune, auto-asphyxiate: my own arms, my own penis, my own head all plopping off into hands that also fall down to the ground. Like soft margarine; everything rubbered by a terrible seasonal allergy to my own self. But only if I feel like it.

I often feel like it.

I am allergic to the greater wax moth. Allergic to freaking beanbags and soy product. A mouthful cranks me up to severe instances of respiratory distress. I ate pancakes once and turned cyanotic, my lovely blue moon face plump with ailing. Hurt me I thought. *Ouch! Hurt me more gently*. I collapsed on a shiny tile floor. Pancakes with a mould count of 23,000 per gram of mix. Spores galore. Dusty flour like dusty words blowing my cheeks. Those stale pancakes would bog me right down to my death if I chose it and then a sprightly epitaph on the grave: *He cracked two eggs and beat it. Battered to the ground. Buttered up, and shoved down the hole.*

Times like those remind me that all I need now is a good Burgundy and a tonne of stimulants. I don't want to be upset with a throbbing sphincter, with a body bag bumped off along the road. I take nothing more vexing than a tin of corned beef. Some tomato juice for vitality.

I continue thinking about my head a lot. My hair. Does my face look rosy to you? Does it look sunny? A sunny-side-up kind of sunny? With its goofy round meniscus flashing yellows to all and sundry? Didn't think so. Don't think so. Try all yokey down the legs. Allergic to my own semen too: a causal incidence when everything crimped off in error during the syntactical engineering of my form.

And yet I don't mean to undermine concrete and all its stability, especially in the business of infrastructure when speaking of a home. You see I wouldn't want my windows pulverised by, say, a bird barging itself into my house, or rats taking over the run of my sitting area. I'm certainly not thinking to bed myself down in rubbish, although surely I would enjoy the momentary rush of excitement as things hurry off towards putrefaction, writhing and shimmering and carrying a general whiff of excitement as I lie tucked in by the mess. I don't hope for this kind of burial or some handful-of-years-later discovery when the police or the children find parts of me petrified, a bit of toe, the lobe of my ear.

I do still have a taste for crunch and freshness. A taste for pickles and caraway. I'm merely opening myself up to all the conjunctions of illumination.

Now, alone in the garden or wet with boredom in the bath, I can think of the great future. With a picture of my little life in hand, I'm a sibyl, a clairvoyant, a seer. I'm a crow in the street with a nose for direction. I can tell you your signs, your stones. I know precisely of the horoscopic flab sweating away inside your cookie, its shade, its flavour: your fortune. Before you can even think of impossible pleasures, I know what's on the telly and which way you want to come.

My uncle, too, told of soothsaying. He always had events cracked open, always had his foot stuck in the door of profitable enterprises. *Look, listen, it's something similar to unfocused microwaving,* he said. *Like reaching out to the future to catch a gust of wind or sand under the nails and from those wispy threads knowing something of the newness to come. A stomach-based ventriloquism; you can just feel it, you know?*

Then I read in the papers how an American rabbi flipped. How he opined. How he opened his robes and poured forth support for Renaissance magic: *since time immemorial humans have longed to learn that which the future holds for them.*

I too can say simply that there are future facts I already know: how the milk in the fridge is sour and if I drink it my intestines will rumple and violate the basin; how when the berries are gone the birds will fly south for warming; how rats can get a foothold in any city, just like dust which never stops gathering.

I practice some lines for what I envisage will be future customers, my future paying customers:

Hello paying customer, let us begin: what about your nymphomaniac mother? Your smothering father? And sisters and brothers with lips all over each other. Cousins with broken necks. All the sluts and sluices of a modern family.

I've been watching online videos to see how to set about rolling in this divination business. There is so much transit to consider: the creaking of the floor, the cracking of the beams, all the city folk clustered on the Persian rug. People joining hands, touching and greeting. Coffee and Cokes. There is the smell of ripeness and pallid light ready to receive a horizon. For music, the endless metal clatter of corrugated blinds: gospel to sweep all the spirits from dusk to dawn. Then an air of arrival. Some shuffled cards and sweated pits. I must learn the clever predictions of a false master and some exiled solos:

Are you alive?

Are you awake?

Is there something you would like to say?

I will become known. I will read for cash and pleasure. *Should I examine the quality of the evidence?* I will never. I will predict a couple are having a baby and they will do just that. A boy.

The light was on, the pounding of urination quite clearly audible in the bowl, the flush, lights relocated, oil a-sizzle, fingerprints, shadows, bobbled excrescences all visible like letters in motion on the wall.

I sat in my own indoor dark on my own indoor seat. But no figures beyond the window were visible in their bushy biological flesh. All my neighbourhood folk kept their volumes limited to audible appliance mode/invisible body mode. They limited their gestures such that I could hear their absence and then again the reunion of their hands with their doorknobs and other life-living accessories. But I rarely got eyeful of their hot-bodied holiness. We were a few degrees of integrity removed.

I think this is set to change, for the neighbours are at it again. They have inherited a baby. Or had a baby, made it, brewed it, boiled away at nine months of bad temper. I didn't toast to their symbiotic colony of bacteria and yeast.

They unfolded him proudly on my doorstep in a gesture of brokering the bad feelings that had long extended between us. As though in employing the balm of just-passed amniotic fluid that trailed over every inch of this child like a bulletin of human nativity they could unveil an exotic male who would be a healer of neighbourly ills.

The baby's tone unnerved me at once, like when goodness becomes so simple it borders on the tyrannical. His skin was plump and portentous as a bean. I wondered, if I painted this cheerless babe, how would I do it? With some magic animals roasted to the point of regret? By grassy burrs and a fruit-like pillow with alabaster reliefs? Whatever scenic brushwork I chose to employ, I knew with certainty that it would be one harnessing full use of the benefits of painterly anaesthesia: I would want this child wedged in, restrained in cotton with pumpkins and other careful ingredients. I would want him banished to my masterpiece.

It is possible that with a small corner of my being already belonging to the devil, I would have hated the baby no matter what. In its eager eyes I could read a savant giddiness. I committed to thinking of it as an oracle towards which I might toss a coin before making my toilet.

Although perhaps it is a humiliation rather than hatred. And I think the baby knows this as its arms appear crossed over its stomach in all circumstances, as though it acts to compress any escaping emotion or intoxicating traits. I expect a weird milky vulnerability to leak out of him, crossing the garden patch and entering through my house into me but there is no such thing. I sense nothing of his small uselessness, no tiny effluvium to speak of. He is a psychiatric camel-baby storing up empathy and exuding all the charisma of a matinee idol. He wails day and night.

I don't tend well to domestic affairs. But thinking much about middle life and that supposed balm of parenthood, this baby has been on my mind. My immediate apprehension was that the skin of a baby should not be green. Mint at worst if the baby is poisoned or corroding, but certainly never has green represented a quality of ripe good health. Pour a glass of water and it looks cloudy: don't drink it. Unfold infant skin and find not a swarthy babe, but a coastal wash or eggy tinge: return it to the cot and run.

Even in candlelight there is nobody who would accept green as the suitable disposition for the skin of a baby. Green is the flag of malaise, of rotten dental tugs. Would you put a necktie over your hospital gown? No you would not. Green is iridescent, a contingent halftone signalling nuclear sepsis. Green is the coward in plain sight. It is not the pasted painterly light of rapturous external reflections, but a pedagogical line of single-cell crumple. Viruses never obey borders, especially where the surfactant oils of skin and paint are concerned. So green: green is no go.

The neighbours are dutifully proud of their prodigious fertility. They have distributed a photo card of their child, presumably far and wide across the development streets, announcing names and dates, as they are prone to do, in a filigree of letters across the page.

In careful studio light the green baby extends his stout arms around a ceramic jug. It is a scene fit for the compassionless glaze of them both. He is softer, naked but for a neckerchief in blue and white checks that possibly throttles him greener and was certainly tied by fingers busy with knots, fingers often tying loops or restraining twigs on the background azalea with a deftness of care never apparent to children.

The baby and his tiny genitals are stoic as a column. He is a general. He is a snail becoming stone. Whether it was the parental wish or the particular slant of the photographer's lens, it is clear to all that the baby has drained himself. He practically glows in the dark with his gradient of green but nobody comes along. What a reckless absent scene. I imagine the parents as peasants presumably busy away saucing themselves in sex and shit instead of pampering with milk or sauce gribiche.

The painted scene immediately around the baby and his symmetrical jug is fuzzily defined and smacked by dark crescents of grey projecting upwards to collide with the sharpness of iconic plants. There are fat sunflowers and I'm not really sure why people like sunflowers: they seem to me the loneliest and most glowering of nature's growths, with their ugly musical tones. I would much prefer a crumpling daffodil in its soiled white petticoat or chrysanthemums as full of ideology as the clouds in the sky.

Perhaps I should have sent flowers to the neighbours. Left some cylindrical pot on their doorstep with lilies and violets, or some buttercups wrenched from the ground.

I have kept the card as seeing the child's face, now familiar despite its glaucous tint, provides me with a pleasurable sensibility, like warm wax over the palm. But like a grape in powdery bloom, I am half-minded to scratch my nails over the image surface, writing in my own evil marks atop the inanimate details. But how can one be philosophical and not exhausted the next day?

I should be kind like a nice lyric novel. I should behave softly, thankful that, under the transparent glow of my room lamp this baby is possessed of all the right openings and closures, some good upright features and enough strands of downy hair to register a terrestrial claim to what horticulturalists would term *groundcover*.

My current dwelling house doesn't offer a particularly smart finish to the outdoors. It reeks of carbon monoxide, and bizarre incidents of sanitation, yes, certainly unfold in the yard. So perhaps for these reasons, alongside the less than comprehensive fidelity of my general character, I imagine I will never be tasked with the care of this babe. And gladly, for I imagine simply touching his flesh would be as stressful as having a dog made of lunchmeat: going for a walk and ripping its head off, wearing out its feet or losing an eye on a low-swooping branch. It would be like getting to know the big hole of disproportion that hangs somewhere between pleasure and sin. How we learn more and more about ourselves simply to get better at knowing our own evils.

What if the baby trickled out a dreadful dark urine, a colour more cruel, more curdling, than any shade of green? Then what? Colour will always be a whore. Even in useless clearings with nothing to live for.

And I don't want a baby. Not a real, hot, wiggling thing. Although perhaps just knowing the kid would be like that moment biblical zealots dream of when God leans in and you see from the lit frenzy of somebody close to you that miracles really can happen if you will them hard enough.

What a sweet fragile little egg; poor little nobody egg! Only when it seems life is over do we learn to live.

In Greece where I have been there is a mosaic that depicts mostly eccentric eclipses of human nature – battles, births and braided ropes whose textural terms are those of pain and beauty. Like my own neighbourly baby, there is a progressive melancholy such that you could say the theme was fracture rather than empathy. Even the scrawny trees and civic squares are washed with an elbow-nudging peculiarity.

And although the skins of the Ancient Greeks rarely appear washed over with green, the general constitution of their malady, whatever it might in fact be, has been mirrored from all angles. The people are hard-edged. I have often thought if only I could change the tone or inflection of my own thoughts towards these pictures, then perhaps the scenes might brighten, might unpack a great grinning sunshine for instance, or a candy man laden with sticky raisin cakes.

But looking again at the parental card with the glowing neighbour child, does it suggest to me the perpetuation of a species? Or rather impulsive emotions of infanticide? Want as I am to project my own character, I see a marital breast filled with wretched domestic affairs and root personality disorder. What a monstrous birth this neighbour boy!

My loyalty to lost causes is sturdy. I can see the boy inside his own house, looking cold even with his private flood of warm rooms. His parents still never appear fully framed in the doorways or window. Theirs is an off-kilter house that I imagine full of stone people eating dried stalks or picking hairs from mouse bones. Isn't tedium just another facet of delayed interest? Some impossible mixture just to prop us up en route to the next frown, to the next clunky point of information. The solemnity of the occupants gives me plenty of scope for imaginative licence.

If I felt comfortable as part of a shapely contemporary scene, I'd scoop up the baby and boom around in a car until the light became general and even again. Perhaps laying some headphones over his ears and tinkling out a sonata or two to put him at ease. Mine being a scene of sorry crumb-like quality, I am stuck again with the unreasonable noise of invention.

I suppose all truth be told I was not so much upset to welcome this child into my daily purview, rather curious how to kick against what, inevitably, was the natural necessity of this boy to lie shrivelled like an evil little nut across my lawn.

More fun for me would be some direct words with this babe or his outstretched arms shuffling through my things, getting plump and less green on the softness of my carpets, near the freshness of my herbs.

Could I pluck that soggy little bod from its frame?

Being a fan of trinkets and the shapely bosom of soft figuration especially, I would surely cover his body in plaster and sit it up with a few brass pins – on a mantelpiece for instance, or a card table. Let him hover on a shelf just behind my ear whilst I cut a pear on some scruffy board, willing me to slice every piece just so. I'd use him as an emblem of all things lost, of the wretchedness and various tones of restoration.

But particularly because I've always been a believer in the symbolism of *trompe l'œil* and its validity as another dimension of reality, I have resolved to take the arrival of this child as a cue to weep to show concern, to weep selfishly for the pain in my back, my broken shoes and ugly teeth. To weep for my sinister urges and pasty demeanour. To generally plough forth with the checks and balances of emotion.

I don't often know why I tell of these things so generously. I wonder if the delights are just born from savage stupidity. I don't know anything about this boy. I still hate him, as much as I hate myself. Or do I feel like a Catholic queer who instead of preaching just tells you they're a poet?

And anyway all that background fury keeps me agile. I mean really I only have to think of all my consumed breakfast carcinogens, of burnt toast or pan crust. I eat ammonia cookies and there is a component of bleach in my sweat. This domestic space and all its chemical euphoria can surely make space for a small patch of noxious green. For a small patch of lovely green and a couple of tiny limbs.

My bathroom is becoming a laboratory kindling suffering. I can't keep up with the suffering, no time amongst the various washes, the various shades of choco pie, clam chowder, bookbinder soup, cheese dogs, devilled eggs, devilled crab, devilled kidneys, garden salad and mulligan stew. All that stuff which repeatedly spills from my guts with water. That sometimes splashes up the wall and just about touches the picture of that glinting baby boy. I should ding my fist through the cistern wall, plummeting that baby down into the flush for good. This stinking green baby in my stinking white toilet in this stinking beige neighbourhood.

I have thought about removing the baby. Grappling him outdoors and into a seat in my car. Everyone loves the outdoors. Everyone loves smiles emitted from parked sedans where just about everything is mingled with high speeds and pummelling sunshine. I would show him the weeds under tall trees, spoon warm coffee into his mouth and feed him gently from the bowls of peanut-and-corn farmers.

I am not an insolent driver and with all those emblems of luck dangling from my mirror any ugly tired feelings of boredom or sickness would be surely fast replaced with gurgling red cheeks all happy warm by my side.

I could exercise great care regarding the thresholds of consistency and constraint, never forgetting of course that towns are correlates for roads and roads are routes that consistently refashion angles of civic violence. I would of course congratulate myself on the resplendent symbolism. The car is a good place to be drilled with pep. With happiness.

The baby seems to age. Growing long and less fragile. His green has softened to blue and the gushes of shrieks heard in the night have lapsed to laughter. He wears clothes not cloth. Out on the porch of our hard-adjoining patios, his face turned up to the irradiation of skylight, he is a picture of endlessness. He is not my analogue.

I will plop down daily, open the freezer to some inexplicable cantaloupe jelly and sit waiting for punishment or inspiration. My white socks, long and hardening, have bobbled to grit around the heel. This is the tragedy of the single citizen, although at least I am dressed. They say it is a success to open the door on another day so I cheer a personal cheer and plod to the bathroom to stare at the original green baby.

MESSRS.
EXTERNAL & COMMUNITY

Invent the underworld

There was a time when community memory was a rough hickory box with a keyboard and coin slot. With buttons in happy colours. You could drop in the correct change and watch a computerised board deliver slices of written prophecy. There were prophecies for birthdays and promotions, for special occasions or illness: stories for the most childish children, stories for the redheads, for the proprietress' dangerous eyelashes, for the suicidal and the Frankensteins with their cobbled-together aspirations.

The process was often one of transformation. Good news or bad, people were often so gripped by their personal revelations as to throw themselves off the nearest viaducts. Or dash moist and electrically conductive to grab pylons and push 25,000 volts through their feeble minds. All for new visions. It was something like the strange language of wind, all its individuality. Standing on the analogue threshold of the apocalypse. The modest and the microscopic, with birds knowing it all. In wind you are never alone. It's magic. Invoking imminence or transcendence through the battery of wind.

If someone told you they knew a secret, it was

hard not to ask, and in this way people always felt extraterritorial, even in their own towns. Comfortable people look out of their windows and say *wind* or *sky* or *tree*. Or they whisper *gorgeous* to the rhododendrons full of God and senseless because of it. Who looks out of a window hoping to say *smog* or *ruin*?

The memory box knew our own giddy urge to listen. To look, always, for the sky because we're lazy and stupid, but ever curious. And so rules often stated that the box be visited at dusk, or night, when candles trailed their sludgy wax straight onto the floor. Candles everywhere, by the way, incessant in their need to be lit, to be lit forever, for every birthday, forever.

The makers assumed that poor light would keep the real future neatly under wraps. That in gloom or the light of a single stricken star, you couldn't distinguish one form from another. In being told *you will die a steamy death*, a visiting patron would not so easily see God speaking to them or see the burning bush where, well, the bush should have been. Instead of malignancy in the armpit glands, they'd see a heron poised on a wetted rock. It was confused. Elaborate allegories all over meant that for all the talk of prophecies, nobody really knew where they stood. The kids hovered about in the present, barely knowing what envelope glue tasted like and the adults felt generally hunted or under the hairs of an indiscriminate shotgun. People developed anxiety rashes. It became hard to know if you were morbidly obese or morbidly deceased.

We like to know where we stand in time. We like to feel the pulse of it beat about our temples and grab our wrists. On the soft underside where the skin thins and bruisy veins tangle hurt and beauty in lilac bundles; this area of body that is neither hand nor arm, but a functional joint whose medial lines make it keen to belong to both.

Well the memory box stomps time clean underfoot. It smacks time in the face with a lump hammer to make it stand still. You watch it wither, watch time crumble.

The designers with their carefully allied delegates at the Town Hall suggested a humble box. They fashioned crude promises with indecent perspective and rolled it all out like a creamy celebration. No doubt the architects were attuned to the precise histories of melancholy and farming. No doubt they had watched millennia of plant life, of forests, shuffle between greens and greys greasy and uncertain. Did they design the box to congregate towns and villages where whole communities were turned to dismal flagellation? Did they envisage everybody living quietly under bushes? Or under stones whose individual weights were proportionate to or smaller than the bodies of their tenants: neither comfortable, yet careful not to crush them either. Or did they imagine prophecy to empower more cheerfully: with everybody leaning in for a kiss and their teeth smelling of sand and the beach?

Knowing of the box only made us imagine noisy graveyards filled with gossip and dinner parties with no curfew in sight. It was lousy in all directions.

We personally have never made a trip to consult the box. We cannot trust the compulsion to micromanage, to get red in the face. We need to keep simple details in mind, need to know that our hearts are pieced together with more than a flimsy elastic band.

We know that life hosts many characters: the lover, the wife, the ghost, the ordinaries. We prefer to open our gateway towards the implausibly gigantic cosmos by route of our own domestic care. Come to our houses and we'll show you the soft carpets and potted plants. The various shades of cream. We can siphon through our patterns together, sift mangy potted junk through gauze curtains: half-sucked gumballs, avocado pits, a Lego head with its face stomped off. A measured distance of things. An octave. A crisis of novelty or rage hidden always behind a smile and the body, which goes along with it all anyway, barely capable of the singular decisiveness of simply standing up, of holding one's shoulders out to keep the arms swinging as they do. It's our idea of desire, all these commas.

Crimes of violence happen with such frequency that it is sometimes hard to know where the dirty ends and the clean begins. One's conscience is a skewed map. And so few have family where bonds of love are not transgressed by acts of incest or feud, that we are all little more than a set of tangled strings, heaving through the dramatics of hours so unremarkable that a year or two may pass without notice. This is a feeling not exactly acclaimed in popular opinion.

And even so we'll continue to plough merciless hours into thinking about that box and its skill. Who could possibly visit that damn box and not see thereafter everything as a happy symbolism? Everything sort of sweet or dutifully cautious in saying, *Can I interest you?* Even a chocolate wrapper or smelly carton in your hand would suddenly seem to rattle as though it had just a few lines of poetry to share. What child or adult could help but wonder if they had stumbled into the underworld, accidentally found some tear in the Earth's pubescent skin and slipped right through? Any one of them could be forgiven, on hearing the box and its manufactured language, for thinking they had fallen quite away from home and into a woody nowhere entirely blank and unplottable.

We couldn't resist the box.

It asked us questions. It spoke, we never knew. It gripped us where we felt it and washed us inside out. It asked about greed and the qualities of a life on the inside, a life on the outside. It didn't even look like a box. It said, in plain English: *Do you take showers or baths? Tell me, just a little something, about this thin bag stapled shut across the seams, strung with brass bells and light branches. Tell me of that bunting of muddied socks and those torn pockets that bump your hips, that knock cups right over. Is there traffic on the river? Or scum and sludge? Are you a fern or a puddle? Are you an over-sexed lampshade? Do you pay for love? Do you pay for sex? Are you disabled? Tell me your strangeness? Can you please, for one second, show me a sense of tactile engagement with this world?*

What would you like?

Have we met before?

Who are you?

MESSRS.
EXTERNAL & BLUE

Shorts, early

We saw much more after that. Our eyes more open, more eager to report. We sensed even in cold air that a great many things could be built out of bounds.

Everything happened when the lights went out. And then how much braver the sun felt than a streetlamp. And how much braver the chlorinated pool of memory was than the infidelity of that desire. Perhaps something stirred in her marrow of suspicion when she found the blue hat hung up by the door. Not his. Ethan. Not hers. Patrice. Not familiar. History is a suitcase filled with money, a schoolboy's cap on a peg, a wife with her smile in the bath.

We watch him of an evening as he walks fast across grass. He eats a banana and flings the peel in the bushes. He moves as though his hands are too big, as though he sees his early self in shorts, so small and barefooted sprawling through the foamy space of youth: *Mother, mother, what is the name of this flower?*

ETHAN

Th Dyssy

I knew that too much recollection would reveal the worst in something. Like how sleep reveals the bug of psychosis and roll out of bed on the wrong side and you are glued in muck to begin with.

Well, the neighbours are at it again. They didn't keep the green baby. Or rather it didn't keep them. It put on several pounds after weaning, milk and matter, and then clamped its jaw shut in silence. I saw utensils arriving at the house for days. Orange spoons and plastics with all their ergonomic hygiene destined for nursing and coercion. The parents wore new white tennis shoes and appeared bright taking packages, but I could see their blackened eyes losing focus.

In better houses the phone would later ring announcing misery and a funeral. The other children were marshalled about, draped in blacks, unusually tall with their hair parted and their tears programmed to fall.

In my own home I simply fell seasick. A sick that no sucking stones or peppermints in the pocket would soothe. The image of life, I decided, was prized to me. Like sugar. Like dried salmon thinly sliced and soaked in salt.

And then I worried a lot. Me being grave and somewhat of a weeper. Because grief is a tilting thing. It strips speech right out of you. Time is a weapon. It makes an imperative of the possession of an alphabet of flexible letters that may stand in should grief strike you altogether dumb. Something like a Grief Pack, marketed to losers and loners alike, where you can simply hoist two S's and an O above your roof and allow those sunless letters to write their own temperature: *send out succour, save our son, save our souls.*

S.O.S.

Two snakes and a great hole in the middle. You always need an O. Our mouths were made to open. You need vowels in grief like we all need a deep notch of love. Rhythms that take you forwards, like rungs, and move you, ill-footed on a decaying staircase, towards a friend with one hand outstretched and a bag of fresh baked baguettes swinging from the other.

Science (old magic)

I didn't open my door for weeks. And not for lack of knocking. I made a man for the fridge, whose face was a *No Smoking* sign, a slash of red from left ear to right chin, magnet eyes. I dreamt of everything holding a cigarette in front of it.

There is an evening feeling that happens

when snaps of light are blown pinkish and fleeting over the flat chest of that refrigerator. It's not often that you see domestic white turned to skin. When your white goods blush before recourse to indifferent cold composure. I find the sepulchral firmness of appliances reassuring. I find them profligate, like weeds.

Devices and science do keep you busy. They give pronunciation to the most horrid of urges, ones you perform carefully with routine and empirical neatness. They bring out the protagonist perspective in you, the science of personal hands. The science of breathing solvent naphtha is one to explore, I think, wondering if I should be filling the car instead of draining blue bottles down the sink. Sniffing could become a habit. The stink of science really summons you to your senses.

In my garage I have set aside a large white freezer box. It is full and diverse. It hosts a community of beetles and branches, some rust and a barrel of ale. Plus a wobbly nightstand and two plastic ducks whose lips like petrified rubber have softened and broken apart. With a heat gun I made short work of some ancient gauge gaskets, melting things so they smelt of chips and vinegar. All this in my garage with the sloping floor, with the plastic table hung high on the wall, behind my ladders. What a fine picnic I have here, I snorted: the fire is in the pots, the wine is waiting. It is clear I should invite someone for lunch.

And then an interruption: a wailing male knocked at my door dressed in suede belts ornamental with nail heads and black silk girdles. I marvelled at the overlapping tinsel body, fabric quick-cut and stacked thick with weeping gems. His shadow grazed the earth outside my door, a mirage in the porch light, his long hair tied and a flashy abdomen – so pretty! A precise reek of spirits dropped right out of his jaws.

Living near an inn of increasingly withering repute, I did a quick sum and figured that the general X's and Y's of being seen with such a spooky sardine wouldn't twist too many feathers, what with anyway my marvellous moonlight excursions being nothing but a little bark afloat on a wide sea of fat hoggish failures: we live and die on the fly, oh what a fun fly to fish that eve!

Well then, no point in concealing the fact: a fisherman in the middle of the night I would be! The door being open and dangling open all days but Sunday we strode into *The Merry-Making Railroad*. Me in a drab shirt, white still but greying nevertheless, and them – the inn and that man – shadowed with a mysterious froth, frazzled around the edges. The result of months of personal quiet, this disturbance might be seismic and I would leave no stone unturned.

We winded the room as we entered. Our feet, partnered in step, clacked out a mechanical beat, heavy on the human air. Sometimes the organ of the skin and how it fits is just a metaphorical stance for paranoia, for its sarcasm and sympathy. Sometimes I feel like my clothes obey this stance, like I wear trousers whose reciprocal campaign for my legs is one of such rigid cylindrical purpose that stepping out in them requires a stride of comically elongated length. This is the industry of walking and I performed well, my shirt neatly tucked at the front.

Our shoes moaned in tandem: *tap tap*, *tap tap*. All those twos and fours, one rhythm intersecting another just to move us forwards towards the bar. My personal shoes shook out a shine. They gleamed, like leather, like my face, grooming the carpet and stirring its fluff. How technical, I thought, how arousing. I didn't feel like laughing so looked instead to their tiny details of manufacture, the stitches and soles, and my personal knots, how tight I'd tied them, cupping curves close around my foot.

People love to mock. That was the general musical way of it. Pots and pans clanged for effect, bread buttered and stitched back together again. All the voices hemmed in with ice cream and strawberry shortcake specials.

My appearance provoked all kinds of appreciation amidst the spectators. But I was confident in my blocky body and colourful outerwear.

I wouldn't turn pale with embarrassment for any of them; I was a man with qualities.

The tavern air thickened nicely. Little white aprons behind the bar moved to service here and there, twitchy with expectation. Looking at us all from above with our meady snouts and rouged chins we'd be denounced the entire world over. We drank beer and wine. We sloshed it over hunched bodies with our pints like clusters of feeding piglets.

Look at all of these blessed idiots I thought, massaging my ankle. Old bastards. For nearly a thousand years, these peasants had waited for an opportunity to throw off the yoke that held them down to the grindstone! And here they still sat with their tenderloin pique, their mushrooms, new asparagus and new potatoes, their *sorbet au kirsch* when the time was right.

I sensed that my companion was riled by my erratic movements. By my feet fidgeting in their socks. What did he expect? I wouldn't lean in to lick his face. Not there. I wouldn't offer a romantic bed or sweet letters in italics. Was I to make myself less of a dying man by telling him of my parenting successes? I felt myself dilating. My lungs drained of volume in thinking about the chocolate egg children I'd stuffed with our mutually deleterious effects. With our marriage. Poor children who were practically sealed up and stored out of the way. Was I to say to this man, *Here is my house, it is mine, although I love you so now you have the key, you can let yourself in?*

I'd cheerily check into a hotel, twist the knob and deliver my body to the auspices of whatever individual chose to have me. A delightful room, mind, one cheery enough to kill oneself in. I could suggest it.

Heck, a strong clear Havana cigar will do very well for a stately occasion or for a late dinner affair especially if you can lie abed next morning, but for regular puffing, real pleasure and enjoyment, also for those stable nerves required in the ageless professional man, there is but one cigar that hits it off to the letter: a good smoke, a long smoke.

What is difficult in the ruins of alcohol is how buildings on the street become endless, joining again and again in run-ons as far as the eye can see. So in describing the way home marked by several waste bags, I could in fact be talking myself towards an abundantly lit wrong direction.

PATRICE

Happiness

My television area is something of a building site. Piled high with designs of humiliation and cheer. A masterpiece in the medium of juice boxes and pasta sauce. There are dirty cushions and drink stains that seen from above might appear triumphant, like my own Olympic rings. All of it is a very British broadcasting.

My two favourite characters both perform nightly every day of the week. The newsreader for one, with his recalcitrant manhood, looks unnatural enough to assure me that his predicament is as unsteady as the rest of us. His face! God his face looks like a dead crab. And mine mirroring it: two dead crabs!

And then the deodorant boy, who advertises a cheap brand with an all-round liveliness that makes me wonder if he were not solely built to churn such innocent emotions. I feel just watching him pass through my screen would be to sully something fine and good. Do they rub ice over his nipples to erect them to that height? He was no crab! With eyes the kind of watery blue that mothers adore, that turn girls and boys wet through their knickers, eyes that incite curses such as *twiglet* and *faggot* on the street. Eternal eyes. Eyes that, one way or another, will keep their happy blue through cruel lust and hardship alike.

My personal grownup fantasies are pictured in dreams of other things. All those prickled thoughts considered too risky are trashed by the wayside only to come back, of course, as all difficult things do, pushing up from the soil. The hedgerows on the edges of towns are fertile hotbeds of deranged matter, cruelly clear like old fridges and radio sets. An empty fucking washing up bottle: what new and modern gems! The towns from afar look thick and silent.

When winter blows in, it sneezes all over. The ground freezes and the gorgeous plump thighs of summer are shoved into wool trousers so legs can go about stamping all over the paraphernalia we just pulled up to inspect. Hardly one season has arrived than another swoops in to muddle it all up again. Modern relationships are just as hard and soft as weather, changing with every locale.

I've lost the knack of intuition. My green fingers have turned brown. Brown as in buggered and evacuated, probably because I am stuck digging subjective black holes with one hand, gin crackling in the glass of my other, conversing with the neighbours, the daughters, the pope and his friends, *everyone*, busy staggering around out on the lawn being merry and looking appropriate and moral with conviction.

I could be roasting a pig on coals in my garden: let's just call that a summer afternoon. It's not that

I'm out every day literally barbecuing myself to death, but the idea of it is there, all laid out on the lawn.

Instead on television are the *Seven Most Frightening Things Discovered Under Beds* and there is space again, all shuttered, cut up and carved into irregular pieces. I've watched over a hundred episodes amidst my cushions on the sofa. Sloshing away the frozen bits of me with some warm wine, with a salad and oven-roasted nostalgia. It feels something like time travel, an endless state of buffering. Of reloading.

That is the great magic of television, a magic not brewed in a laboratory, a magic without molecular structure. It enables us. Electrical light, like the pure vision of souls, can be seen escaping from the tops of houses. And that's television. When the room goes shadowy and the light outdoors has sort of sifted down to the bottom of the sky I know it's time to turn on. The light that pours from its screen is soft-blue enough to fuzz outlines and merge my own self with the bodies of those on screen. We move together. Nothing is hard edged. The navy outside licks against the windows so thick it would knock you over. And yet as soon as the indoor lights go out and heads hit their pillows, everything is orange and pink and green.

Together we know that I am the passive

spectator; television and I, we agree that neither one of us need do anything other than exist. If I leave to make a coffee or slap something on a plate, our particular thrilling brand of agreement firmly ensures my TV will continue to puddle out its image language, business hours or not.

So I am building up my own homestead fortress to provide a comfy place for my TV guests. We're hosting each other. Through the cartoons and soap runs I'm amassing quite a cast of itinerant bodies. As if we are communicating! But I am quite happy to form a personal response to trash, to melodrama, crime, news or skinny commercial glamour. I'm happy with or without my organic food exploits and the telly protagonists with their general *joie de vivre* for just about everything. I'm happy with cold toast.

As I eat my snacks and watch my television I picture the food stacking up in my stomach just as the commercials are stacking up in my brain. Pulling up new behaviours through the crust of very old behaviours as easy as switching on a television.

Great is wickedness

Sometimes a huge car pulls up; its occupants get out and the doors slam. The disturbance shakes my walls. There is much animation around my coffee table as I scramble to see, to restore circulation in my legs, but I rarely know the people. They haven't come to see me.

In school they warned us about strangers in maroon cars. Always the Mondeo wagons or Land Rovers with modified car boot horrors. Cars with no regard for the binary ends of the spectrum, but rather the sludgy leaf colours you'd never choose for yourself and would be wary to kick through anyway – as piled leaves in these actual colours – even in rubber boots. Teachers said these cars would be out when the sun set but we needn't worry as the spectrum of our young days would be near finished and off into bed by then. Plus anyway, they said, you can always tell a villain a few hundred metres off, their sleeves and trouser legs are either a little too short or a little too long.

That you could turn many of life's big questions into easy hemispherical splits was of great curiosity to me. To think that the classically understood *right and wrong* was as simple as not driving a maroon car or being around when the sun set was as radical as to suggest a kind of ceremonial rigour. It was a crazy simplicity of thinking that instilled in me a deep apprehension of the colour crimson. I'd see a colour tone on just the wrong side of itself and would always be seeking to add some yellow, to brighten it up a bit or make it darker and dirty. I would press my fist into my palm and imagine somewhere on the other side of the world where I could drink my milk in the bright stream of noon.

On more wizened dismantling tools

Go on, I thought, I'll post a classified, only to clarify, only to get me out of this spiritual torpor:

> *Good-sense-of-humour seeks bottom-up takeovers focusing on cyber soft-weaponry and metropolitan trampling;* GSOH *seeks worms who burrow for a tear;* GSOH *seeks metabolic stasis.* GSOH *is a broken heart crossing the room at the party; a body entirely covered by glued-on sections of the world map, a body exuding chemical fumes and a general need to be plastered in phrases of desire.* GSOH *seeks a firm chest and fingers light on a bow.* GSOH *makes a lovely Sunday lunch, is a happy conspirator dishevelled in the Sabbath breeze.* GSOH *seeks similar.*

MESSRS. EXTERNAL & PEATY

Rotten earth

All over the world bodies are wrapped up in themselves pursuing an ancient utopia. Pursuing flavour and experience. Birds too are part of it, part of this wild wheel of anthills and deckchairs. Picking out crumbs left by strangers with blood in their shoe. All over the world we're disappointed to find greens packed with too much unhealthy skin. We are no longer astonished by the seasons and their glittering parks. Even the rainforest suddenly stinks of skin. The forest seeds trees that are barely grown before they're cut down again for paper and houses or money. And the price of timber rockets. Birds and worms begin to die out all the world over. Migration patterns scramble, seagulls constipate and drop right out of the sky into the sea.

Even the delicate whorl of wood grain becomes as coveted as the fingerprint unique to all digits. It's replicated on ceramic tiles where the legibility of the pixels from click-print breaks hearts and the skeuomorph becomes a tragic king of trade. Nature and its original patterns are pulled into scarcity.

Everyone rushes about wincing at the VAT, mumbling about trade discounts, but jolly too because of course, *of course*, doesn't everybody know that wood grain is *added value* even if its value is just some pimpled adolescent newly skilled in digital cut-and-paste whose family kitchen store is doing a two-for-one on laminate flooring and matching Idigbo push-and-swing cupboard doors. Even if the wood grain didn't actually come from its native Cameroon or Ivory Coast or Ghana or even Nigeria. Even if it wasn't ever sprayed for bark beetle, fumigated with methyl bromide and stamped up with a cheerful ISPM-15 to satisfy the most rigorous international phytosanitary measures. Even if the wood grain came from a low-res Google image session somewhere between a jerk off and some soggy tissues, even then, the value my friend, is added. Even then.

Even when the world behaves despicably, when our despots are their most despotic, when slaughter and fraud and miserable housing with asbestos roofs and broken taps, with dead cats in gardens and general wolves in sheepskin all the planet over – when the world rains down those long dark days, still the sky always looks so innocent.

Our people are rotten. Are we proud of our rotten foe? In institutions there are dark museums with their collections of hideous deeds, notorious poisoners and inspired assassins. There are the umbrellas firing ricin-filled pellets and letters of killers in scalloped scum to hell and back. All are secreted shrines of the most commutable filthy things at arm's reach: tissues, pancreatic acid, murder.

Newspapers are always cooking morality down to a filthy bile. They discover caravans in forests where instead of birds and worms and people happily cooking with their propane and enamel spoons, little scrolls of human skin are found sheared off, rolled up and wax-stamped with Masonic seals.

Cheese moulders in the fridge and not disposing it, somebody films, cultivates and disperses the mould spores onto the clothing of strangers on public transport. It becomes a top hit on the Internet. It reaches download figures in the millions. Internet service providers engage in deliberate bandwidth throttling, they regulate network traffic with an intentional slowing of their systems and everybody is suddenly concerned at the prolificacy of real-life humans interested in acting out small deeds of harm on one another. People collide and continue on their manic tilt. It makes cohabitation look serene.

ETHAN

A tobacco zone

My own contact with quality has been reduced to such a bare minimum that any unsolicited visits might conclude in murder with a bread knife. Even my ice cream, so cleverly named, oh so carefully enjoyed in front of screens not quite divesting UV light although perhaps soon powered-up to deliver a suntan so I don't even need to go out into Nature anymore to perform the dermal synthesis of actually making Vitamin D, even my ice cream name curves its comedy edges around to morbidity: *Raisin Hell*.

I am obsessed again with the weather and the condition of my head, its architecture, which is falling down around my shoulders, and I'm committed to liquid dispensation.

I drank exterminator moth solution: one quart mixed with water, with a smart cocktail umbrella and a maraschino cherry reeking of sulphur dioxide and Red#4. I practically bled sugar.

I was playing a new computer game – *PUNKO!* – fun for drunkards, this latest American craze, still in prototype. Four players were diced in – Owner, Architect, Engineer and Contractor – all figures cast with a remarkable absence of grace and the roles changing each round. All figures were hunted, bagged and bodied before midnight, befriended from the great mass of online men-for-men teeming in their millions out there. I clicked with persuasion.

The game was designed like the remains of a phonebook. Some thundering enterprise would be proposed on behalf of the Owner by cards summoned forth from electronic piles. We built and pulled instructions, not stammering with any self-consciousness at all.

As players we plundered each phase of a project – design, planning, construction – with possible actions and their narrative impacts determined by theme-specific preparation. We exchanged sandbags and meat choppers, feeling presidential with our many illustrious pockets busy on the open and close. We alternated actions that benefitted some but not all participants. We built walls and great prisons. We played roles suitable to our general conditions, to our eloquence and zeal of general office life.

Our imagination was key. Us judicious authors of new plots, new malls or Burger Kings in our world otherwise lacking in what we termed 'good judgement'. We spent big money and the lots increased in value while we slept. We built sugar plants and new forestry schools. I felt myself to be very wise and restored with a great sense of judgement. My kidneys twinged at the sight of all the pretzel ends strewn across the living room floor.

This was a game of great artistic freedom and I amazed myself with a development of spa towns in blossom with great limestone facades. I rigged the piazzas with fairy lights, unconcerned about towns I'd razed en route. All the people who'd made space for my plot just stood there in miniature shaking their digital fists, left in clumps outside grocers whose cabbages had long gone sour.

I oversaw popular pine- and spruce-planing mills – my holding bays with floor-to-ceiling stacks of the country's largest red cedar shingles. I bit my nails raw over the cost of metal and cement, almost blowing my chest out when the exchange rates flew in a tumble. I bloomed a rash across my face but in the dim light of my screen you couldn't tell at all. My attitude was not one of indifference, but part of an inner reawakening.

The game was so long and expansive it was hard to know whether I was obsessed with horizontality or with the thickening vertical plumes of my skyscrapers and cranes. I wanted to experience space. I ached for it, feeling like certain birds that can also explain territorial fears because they have crossed whole oceans without once taking pause from the beating of their wings. I sat without clothes, ensuring my routes, even with hard shoulders and bending roads, were the greatest and I made progress, which all clever people will tell you is a specific type of vertical chronology.

There were no ordinary espressos, just everything blown up big enough to keep caffeine and virtue in one breath. I apologised for nothing, seeing that really I was acting with quite paternal kindness.

The game raged its unending timescale. It made me feel as though the only way to move through the world was to click my cursor on *demolish*. I mowed down Inca crop terraces, earning big profits. The cards sent a cloudburst and one town flooded. They held a horse show and fine steeds entered. I was buying and selling tableware at economic prices. There were simple vouchers to gather the poor and medium-poor peasants for a newly urgent wickerwork; a liberation of the proletariat from glassy to clear-seeing. Lawn fences – I built them, neat fences for neat homes that would last for years without painting. I was proud of my farms and being unable to tell a lettuce from a cucumber, I was generally proud of the produce too.

I had many fancies and was sure I was attaining a mastery of this craft. I almost didn't notice the contractions, the cruel pricks that rang in my ears. I sweated dead shell stuff whiter than any moon. The silence was the loudest of all.

What a sprawling bear I'd become, spilling red and raging out of my pants, a smouldering rat, a man, a man! So singular was my devotion to original sin, to a situation of pleasure. To a situation: that was the intangibility of the thing itself. I hadn't felt so pink and clear since birth. I was personally driven towards a future, any future.

Perhaps I lay there somewhere between pillows and puddles. One half of my jaundiced face clearly minus a few vits; the other half coloured with sodium streetlight. Outside noise spat through the doors.

I was beyond seasons, imagining September, possibly England. Objects were scaled beneath me, beside me. Shaven I was not: sneezed out liquids, yes, a thin jumper, dyed. There was music with the tenor of genius. A soundtrack. Something throbbed. Headache, known, and then muscle pain stealing its thunder.

I see well enough how sufficient my judgement was. I was as huge as a horse stuck in a shaft. A panting fever. I was a free man or nothing at all and, game or no game, I would continue to drink myself beyond the wide empty field I called shaking hands with death.

MESSRS.
EXTERNAL & SORRY

Witch grass

There are many categories for the players: money, skills, service, entertainment, romance, shopping, leisure, politics and residence. Each of these categories has special items. Hopes are pinned on some ungodly transmutation. Sometimes a glitch wrecks the ship. A virus blows the system apart and categories malfunction. The economy splinters and people weep as their land loses value. The people wave their arms about wildly. They create custom content and sell terrible things at a higher retail price. Mothers weep and fathers bury their shame. Children lie motionless in trenches. Furniture can be created and uploaded, single-tile outlines with sculpture and nature universally non-specific. There is not enough salt and no soup to season anyway. It is a crisis of vision and all that can be heard amidst the many onlookers is the sound of enormous canvas suitcases being dropped into the sea.

We now are quite sure: it isn't us who have become attached to the place, but the place that has become attached to us.

ETHAN

Ichnos frog

In the kitchen shared by these two rooms, I have been known to leave the oven woefully unattended, finding days later my fortune blackened in a pan with a high carbon stench: an unhappy cat or a pair of scales. Like my brain, which with its two hemispheres is also weighted on a tilt.

I am still on the floor. I am a current leftover holding his own liver. Inside architecture, but outside too. What a suspension. This hangover. To be hanging over oneself. My eyesight feels limited, rolled up in a cylinder whose wick has not been lit. And right here beside me, yapping like a dog, is what looks like a brain, my brain. It's rolled out, a flattened chicken paillard, all griddled and walloped and grey. It flaps for attention.

Of course my head is here, my lovely head, still attached; the sinews are soggy, but I sense my lollipop hasn't rolled completely off its stick just yet.

At the window small rain is wetting with innocent motives. Wet stuff full of colour and clamour. From this lateral position down low I can see clouds passing overhead, all those creamy shapes with their proper Latin names ending in '*us*' which makes me feel closely held in even though I couldn't tell you of their structure.

It comes back to me slowly, the physics of falling. This miraculous expanding universe surprises me all the time. I am so routinely off course. Sometimes I feel at odds with almost everything although with pleasure I taste that Red#4 still lingers around my lips.

It would be impossible for anyone to enter without a key. If I roll my eyes back far enough, I can see a small patch of blue foil flattened into the carpet. I wonder what it would be like for another me to open the door right now and find this alternate me-figure mapped out with an expression that was simply a reflection of its own broken structure. How there might be a gasp and a voice only just hinged together, torn: *I see that you too, like me, are glad to be punished*.

I am having an experience of space that is tapering quickly away from conditions of matter that I had before gladly assumed to know. I want to laugh because all the feelings nearby have suddenly changed direction and a big gush of them is whacking me in the face and it's hot like irony because for the first time in days I feel alive. Like when the death of a loved one reminds you to feel and you're suddenly opened up to weather, to how skin sticks on a body alert to sensation.

I love how my relation to fact arrives in wavelengths of feeling. If you look and look for long enough, profound motionless whiteness becomes quite the summit of activity. Enough to see the outlines of animals, many-hued and full of heat, and all of them symbolic optimisms.

I wonder if mice or birds are perfectly wrought parts of some mechanical symphony I've habitually overlooked. If twigs and money are in fact forged from the same stuff, just painted over in military application with miraculous skins that feign a suggestive difference. I must get some work done on my face, must plant some poppies to commemorate, must be a good little guy.

I have now only two rooms, left and right hemispheres. They correspond to a singular hallway. It works without me. The clump of skinny ferns in the corner never dies. I said, *look, it's only a glass of water, what's the big problem?* and suddenly they'd shrugged off transpiration worries and were living pristine as a printed picture.

I am a blood person; this is a blood building, of course. A drawing of a floor plan is the abstraction of an idea, so we live inside one another endlessly.

At least the books are down here. I like to see books. Facts on the contrary are stones. Like bodies, just a collection of lines and weights glued together by contingency.

Am I a weapon? Or a tool tied to conditions of gravity? I feel more like a floppy sausage snipped from its links and left to grey behind the sink. Like that damn laundry-day sock held in equilibrium of forces between action and discovery, getting steadily shabbier because of it. Grey skin in grey pants on grey floor.

Well, certainly we are all under the glut of red meat and wine such that we will be unanimously wretched soon enough. The velvety iris of planet Earth as it smokes and frazzles away. I'm too ashamed to look at myself naked for long. I am convinced I will die a symbolic death. My neighbour's son, the one of two, seems to share the conviction: I can see him performing a hex sign with his fingers and practicing a little death, rolling down dead on his doorstep.

My telephone is lit across the room: artefacts everywhere, fluffed and cluttered like mail in my hall. Each time I peer into the mirror hung there, I think one day my eyes will no longer discern a real face beyond the fuzzy logic of whatever digital light I have stapled to my fingers.

There is something moving on my desk. Didn't the Greeks insist that to view rare animals is to drive out evil spirits? The body I can see is a turtle with the head of a monkey and limbs of a frog. No bigger than a rat in grasses. He is upright, back scratching a metal tray smeared with sauce and smokehouse bones. Last night's dinner has limped loosely back to greet me. A complimentary vision with a passive voice. Perhaps he will climb the tray and sit inside like a bath until I venture to towel him dry. Perhaps my boils will heal. Perhaps my legs will straighten.

Am I accused of assassination? Of my own pleasant optimism? Where has the almightiness of my meanings gone? What wildly capable hands have written a visitation of such spookish insobriety?

I can see a saucer-shaped cavity at the top of his head. It is full like a dish with liquid. Not fierce as zinc vitriol in medieval painting, but shiny enough. The brim is heavy, hanging felted-over in a weary curve.

The frog thing jiggles up and down, bowing his head, kissing his arms in a way that dribbles liquid all over. Between my biros and mechanical erasers he spills almost everything from his dish. So much liquid, so much punch, all that pickled junky juice: *For the ailing stomach, fine lady, good sire, here is alligator soup, a broth of stones*. Perhaps it is a hunger pose. A blinded-by-silverware stance. A test of endurance.

The frog-monkey gives me a queasy look. What a top-heavy hat he wears. I couldn't say at all how the replenishing might occur. If I could reach my phone I'd snap a picture and on the beat of that mechanical click, that no-pleasure-or-pain policy, he'd surely spin and be gone.

The signs are collapsing. I'd murder a soda and its violent brown fizz. Will I vanish if I dry out or cool below zero? I stare at the door as if in persuasion, at the entrance where a crop circle of screws has been pounded into the wall by a manic somebody sowing a bubonic harvest with their drill. This entire building is so parched of moisture that cracks thin out to a nothingness so chalky and precarious that my windows could fall at any moment from their frames.

And I'm thirsty too, still a little poisoned. My qualities are so shapeless and foamy they slip through the fingers. I am a seamless unending horizontality.

Tomorrow I'll pull my shoes back on, dust off the legs. I'll talk about the drinking. Ration the smoking. For now I'll play the utility man, like a utility room, big and cold and vacant.

PATRICE

Jogging to the sister library

I don't ever design campaigns for my life with Napoleonic rigour, nor does my sister, but she does offer espresso after every meal, which provides us both with the stimulant emboldening we crave. There is rigour in this gesture alone. It is these small proclamations of control that make me understand how thoroughly life sits in her grasp. We ate mostly bread and butter, but the food was noticeable for its correctness, the spring of the yeast unbeatable and the butter relaxed to just the right degree of soft.

So I am all over the happy wagon. Back on it. Riding forwards, no point in anything behind, reversing, no point in backwards anymore. The front is definitely a thing; on the back-to-fronts, the behinds, there's always a predicament more grave and startling. I am moving on.

I pulled on socks. Two of them. Only slightly different textures, similar colours, and today I ran. Not a jogging situation, but a running-for-the-bus situation.

I had worn a silver necklace with my socks, a sailboat fashioned from tiny vertical strips like a garden fence. I won it at a fair and the cheap metal performs the unsettling irony of greening my skin the shade of money. It is roughly finished and dots of miniature weld blacken the overlapping segments with tiny burns. Even seeing the little boat sway under my chin, I feel a tug of seasickness rising so I tuck the chain under my sweater at the back with the boat drifting along my spine. The boat snags on labels and long hair like a graceless whaler.

When I ran and missed the bus, I saw the judgements and opinions of the bus riders adhered to the glass of the back window. I saw people pressed sweaty against each other with their necks numbered by moles.

The boat bumped softly against my skin. My back, I thought, is an open wild ocean whilst my front breeches the air, a figurehead prow going god knows where.

I felt no embarrassment for my breathless run. What an easy escalation of progress, from immobile to panting on the curb. A busy dog in sneakers, a jam-packed handbag. I am happy to wait under the open sky, tissues erupting all over onto the floor, which was excellent anyway when my nosebleed arrived.

The small man next to me pointed and said *bleed* as though you might say *plaid*. He said it over and over and I imagined my blood turning to little intersected squares before it hit the pavement. It just dropped like spiders, my nose hanging over my knees to splash onto chewing gum and paper packets. The cracks in the pavement held it all in, infinitely deep, and infinitely shallow. Maybe there was blood inside them too.

When I arrived at the lodging house with a baggy rucksack worn bouncing low against my bottom, the check-in girl described how the particular weight and direction of the bag emphasised the droop of fat around my middle. I was shaken by her honesty. But when I later poured an angry glass of milk, sloshing it onto the floor, her words had triggered a new sensibility. I newly understood the liquid's relationship to its glass bottle, how it is only in a single moment defined and bracketed by the idea *cylinder*. How its meniscus is quite temporary, can be curved up and out as the escaped runs of a smooth spilt edge. How miraculous, I thought, are the atoms that stick us all together, that flex and flinch under friction with other things. The puddle of cool milk on the floor was not exhibiting a new fetish for flatness but was representative to me of an exhilarating crisis of volume that at that moment dissolved everything I thought I knew about subject and object. My own elastic materiality, my own rubbery guilt, it was all connected to this spilt milk.

I am here only one night. To speak with others. Like therapy, but not composed of that old myth of bawling, rather something equipped with weapons and big hair broadcasts.

At first I felt ill-prepared to speak honestly. Hesitant or at least not able to talk in truths or wishes with my outdoor voice. I felt so tentative in my skin. The others smiled, taking books off the shelves from the walls of their dark library.

They showed me illustrations of hell and we'd discuss our favourite modes of torture. I looked at pits filled with naked sinners, all of them poked or boiled or skinned and always exhibiting these funny round little mouths, which I found curious because the sound of pain and eternal torment I always imagined to be more stretched out of the mouth, as though pulled apart with two big clips east and west of the lips. A thin grimaced line, not an O. These people looked like they were faking. I was surprised how many gruesome books could be pulled down together, excitement animating many arms and their biceps like happy apples.

I particularly loved a boldly outlined drawing of a bald man curled on his side whilst a dark blue devil shot an arrow straight up his ass. It made me look up things like *endoscopy* or *colonoscopy* where I'd scan the images for patients with faces exhibiting pain. I was looking for those same round circular mouths, for bodies undergoing the mild hellish torture of medicine whilst living. They were mostly all asleep or sedated beyond muscular capacity, as though pain were simply not possible in the unconsciousness of the dark.

I looked too at long tunnels of people walking to hell, at metabolites excreted in urine. I looked at hives and widespread rashes. I found myself newly interested in all of them. We were sordid and knew it, relished it. Our words were associative; they brought on *gatherings*. I felt a stillness, a certainty that I could thrust myself forwards and my reluctant gravity would change: I would not topple over. Tonight I would not need to cordon myself off under the blanket.

For lunch we laid tablecloths on the grass eating eggs between our fingers. The eggs had boiled so long that their clean white heads felt warmly optimistic. The long pines encircling, the silver birch, so much white on white. We looked like bones at play. And surrounded by those trees sitting out on the grass I was calm and silently enclosed. I would not achieve the hysterical stereotype, I prayed.

My hands on the picnic blanket felt new and the harder I clumped the rough wool against my palm, the more granular the egg became on my tongue. My perception of taste and sound were confused by this pulling of strange new roots of feeling. Like a great synaptic pruning of my brain, speech and meaning no longer seemed correlate principles. The word *woman* fell through my ears and I shuddered with pleasure.

Some people looked at the soil and spoke about family, about gods. Some had dreamed of marrying cowboys. Some denounced the thin and heterosexual in favour of off-piste fornication and bodies built like winter huts for large families. Many lay happily in the commission of sin, bare legs stretched to receive the sun. Some were silent or would whisper when reading so that when they did raise their volume, the body of speech was deliberate, a bold nakedness rising to meet high noon.

I'd married a man who carried his briefcase as though it were simply an extension of his own arm. He'd never looked quite right without it and when he finally left the house empty-handed, the briefcase slightly limp by the door, I didn't say *don't forget it*. In this way, I was the cowboy, lassoing all the artefacts of my life tightly in place.

MESSRS. EXTERNAL & WATERY

Sailing alone

The brain receives a tonic signal from white noise. We have pulled up the collars of our oily raincoats for heavy rain is coming. Its rhythm is a white water, an omen. There is something difficult about being invited out into the rain, something sticky like bad breath as it drips down unprepared necks. Perhaps there is fun to be found in adventure.

We watched the wind roar past as Patrice skipped into a taxi. We watched her bent like a sail to balance and open her door. A simple coming and going towards shop windows that would refuse her, that would bounce the narcotic of seeing back off the glass and towards a penniless purse. She knows she should walk.

Rain makes everything quite the calendar pin-up with its rushes of colour and enlargement. All the usual signs are plastic-bagged and fogged by temperature change. Outlines blurred in an instant. The American-style steam laundry is packed with busted hairdos. Its machines are gurgling washes and their endless vapours curling a secondary hydration shell out through vents and back into the drops. Broken waters and a million marks more.

Her passenger window is flecked with gummy

bobbles. She watches as the wetness sticks and stipples, static charges in cones and wicks. This wet world where the creases of clothes depicted on the marble statues downtown are hewn with a realism so preposterous they reject nothing. Their liquid faces appear lit by a monumental world of stuff to be loved from within, stuff you find when you walk off into weather. Time is circumvented.

She feels like a duck returning. Glad to be caught in a downpour, watching from the inside. Everything looks bound together by events that more and more mean less to all of us. Her taxi glides through it, this primordial formlessness, for there is nothing as abstract as water.

And now rain comes slowly like the inflexibility of pulling a paperclip apart: a mockery of straight lines. The rain cuts and weaves. A sudden floundering tempest and everything reflected back off the floor.

Ethan is also out in the rain, his pearly body busy at the side of the shed. He bounces a rubber ball against the wooden slats, its galactic swirls spinning into his palm and out again, usual and unusual modes of impact. Its springiness threatens his face, one slip through wet hands and there will be a new point of collision off eyes or nose. The sound against the wood is hypnotic, a rude puny thunk amidst the swish of rain.

We say it rains but what about the *rain*? All those constituent parts, all those drip drops – are they *rain* individually? If only one fell from the clouds, squeezed out on its own, would we say *it rained*? Or can it only rain en masse? And when the sky is green and full of light is it still the same kind of rain?

Ethan feels there is adventure on the open sea, out in this great sheet of wetness. He had been digging when he found the ball, partially buried in thin soil. His spades lie half submerged in a shallow pit. Water darkens the handles and he wonders if the wood will split, if the varnish is enough to protect the grain. The rhythms of digging and throwing are similar, he thinks, like sex and breathing.

The post-rain kingdom is stirring. Tiny flies rise together in ropes of vapour, knotting figures of eight that signal the passing of weather. The world is washed.

A health-care professional might say glycerine soap cleanses the skin and clears the face of pimples, keeps the face pure and soft and delicate. Ethan and Patrice will both soon turn their heads towards the sky, with a mutuality of feeling that spreads hot across their cheeks. They will feel the last fine bits of rain gather on their skin, patting the little hairs on their lips. She will wipe it away, taking lipstick with her. He will let it gather against the clumps of growing beard. Rain is always dutiful and sexy, that swill of water, drip drip, drip drop.

Soon bored with its thunder, the sky will blink and shake itself dry. After the suns and moons, dews and wettings, comes sabotage. This was a forecast made across old centuries: the weather was bad and we didn't enjoy it then, we certainly won't enjoy it now.

The beasts shelter out in the provinces and our morose families, our ones and twos and fours, go about indoors with their crooked moods and blistering soup. Ethan will sniff at the air and correct his soggy fringe. Patrice will signal to the driver that her journey is ended. They will feel, for just a minute, the exquisite presence of the absent other and they will hold on for dear life, with fingers and toes and feet.

That is our rain. Rain like words like ants like peaks like spores. In every scripted century rain writes us off as phoney. Every drop is a soluble paradox. Rain is far flung folklore of the friskiest fisherman we ever knew. Rain will see you squelch up nicely in bed with a whelk of a man, a waste of a woman. Rain's nice and worth a trade for a bottle of Sauvignon. Rain's a quack's meeting, oxides on a shaggy neck. Rain's a sweet corner with female associations. Rain doesn't give a thinker's damn, it knows all your business, everybody's business, each single drop an edifying of gambles elsewhere.

And just when we think we've had enough rain and somebody beckons us abroad as the lilies are about to flower, we worry that everything might dry up and blow away.

ETHAN

Chopped hands

My body sags now in all the wrong places, ready for demolition. But I am not a mouldy shack of plywood.

Yes I've been hungry. I've retreated to my begging bowl at night, my swivel chair winding down. And no renunciation of soccer, sex or sin has soothed the ache.

Is it useful *not* to find pleasure in that which cheers others? I have envisioned how the pleasure centres of my brain look clammed hard as a nut. How a drawing of my emotional competencies would be exercised in dried out felt-tip pen. I have envisioned how much better they would feel if tossed high in the air and smashed open with a bright flourish, out of their certain depths of sadism. Is all *that* common pleasure?

I do believe I have sufficient power over myself. I believe in my sticks of arms and legs to keep moving. I'm not ready to join the ranks of those none-eaters whose skin falls slack over their heads like a great hairless rug thrown over, whose cheekbones are proffered up to whatever rotten raven fancies a pecking.

I have cracked it. It has been explained to me by figures of shared austerity: the laws of trauma dictate that *feelings* about feelings offer only a shaky scaffold for healing; it's the *doing* of feelings that shakes them up and breaks them open.

There are many names for it: Yarding, Backyarding, Torso Mania, Hell in a Cell, Big Evil. Underground wrestling is a spark of inspired faith for any misery figure. Flunked out teeth and woozy mornings. There is so much gel on my head it looks wet, like a big rock splashed all day. I feel like a big rock.

I began with flavour: whey with cookies and cardamom, drinking muscle damage under the table with bolstered proteins in happy colours. B12, B6, HGH, Creatine – all my anabolic dreams frothed up in a juice of chemicals. A buzz, injected in, down on the rocks: my sweet and sour margarita.

Like any example of un-anaesthetised brain surgery, my one o'clocks and twos and sixes were delirious but at least I was growing stronger. Muscled. My orbital sockets dampened and exploded in a continual rose of bruise. My hair, no longer beautiful hair, was a stitched-on clump, a hood of sorts.

My wife was long departed. My children gone from the nest. The neighbours and my house were never far away. The whole business encouraged odd swellings and holes with their rotted portions. I was a sports ground in my own right. No matter how many times I recomposed my damp shirts and dirty-coiled legs, my body hardened in witness to an age of horror.

It was addictive. Power and money and violent insanity.

I gathered so many rosettes for the fridge. And how pleased I was to see the silky chords, so pleased to see them wave as I pulled the door open and closed, so pleased to see them wonderful like a human voice.

Forget Swiss chards and seeded bread, my Darker Me ran a gullet hectic with fats and liver meat. I wore black, acting with substance on behalf of shadow. I battered a man named Brick. I ran Casket Matches stoked on inappropriate touching. My cartilage grated into flints you could flick off with impermanent aim but permanent harm. I bled: gums in the bathroom, nose in the street. I worried endlessly about the distorting limits of my head, my skull and the deep long breaths that soared out of my lungs.

Joan the Wild Salmon and Megan Danger; Lolita and Jake the Snake. Hogarth the Executioner; the Satchelled Schoolboy. We were siblings of destruction running each other into puddles of distress. Our untouchable psychological matter spilled so we invented new vanishing points to scoop it back up.

The mere consideration of having allies launched me into social action. I shovelled earth without mercy, working hard to train trees and clematis into an ordered ring around our pit. There were cables rigged up and dipped under short poles. The bobbing birds on those wires were natural grammars. I could see it all from my window, a cruel kind of arrangement whose prancing lights shone at night with such natural harmony that even the wild animals joined our sides.

I wanted seclusion from car connections. I wanted the houses that shaded us from skies above to keep the light keen and hemmed in. I wanted everything to feel small, all the problems, our gadgets, my waking sleep. I wanted my heart to feel flexible in the shadow of these curious houses that both fastened and unfastened us like latches. We needed our backs protected and performed at our most exuberant when an audience gathered close about. Any aggravation of evil was teased out by strange moves that choreographed the wind into pathways of direction. Sometimes we made the air hang so still it cultured an ambiguity between the outdoors and indoors. All this stopping of the wind acted like a cushion, a silencing tool such that each time we rapped our coconut skulls together, smashing all the sour liquid out of our heads, there would be no blown-in risk to muddle us. We made the wind a pillow to lay right onto. We blurred. Any inveterate sores practically healed on the spot.

Although we did contract with something. I'm not sure if could be called focus or pleasure. There was digital photography and dinky cameras. The pictures made clear just how much space everyone was taking up. You could suddenly see us gasping or crumpling to connect. It was documentary evidence of our mutilation.

The neighbours realised that you could capture the boundless extent of time and space with just a little film and a careful finger, so people went wild preserving their own vanity and all the heaps of stuff around them. The present face of the world became the future face and the past face. In the tight little body of the camera we were local evidence of the grand pastoral. Everyone snapped horses having great hair days or fifteen places in the neighbourhood to view beautiful wildflowers in spring. Boys and girls and willows and windows. Images were made quick as a dog: hasty, barking, frantic.

I was reminded that 3mm of water is perfectly adequate to drown in and the ridges of dirt all around grew spackled with skin, layering up piles of desiccate and sometimes teeth. Perhaps it was simply our lack of imagination to think that death was not desirable: it was so easy!

The whistling and cheering soared for the extracurricular details: bat heads and buckets of simulated human shit flung over the audience.

Brotherly Love, we called it. We were truffles with stinking plums inside. Peacocks infested. Even tiny blonde children twinkled encouragements with monster glee.

I was amazed at the energy and timescale. The present face of things slipped quite away whilst I lived in it. Sometimes I held my breath taking a picture. I waited for my lungs to burn and feel the tiny atoms of my past silently tug away. I flashed body parts, the rudest parts. It was a regeneration of sorts, this person-in-progress. My cape was a ghastly dirty sheet called *reality*.

The pit taught many people how to close the breach between the universe and their own sensitivity. It harvested abundance, with our trees and smoke, with communal spaghetti dinners and candlelight never wiped out in distress. It was acknowledgement of our closeness, our neighbourly fondness, a reminder that our roads were black and they too had their usual points of reference.

Nothing lasts long. The pit was closed and filled in. We didn't have a licence. Never mind I had been briefly gorgeous. I waited, still feeling somehow part of it as newspapers flapped to explain rationally the coming of the world and then the going of the world as it fizzled out of itself. In and out and totally obsessed with the practicalities of capturing a dream picture: a prize-winning picture.

MESSRS.
EXTERNAL & STRICKEN

Memorandum

Ethan. We have travelled abroad where different currencies hold sway. We can touch them whenever we please. We can sit up half the night should we choose it, counting and recounting, polishing coins until they shine.

We have looked at that all-seeing eye etched onto the one-dollar bill and it reminds us of you. We see your own shirt-popped stomach, a triangular wedge of fat between the seams, with its belly button a poor Eye of Providence in a nest of curls.

This is a mere reminder: you are not an architect of guts or glory.

PATRICE

Luxury

My early adult's pleasure saw everyone at my door: the drunken boys, the prophet in sackcloth, the whores, tigers, snakes and shakers – the whole town in its merry troupe.

I'd do feasting and pies. I'd be in the bakery cross when they ran out of boxes, nervous that the tarts would crumple and beggar my respectability. I'd line up the glasses at home, crystals crammed with ice and everything flecked afresh in my new kitchen with its slanted tiles.

There was kissing everybody. Everybody who ever lived and was touched by the world. We'd be a live tumble of bodies dancing by the light of gin and getting our hands sweaty. Even on level floor we'd slope straight into each other, not falling apart but smearing ourselves flexible into the thickness of night. I've had parties where night would tread on the heels of day. I'd enjoy it all on my full-breasted carpets, dressed tight in my coat with the gloss of nail varnish and there would be the gate again, squeaking arrivals with its sound composed by temperature, high hots and low cold.

What I held in were those voices branching into sequence. People were pricked by laughter and opened up, their bodies suddenly strewn on gutted sheets. Their impact on my walls was part of the definition, part of the party and what we aimed at beyond.

And now I find myself remaindered to a hotel. There is nowhere to sit. Up or down in the lift and I am choked on rooms of non-returnable furniture. Space is differently framed. The religion of surface is smaller and meaner than I remember. There is no laundry hung out. No detached husband to leave you fawning at a shop window: *Say it with me: only diamonds do the trick, only diamonds do it. Say it.*

Before my money ran out I would frequent bidding sales in chambers of the district post office. Mahogany everywhere, trunks like questions and legs like benches, chairs and the like.

Kicking the fat load from his back and ascending a small dais near the front of the room, the auctioneer would begin his calls:

Any offers for these stones? Any offers for the lobster tails, the scallop shells or olive pits? Any offers for the chicken feet or salad? Any offers from the seat at the back? Any offers from the sinking world? Any offers from the smoky trees? Any offers from the insurance company? Or the lady with the failing husband? Any offers for my body, may it lay, where my wife moulders in decay?

The auctioneer always roused great emotion. I am a firm believer in hell and witches and I was convinced that people gathered there to listen between the lines. To hear a hitch in time. I waited alongside everyone else, breath held for the moment the auctioneer's words would turn and deliver us.

The flat speed of his sales voice rang out and how we stiffened. My body was furniture. And the vowels rushed past it all, out of the auctioneer's mouth, off the plinth and towards us, towards *me*, always aimed at skimming past the infinite blackness of my hopeless wanting, making a beeline for the nectars of my wallet.

I was soppy like a dog. My black hair, red vest and drab trash plimsolls. We dripped together. Loveable. I waited patiently alongside faces in shiny running suits. I could have been on my knees, on my ruined limping knees touching the floor in a holy position. I was desperate to perform with my body the task of touching everything, just a little at the edges, just lightly with no pressure at all, so those things too would pronounce my bodily existence as integrated and important. The itemised buckets and ball-bearings offered up found takers out across the floor. I would watch and want. And with my flimsy sleeve stuffed in my mouth I would feel once more the faith of being physical.

In those moments of bidding frenzy, I was a brainwashed ghost of love. I was a higher creature, a body all litheness and energy. The auction visitors sought something to squirrel away: a person will put more into their home than themselves. For pleasure and posterity, it is true that anything goes for a banister-back side chair or tapestry sampler. People are ruthless.

Dead Badger

Now the discount coupons rammed through my letterbox are fattening by the day. There is a great pile wedged on the side table. I assume the universe understands my sharp distaste for recycling. This is vengeance, these coupon booklets and their preppy sketches of aspiration. They encourage mini-mart haemorrhage so that my money earned can be exquisitely burned in the most degrading manner possible. All this pastel toy paper selling me half-price beans and fluorescent scooters with ill-conceived wheels.

Don't think me churlish.

These dealers of import-export could shit in a boot and sell it to you, dirt cheap for a grand price. I'd be very sorry indeed without them, eating raw sludge right out of the bin. Instead, look here, I have pages aplenty offering exciting oranges and seedless grapes, some sagging Sicilian pizzas, not warm but dripping in toppings!

I can buy it all at half price.

Less than half price!

I should buy everything and fill my home once

more with the personal constipation of many hundreds of unappetising gadgets. I wouldn't want to lump myself with flatulence and frostbite. I should sign myself right up, right away, and put my vulgar vocation – *purchase on demand* – to good use.

My recycling bag is ripped open quite ceremoniously each morning. The badger – soon to be dead badger – is a devourer of jam, scraper of my jars. This cycle, the repetitive process of process, of re-cycling my recycling, only adds bile to my loathing of the task.

What popular songs do you like, dear Badger? I will put on a waltz and dance for him. I will scrawl a message on the bundle of paper coupons and hurl it out onto the grass. To the badger who buries my intimates under a bush. To the dear Badger who will know my feelings sooner or later:

> *Good morning dear Badger,*
> *I'm writing to you today with offers of the best wine and the best jam. Sir, I'm writing to present an offer of an onion bulb and chops. I see you have already a smudge of butter thrown down on toast? I trust, Good Sir, that the sweet tarts I suggested last week were grubbed down so fast you could barely discern a shape? Most excellent, dearest Badger. I see your mouth so dead, your stinking pocket of darkness. I see your warmth, your snuffling claw, your clips, the*

nibbled tree and trembling head. I note your black hair, dear Badger, dead Badger, has turned white already, with age or desire. I offer today a single-day deal, an ex-voto cutlet – you see this soft slab offered in lieu of a life more majestically lived? Tender of course. Better diet, more exercise. It's yours to accept as you please. I wonder, dead Badger, whether you'll pray for me as I carve up my career? As a business figure myself of course I understand your comfort in taking stock, but I must ask that you please respond in forty-eight hours or consider these offers voided.

MESSRS. EXTERNAL & WEALTHY

Always Christmas

She used to be a merry traveller. Now she sniffs the linen when she lies down, rubs the sheets between her fingers and tuts that no, the thread count simply isn't high enough.

Our Patrice. She has thought of leaving through the window. Many have. Running fingers across the sun-warmed aluminium windows before razoring wrists and diving through red spray into sunlight. Warmth on warmth then black crumple down on the ground. The hotel is accustomed to it. One girl drowned in the water tower, left her body toneless with indifference or fatigue to float in ever-smaller particles through the drinking pipes of every room. The roof baked and swelled in the heat, ruptured at the seams by its own kind of boiled black blood. Some guests said the water tasted like eggshell. When maintenance workers carried out the body, their movements were as compressed as possible, not to save time, but perhaps in efforts to respectfully align themselves with her lifelessness. The news travelled and then disappeared.

The front desk in the Carmen Hotel is always Christmas. Tinsel and prickly evergreen. All those stems bending out strange angles across the tiled desk unit even though the heat outside is clearly ravaging, clearly magnifying calamity, clearly not winter. The sunlight is political. Its scour is a conceit, a wrap of light that rakes through dreams and dirt, pours over sea and sucks haze right out of it. Perhaps it's what once drew money here. What brought television its saturation and colour bloom. Or tracked every little car like a sad smudge through a city where voices of all kinds are voluble if you listen. The light here is a language all its own; it is science and god alike. It is a poison of sorts that glows, then dies softly with a shrug mostly pink and gold.

As far as we have seen, there is only one employee, a young man with a brow like a spatula. The flaps of unruly pores are pinned in place by his eyes where enthusiasm dimmed long ago. This boy is a living scribble: tangled and greasy, an onion ring left to wrinkle in the fridge. Even his aura is soggy. His body with all its compact distortion holds a kind of sexual perplexity, but perhaps when you are surrounded by dying, all that extra skin, those needless details just feel like life trying to assert as much body as possible. Like pigs on a farm. And when you're dying, of course, why care about being pale, about sweat, about hair. Why care about anything at all. The dying do not have enough air to fill a birthday balloon.

To say she was a guest at the Carmen Hotel would feel like hyperbole. She has a room here, in this big swell of a building. Our Patrice. Each time she glides up past the front desk, she touches the gaudy roses with their petals polymer sprayed, sometimes stuck together and the sensation prepares her for her room. Furniture there has suffered the same potent cosmetic of sleep deprivation as most of the faces around. The carpet is a crust, not soft-tufted but raked in grime left by wearied feet, feet with toes and heels squashed out of usual geometric proportion. Perhaps that is what all feet are: testament to our gradual misshapen destinies. There is a bed too, a basin and a tight pouch of window, but being only sad squares of mostly grey their very existence seems unkind.

Legs up on the rim of the sink, her own hands put the curse into morning. Stripped hairs scatter. How bitterly others must have shaved at this mirror. Even the white infallibility of toothpaste and shaving cream has lost its benevolence. These rooms with their calculus of variations have splatter dots all over. We recognise the feelings. It's as though we insist in error when brushing our teeth, hips deliberately offside so you never hit the basin and can rinse away calmly. It causes us to walk differently than before. We limp with deliberacy. We do the same with coffee in diners where people sit still and alone. Drip it onto the floor until the waiter arrives with a cloth and our round beige cup is an empty vessel, dull as soil, dull as potatoes.

ETHAN

Browned off

Just like the tongue's pre-emptive anticipation when eating holey cheese straight from the fridge – the dark aged kind – that the innermost curves of the holes, the round barrelling walls, will be full of a salty wetness more flavoured than the cheese body itself, just like that, it's often possible to know on a morning when something bad might occur in the afternoon.

I usually bring a lunch wrapped in paper but today I was lazy and the food was spoiled anyway.

I'm all for apocalypse, so I understand that the happy land of convenience shopping ushers in emotional weather I find both violent and unpredictable.

The snack market is swamped. Bigger, fresher, tastier. There are modular flexibilities and cute cardboard flanges to hold out, inspect and pour over for provenance or discovery. The inherited systems of supersize, mix and match – all of them are rammed with rhetorical appliqué, and fugitive symbolism, and then but wait *salad has no system of function*.

So salad box take note: you are not a voting booth, an office cubicle, a toilet stall – your compartmentalised privacy is lunatic. You do not need real territory because you will be gone in seven minutes, swimming through the gut. You are microtexture. What is this puritanical procedure of concealment and cover up? Tomato, why pretend you are part of a composite picture, portable imagery like the wheels on a car? The cucumber recognises its roundness and refuses abstraction. It refuses to lie down flat and just wilt in peace.

And the employees? They're practically powdered people, artificially irrigated behind the counter with their sweated maws and opposable thumbs or some ungodly third eye, with pimple-flapped flesh pounded to diamonds under hair-net stockings, too tight, as if all that could alleviate my hunger in the best most pleasant and satisfying way plausible.

And just like that, it's often possible to know on a morning when something bad might occur in the afternoon.

Delicates

They told me to wear the leather or leave the company. I said it was an indignity to cram flesh such as mine into tight and chafing quarters. To reduce myself to just a few marks cinched around the waistline.

They said wash your genitals on your own time, get some flour down there, wear stockings or bring a padlock and latch yourself into seven years toiling doing something excellent. So I stayed.

My parts are all but exquisite and I feel lately that my indignities flap open and shut for any old beggar tune. They said *find your opportunity by working!* A neat advertisement. So I stayed. And I spent lengthy carbide days ankle-deep in soot and snipped straw packing.

The company literature in its signature marigold cursive described the greatest business relations. It said: *Calling all epoch-makers of the world, all willing slaves of the moon – sleeping foxes catch no birds!* It said: *Plough-deep-while-sluggards-sleep-and-always-eat-lah-lah-lah*. So I stayed. And instead of my own good clothes I wear costumes designed to propagate a company-wide attitude of elfish diligence and good cheer. The job is not hard; I am equipped for better, certainly. Right now armed with scissors and parcel tape, with so many zips and tassels on my windbreaker, or whatever you call a jacket with so much utilitarian gusto. I am late and plain, not harmonised to the blank hold of night.

The last inhabited structure before the cabins turn to rot and wreckage, our space is a tin mountain on a near collapsed road. We are all busy I think. I open and close boxes in a room sodden with artificial light. Boxes of such density they narrow everything with an infinite hush all over so that some feeble minds even forget to move.

The packets suggest a labyrinth of recipes for escape: a young pig posed in a cart; a cute baby and rustic vegetables; tides of snow with their thick white mantle. I am growing weary from the constant crouch but I like the pictures with people in them and keep my back to the wall.

When dry August burned over and everything outdoors was dirty and dangerous, my room here felt cold. It occurred to me that I could like boys. It occurred to me that I could like girls.

There is a selection of pens for our operator shifts when we mark great evaluations of contents diverse and beautiful:

Today there are hand-formed vessels, turned, lathed and shaved: smooth. White parts and colour tint blown from atomiser. All whilst wet, tree patterns dripped on with camel brushes, muddy with tobacco, turpentine, urine, hops and acid. Seaweed on pinkish tints. Fantasy slip and cocktail rings: twigging and fan decoration. China with all handles gilt, smoked and corn-flaked, soft paste with good crazing lines flanked by dark brown stripes and green-glazed herringbone.

Often I'm kicking around with foam peanuts and gossip or questions far removed like how much oil is left in the ground when distant corporations plunder for fuel? What are the fastest beats per minute audible before we hear only a continuous note? Do centipedes have more than one gait?

I've been here because once you lose one job, once you're dead you're dead. So the dropping into one kind of economical hole and lying a little about my Christian name was a quietly exercised compromise.

But today is my last day because I stuck out my tongue at a driver, shook my dirty trousers leg by leg until he pumped the breaks and cargo rolled to crashing. I'd kept my head down, but those crates were packed with Cornish calendar mugs, all of them hard-baked with red enamel glaze, obese and excessively rounded, the epitome of ill, so I suppose I lost control. I remembered people and their faces sucked quite out of my life. The density short-circuited me.

The company believed I'd performed a psychological obliteration. So they performed one back on me and poof I was gone. Overalls in the bin. The post-mortem on my career: that happy packer with a bit of bounce about him.

After that I went away. Back to warmer weather less maddening and black roads so hot they rose up and socked the breath out of my mouth. My third day was one of burnt grass and cicadas. The wind was effortless and grasped me about the waist. I drove my scooter too close to a dead dog on the hard shoulder and his fur pricked and stuck in my sandals. He lay on his back, legs frozen, sprawled unkindly at a painful angle. There was no blood, but a pool of stinking clear liquid that flowered around him, marking out the difference between his dead and my boiling alive. A boiled in between. I saw his paws and anus, haloed with flies, all black and pink dried up.

Driving on through hot walls of fig and perfumed jasmine, I had that ripe dead animal always close in my nostrils. I sat carefully on the white plastic chairs handed to me in restaurants, afraid that the stick-and-rip friction of my sweaty thighs on their surfaces would jerk the taste back into my mouth.

I figured I had witnessed full malice. I had been a lousy pedestrian with no gentle language to lay over a dead dog. I can say in that short week I knew wine-drunk better than I have ever known it before and food faded away from me, as I knew too would fat from that dead dog's bones.

Customs and declarations

So what you found a USB of pornography in my backpack. Did you find the cable ties and chapstick? Did you notice that the time codes match her birthday? Her height and weight? It's all research.

MESSRS.
EXTERNAL & BREEZY

Old wind

High past the steep and dirty lanes, above the foaming billows of sea and spray there is great wind. Sometimes it is a warm wind, the west wind, full of birds' cries. We rarely catch its breeze for long, but tears are in our eyes for it comes from the far warm lands, the old brown hills. April's in that west wind with its waves of pollen and daffodils. It picks up the annual herbs beginning to think and stretch. That west wind has caught us too, cleansed us, made us grand. It steams and shrieks a little, a boiled kettle wind for a favourable gale. It is a wind bought and sold, a good wind, honest and cheap. We love a west wind. And when that wind is high, when the sky is taut and hanging, we look out across it and see a figure fleeing. A man goes riding by.

PATRICE

Hot shells

I unpacked two ostrich eggs from the postman. He always brings a delicacy. I wonder what observations he makes of us TV fundamentalists, us liquidating our property and filing our divorces. These eggs were remnants not carriers, decorative, not sloshing yolk yellow but hollow. Insides breezed away. A small hole at the bottom. A hole as big as my eye through which you might see a flicker of action, a thick mellow dream – my dream.

It was a warm day, horizonless, and nested in cardboard tassels, the eggs felt baked when I lifted them, heavy with slumber. The box was symmetrical and dusty. I sniffed at the holes and dipped the tip of my index finger inside. There is so much I could do for the person I love. One of those odd twists of desire, my just-painted nails, black tips, curled into the immodest scent of hot protein. My nostril sniffed like a great hovering mollusc, one dark hole mining another.

Holes are openings which invite invasion; in pairs they are eyes. Fingers are intelligence. People recover. There should be an erotic classification assigned to the impulse to poke fingers into indeterminate holes.

You said I made a small hole in you. I watched as all the stuff leaked out and didn't poke anything in to stop it. I let it run right away. You said it was mean but what it was, was evil. A new pain evangelism.

Lobster, a season in red

Tonight I shall make lobster ravioli. The glutinous kind where the sauce is fragranced just so. I am gentle. A thin person. I love pasta so shall show myself gratitude.

As I get ready to boil my languid crustacean, I think lobsters give me comfort. Theirs is a voluptuous beauty, staunchly un-evolved. For one hundred million years, rattling around in scorched bodies, sopping sweet, sopping salt. Milky emulsions and the same soft concentration of ancient, wise matter. Beautiful red, beautiful pink, beautiful orange. Those footnotes of corruption. The lobster is one great erogenous zone.

The water bubbles, its curly drum head pounding in the pan. I run my soft finger along the inside rim of the lobster claw. It looks like a giant gum with knobbled wisdoms. I am a careful ligature, knotted in strokes. Me and the lobster together, both ampersands in a landscape. It smells both sweet and sour.

I feel a tic in my eyelids. I remember eating liver and marrow, stewed fishes liked striped awnings with their wide bands of pattern. Things potent with colour and heads snipped off. Glassy cheeks from a cod. The stink of meat and its buttery temper. Beans.

I catch myself through the steam of the kitchen, feeling moisture on my skin that reminds me I am alive and breathing. Am I still a mother who believes in nothing but fattening her children? Who believes that the most beautiful house of all is made from icing and gingerbread, that her own greasy kitchen will one day fall away in a grand reveal?

My pasta is overcooked. Not how I like it, your honour. Lacking instinct, lacking the principle characteristics of a meal made for one: stability. I hold my soggy pillows up to the light. Little tears have opened up along the seams and rubbered bits of meat dribble out, as if by way of entertaining me, of illustrating that this lobster hasn't finished just yet because its flesh is potent, rich and insolent.

I put my tongue out to touch it.

Explain this muscle to me, I ask, *but say it slowly so I hear every syllable and feel bones extending to press me carefully against the thick atoms of air. Hold me in parentheses of pressure points and let me feel the extraordinary experience of being a human wrapped in skin.*

I am a firm advocate of the fact that every statement we issue bears witness to our being here.

So many things I don't say aloud. The real challenge is to tame wickedness. There has been a scarcely decipherable change in the skin of my palm. A slight wearing away of the inside edge of my index finger. I bruised my nail when I hammered the lobster shells. I see them, cracked and trampled into the floor. My knuckles hurt. An inflammation from all the scratching and wiping, all the waving goodbye. I am at the mercy of my own swollen self. The ravioli floats on cold water. It looks like the wallets and passports of dead businessmen, some frothy white weeds around the oars of my utensils.

I would like to see this situation with somebody else, someone with a tender lowered face who can hold my chin up to the window and explain it is not wrong to want a clearly visible picture of the source of all beauty. The kitchen will wear you out if you let it, with its table covered in coasters, dirty and irregular, that reminds you of how few chairs are full and pulled up tight to its edges. In such a mood I cannot guess if I open my mouth if I will laugh or cry. The feeling will deepen if I spoon food in there.

There is a new pink glow and a yellow flicker. A sound like mating dogs, barking and scrabbling. Something whirs and silence is closed upon with a hollow ping: my cup in the microwave. There was a time when I would cook with success and originality. With decadence. Now a cardboard image of cabbage and carrots curls under the tray, still warm, still wet. Sun damage has turned them pale blue. The last days of packaging like a sea of radiated weeds. I want to suck the feeling out like I would suck a mouth.

Pleasure and pain.

Pleasure in

Pain.

ETHAN

A wretched macaroni

I recognise my voice as my own, yes, but there are colours where there have been none before. I'm having wide-ranging bed conversations. With the squirrels in the limes and my dead father; with the diabolical lawyer next to whom I ate a steak slowly with its little pitcher of warmed blue cheese gushed over the top, smoking throughout so the cigarette ash dappled around and we swallowed as much smoke and paper as we did raisins with our pale dairy puddings.

The opinions of all seem to be that time is running out. That I might be more fastidious from my speaker's perch to describe something that actually pleases the audience. Who have remained patiently in their seats.

Well I can describe the sea, or a headless man, a woman or a dog. No longer a cat, not maternal tones erupting at night, rather neighbours cold on their sofas and a handful of trains with their fixed arcs generally designed to disappear.

I make myself out to be very tough but the house has become a bit of a tip and my fear index boils way above yellow. Yellow because the shade chart I received with a recent spamming email asking if I *LovedDesign?*™ provided a psychology breakdown of colour symbolism in marketing.

Yellow, it said, was evil and brooding.

Here every day now smells like chlorine and the mice have surged in low-level noise, turning the floor into a lava of excrement. Between the wind, the clocks and all their sorry gesticulations, there is little time to bewitch the furniture onto the ceiling. The urine of course is also piss-yellow, so you could consider the symbolism of that too.

Call it sulphur-induced, call it unpopular, dirty, mad. The specifics of colour that surround me feel like a chemical pond. It is true that small things running about, unlatched, running about the base of a curved stone wall, running about your cake and crumbs and satchels dumped with no musical order, it is true that a small pestilence not welcomed in will turn your home to a tangle. It feels like a machine, all these tiny feet scattering dreadful spirals all over. A growth that modifies with each stage. A growth with a metric like wild writing that leaves pieces of food and body parts in undigested assembly.

Mouse, plural mice. A house mouse is different to a field mouse, different to a street mouse, different to a lab mouse: aggregated together by virtue of their essential reducibility to vermin. They are quick snakes. I would have left them well out of the ark. All that merciless multiplicity, it withers me in front of any witness. The devil may have his favourite pet, his contagion, but these non-Oedipal beasts turn my history to a redness of fear and disgust.

Naturally I'm convinced the trail of warmth my body leaves is an invitation for access, a radiating borehole. I am simply biding my time until they will surge, chewing up against me to reach the fleshy curve of my insides, commencing with procreating and scrabbling en masse with their own squeaks and clicks until my internals are nothing more than a shred of wailing ribbons, burnt curtains across the marital bed. At that point, you will hear no more from me. But you can't hurry the mice; they circle then change their mind.

There are whole categories of strange medical people. Those who blow their noses and swear they see mealworms in the handkerchief. The planet will certainly feel heavier if you drink a lot. If you begin to see systems of creatures cocooning fibres on the surface of your skin. If you persist with rotten tasting whisky, tasting like it has warmed then boiled in an abscess of oaky barrel decay. Ah these mice. Let them eat dirt and perish in the cold. Let them slink their greasy tails off to the ash pits. It is hard to push them away.

I am sitting with my granola. With my white milk which has browned whilst I wait. For what? The alarm is early. A black hour meaning I am slow to wake my face. A huge plane has just lifted overhead: I can feel the shudder of its engines suck something a little tighter in my chest.

I am naked to the waist. I am entitled to drink as much gin as I please because as my own understanding of social progress has it, Hogarth's impoverished people of 1700 gargled down tankards of sulphuric acid and turpentine and lived to preserve their essential symmetries well enough to communicate moral warning to me and my kind.

My tools are in the corner, what am I to do? My spades and my ball. They are so equivocal. Like the table and lamp, they precede all beginnings. They are cut off. I rest my head down on the table. My hair disagrees, rustling my ear rough to touch. My own severed head on a platter just a point of polite disgust. A point of discussion. Another hot pink baby mouse. A newborn.

MESSRS. EXTERNAL & DARKENING

Fishing

Reason looks for two people and pushes them together. At night the stars with their shapely congruent points, their arms, wrap around them. How quickly passion becomes a question of economic mitosis and suddenly there is restlessness: it breaks and is gone. Consequence is narrow. Mornings no longer feel maternal. Work is work and wood just flat awful planks with their bland surfaces that represent the world, that chafe hands held together with glue. For the present singular person it is hard to scrape at bread and not feel like a rodent. To drip milk from the carton straight down a chin feeling that maybe these eyes have yellowed or newly wander in two directions and the only source of comfort is abstinent days spent in a small dark room. To try the dark on like a glove, bare your teeth in it and sink down low like a louse. The prison of time. The freezer box is full of fish, frozen, small pieces in plastic. Sometimes he fries them. This is how dehumanisation actually works, thinks Ethan. How it works, and sometimes it does. What he is not is a bruiseless child.

MESSRS.
EXTERNAL & SALTED, OPTIMIST & OILS

Out

The sea and its salty simmer is a catalyst for feeling. The Ocean's own peculiar economy moves us. Like ice cubes that have lost something fundamental even though their melty decay is a concentrated focus of the world we call atomic. Everybody likes white sauce, blank froth, and the reputation of a broad mind.

The beach is not human although it reeks of entropy with its avian aesthetics so bleak and cinematic with only a few people around. A few people and the tide and arctic giants of cloud. Holiday landscapes amaze in winter when their blackened trees write out a calligraphy against the creamy emptiness. Summer stretches bring forth cars and an agitation of bodies with their all-too-visible emergencies.

The two of them used to practice on the sand, walking, feet no longer feet, but extensions of a moral force, a pride in that force contained within two solid bodies. The details came out then: one leg shorter than another, a vague ache because of it; the sand itself groaning and collapsing all its billions of silicate granules, little gems between their toes.

They might look at paintings together in lonely caostal towns, postcards of beaches and shipwrecks. All those soft-breasted landscapes where tiny dying suns poke at skies and suddenly there is a memory of rosy nipples amidst sheets, licked in mornings only hours ago. There is context for it all.

We remember that we too are made up of dusky shadows rolled over with bluish pigment and paranormal whiteness. Painting is so vocal. Full of faces and sappy pastorals that say *what is the matter with you today?* Full of people who move to the shadows and say *oh yes we should, I haven't seen you for ages*. Faces that compose elaborate lies like halting and greeting and grinning.

The problem with order is that it rarely comes on its own. Nature and painting share our peculiar denial of participation in the zone of practical feeling. We talk about the weather to fathom some grand ecological algebra that might be applied to our own weekly erosions and sedimentation. Earth and snow are given credit for our beautifully preserved conditions. It's nice to have a condition. We spit and sniff, piston down on the world's pavements and call them our own.

It's true: people get messed up a bit. With opioids and amphetamines stuffed into socks. With children and parents stuffed into houses. We see them literally drop dead at our feet. We wipe them away or pick them up. We see spiritual paths set such that bodies are flung forth in the air. Faces crack and petrify, because everything noisy happens at the edge of a crack. We try to pin down terms like *body* and *feeling* worrying always that the crack has entered us too, entered us intimately and is widening at the edges with few lines of resistance. We try to save ourselves by saving the surface, by keeping our feet on or near a shore. By shoring up. With sandbags and language. *It's only politics*, we whisper amongst ourselves.

So we sit tight and watch great loves become remote and hard. Sometimes the sensation of pity is so amplified in the bare earth that a mere acorn on the head might split us right open. We witness desperation that is the beginning of the end. A feeling that there is nothing more important than being alone in a field of corn. We measure distance that begins hand in hand on a city stroll and ends with an urgent need to rip off an arm, to do anything with hot coals or guillotines to avoid the touch of that other person. We attempt an organisation of feeling where the only clear imperative is to be one singular noun amidst all the furious plurals.

Ours is a conventional blind obedience but sometimes lines cross us with fatal points and we look amongst ourselves, all of us set to sobbing on a mound in some gloomy town with our intimates up around our waist. Perfection never comes to pass. Rather our people are blasted with years of moving and window boxes. With cold coffee living life in the pique of emotional untidiness.

And then the abominable wound heals. It's a cultural event! And the gallons of booze dry up and the crack begins to narrow. We watch again from afar as a stranger in business hours suddenly appears like a great god on the shores of the universe's most glorious beach and life is struck with more touches of brilliant colour than we could even give name to.

And everyone can be satisfied simply with clean hair, with deep night, good sleep and wine. Personal living is no longer dismal, full of good warm things to wrap even the most insouciant creaking bodies happily about.

Our women swig at highballs with their joint innocence and deceit. They lap at the sureness of rising good feeling, hold it against their suits and beckon in friends with fingers wide. Our men lay their palms flat across it all and feel the thick silences of impotence moving gently through them and away. Tension unravels and the crack seals itself deep within history. They can speak freely and they do. They say, *my body is mine and I am not the prisoner of such a space.*

Big sky

Winds frisk me to the bone, bone thoughts, all gurgling directions and great arcs of pine and geese. Leaves fall to the ground. They know their rhythms, aided by rainwater or mud, sticking fast together, gummy stalks and green moustaches, nodding off like practiced husbands. Both the sticks and husbands are blind to altitude, to weather rolled out in rampage. The outdoors is full of verbs.

The outdoors makes me hungry. A few minutes of air and I want to feel my mouth around something, coarse salt and butter between it. I wish to cram myself with as many baguettes as I have fingers. Or replace the fingers entirely, with oil and ham and cheese.

Near the trees beyond the empty house with its cold sheets and pointless neighbours, there is what they call Big Sky. It's like an arena for nothing at all. The opposite of our clinical obsession with stuff, with its *thingness*, its transactional, paranoiac conditions. Looking into that sky incites a desire to shed it all off. To be myself, my biodegradable self, with no plastic or drawers full of old batteries. It is not a sight, but a feeling of open angles inside you. A principle of gliding on wind with a body stretched out as broad and flat as possible.

Striding around that sky I think, Christ, wouldn't it be great to remove all my clothes. To wander around bare as the day just picking herbs and harvesting. It makes me believe I'm an apothecary. Somebody who knows about plants. Somebody who knows about pure affirmation. Practically speaking, I couldn't say which mushrooms would burn a hole straight through my oesophagus.

Do I claim to be gesturing my way into history? Walking my way in? Talking? Fucking my way into history? That through my collision with air and hedgerows, or some simple folk or simple mud around my boots, I am opening up the way towards the *real me*? I like that fine but lethal suspension of knowledge. It's acting as though you're made of literature.

And don't we flush fondly for this natural chronology. It's comforting to know more or less where we are headed.

ETHAN

The farewell head

My best friend in high school was nicknamed Death because he lacked melanin everywhere, save a line of red hair from the middle of his forehead right down to the shallow dish of his skull's bottom. He looked permanently cleaved apart. As though the concentration of any conversation with him was a contribution of just enough static friction in the brain to keep the hemispheres intact, and as soon as the sports talk or band talk or collection talk would stop, his head would split right in two.

I asked Death if he wanted to be buried or burned. He said, *I don't think we should do this over the phone.*

Instead we walked out to the trees together, beyond the house of the weird sisters and out to more open land. Because Big Sky is just a way for the body to feel elemental. A way to feel the pierce of being a person smacked senseless by air. A way somehow to return to whatever the very beginning was.

Death held a shell to my ear and on hearing my own blood fill its chambers he told me: *If this white noise is the sound of living, of the beaches, of the sea, imagine how that sensation retires when we die. Our bodies crumple into earth so we cover the abyss with grass and plant flowers. Tombstones are sewn like teeth. They chomp down on us. The earth compacts and presses. Things dump little bits of themselves upon us to fuse with our own peaty remains. Our bog bodies. I would rather be lumped on the compost heap and left for the birds. A pack of starlings on my face, pecking out their own expressions or carrying off a jiggling reconstruction of my better-known self to warm on the plains of Africa. Of my body I wish for big geese to take up the limbs and somewhere around the Pacific seaboard or crust of Mexico release them to splash into the dark blue below. I want to hear the rush of blood in death, too. I want movement and air. If my heart is destined to end its beat then I must know that some reckless bastard will carry on with the performance above ground. That something, anything, might fill the resonant cavity. I'm not asking for butterflies driving chariots or tap-dancing weeds but maybe for some mosquitoes to buzz nearby as if I were still there. Make ink from my burnt bones for all I care, just don't let me drop out from under that Big Sky and rot to mulch underground.*

Death showed me a corner he'd prepared. *In full view of the sky*, he said, pointing to a heap of tyres and a bucket steamy with baking soda and vinegar. The gas poured off it, pulling mosquitoes into its mist.

He unbuttoned his coat, pulling out a small blue hacksaw blade and holding its end out to me whilst he placed one leg carefully inside the bucket. *Cut my arm*, he said, *just to test the mosquitoes.*

His eyes fizzed, not like a madman but in a way that made me think he was wild with exchange. This was acute awareness of pleasure and pain. A sort of attenuated derangement. How long did he plan to stand in the bucket? Death waiting for death at sixteen years old?

I took the blade, hacked off a downward dangling sapling and whipped him hard across the cheeks. The force brought a red flush to his otherwise albino skin and I knew from the marks it made that I was destined to be a conscious steward of his life. He was lumped with a namesake whose fixations were entirely morbid and irrational, whilst I would extend myself again and again to look out for the matter which trumped the soul.

He pushed me in a headlock, both of us tumbling neck bones pressed into the soil. My teeth hit the grass and I smiled. Both of us returning to the elementals. The mud was wet. Softer. I wouldn't weep him a fig tree, but I would, under sky of any shade, have his back.

PATRICE

Home

When we had, we had lived together near a church with the house backing on to the garden of a preacher's family. Sometimes I threw my shoe over the wall and would whisk around to their front door, eager to receive back a sole touched, by extension, by a hand of god. I knew that if the shoe wasn't returned, I would be straddling a limbo, one foot scraping bare and close to the soils of damnation and the other still sensibly strapped between leather and a cork wedge sole. I wasn't a pious woman, rather mathematical. Ready for the expedience of a transfer into whatever heaven might open to have me. Yet primed too, giddy even, for a rapid pivot into hell.

The wildness of that house was always comforting to me. I had taken a loose-stitch tarpaulin from its windows and unfolded it to mark out a plot only yards away from where my husband might have sown his plants. I weighted it with stones, taking care to pull the corners taut underneath. I knelt down with my knees on the earth, one darker smudge of scandalous girlhood with skin pulled tight, the earth again a lyric platform for the sake of filth.

Together once, we'd hammered silver pennies into an old pickle box, as though we were decorating a headstone with shining manic teeth. Teeth with different impacts of term and consequence. I unwrapped that box and a little packing paper still adhered, distrusting the condition of complete abandonment from the wood grain. It still smelled like lemon, like the hard dust of long-fermented coriander seed.

I creaked and the soil received me. A complex contraction of the muscles in that bend of surrender downwards. I arranged the box at the head of the groundsheet, one smaller rectangle making a compound path atop a larger outline. It looked like a pillow resting neat and still on its bed.

In light of wearing both shoes, I looked upwards, feeling the contact bearings of my feet and wondering if this historical consciousness of possession – *my feet* – would contain some principle for rejuvenation of my world.

I poked my red finger down into the mud, feeling little resistance or any displaced weight of the great deciduous forests or vegetative existence that had surely once rooted there. I spat inside the hole, putting my mouth right up close to the ground so I could feel the cold water vapour rising brownish against my face. My spit might gradually raise the temperature of that tiny hole, just for a moment, whilst it was absorbed and nudged away through silt.

I rose quickly. I was not one for squatting in fields waiting.

Words have always been complex signboards, chipped and pleated on road bends, always a little bloody. Brooding. Something of our mutual speech was held tight to that pickle box and resting it silent on the grass we would finally take leave of one another in many double reverberations of material: all their peculiar weights and volume and density embedded over and again all rich and slippery but left out to decay for good.

I could leave everything just as I decided: my final handoff of aged wood and scents in this landscape as blue and green as any other. I could smoke a cigarette and drop broken matches on the ground, feeling the conjunction of their own selves as slivers of wood once part of these trees and their roots down deep in mineral volumes. I would leave everything to water and land, to sparrows and starlings with their clever eyes. Everything entirely of body or soon to be body in all its useless delinquency, all of it folding in countless luminous signs, this way and that. I could count the silver coins and with that sum total no longer have to answer for what was lost with anything other than a figure on a scrap of paper.

I could simply nod my head and turn to leave. There would be something to fathom from the change of air and how I moved right into it.

Gripping hard onto the hem of my shirt, I tasted the faint warmth of eggshells. My face was wet and through the peripheral thickness of my glasses I could see a crescent shaped slot of land altogether grander and more elaborate.

Later there might be a postman's knock and a letter or some careful aggregation of foam on my leg from bathing that in its complex fuzz would provide a better explanation of the day's unfolding. How I would slip into bed with the dreamy cream of linen all about. And how I would remove the last black olive from its jar with the arm of my glasses and lie blindly in the light whilst the salts of its dark helmet roundness filled the whole of my mouth with a carefully cleaner sensation.

†

pp.17–18, *There are people in the world who appear not as primary objects, but as incidental specks or spots on objects*; Nikolai Gogol, *Dead Souls*, 1842.

p.42, *These are my paths and goals*; Christopher Alexander, Sara Ishikawa, Murray Silverstein, *A Pattern Language: Towns, Buildings, Construction*, 1977.

p.87, *The inventor of the mirror poisoned the human heart*; Fernando Pessoa, *The Book of Disquiet*, 1982.

p.106, *It is no semantic coincidence that the word for colour is rooted also in drug, remedy, talisman, cosmetic, intoxicant*; Amy Sillman, 'On Colour', in *Painting Beyond Itself: The Medium in the Post-Medium Condition*, 2016.

p.106, *Maybe dust never settles, only clears briefly from the last failure*; Don Delillo, *The Names*, 1982.

p.139, *The art of construction has been claimed to be the only true art, an art currently deployed by the mathematics of machines since the human spirit is currently too clammed for acts of such deviant delicacy*; Fernando Pessoa, *The Book of Disquiet*, 1982.

p.274, *After the suns and moons, dews and wettings, comes sabotage*; James Joyce, *Finnegans Wake*, 1939.

p.284, *Any offers for my body, may it lay, where my wife moulders in decay?*; William Combe, *The Tour of Doctor Syntax in Search of the Picturesque*, 1812.

Deepest thanks to my agent Harriet Moore and publisher Jess Chandler for all your tireless guardianship and tender consideration – this book would be nowhere without you both and I am grateful for everything. Thank you Matthew Stuart and Andrew Walsh-Lister for the love affair with typography. Thank you: Sadie Coles and Pauline Daly for the deep magic of friendship, Carol Greene for your kind and brilliant brain, Johann König for your trust and energy, Hilary Lloyd for everything gorgeous, Tom Hardiman forever my best wingman, Charlotte Prodger we wrote the wind, Beatrix Ruf for endless care, Susanne Pfeffer for Bach and night professions, Hans Ulrich Obrist for a tireless spirit of aggregation, Daisy Johnson my dearest stoic, Flint Jamison for cats and circuitry, Frances Edgerley for pep, Emma Astner the bread to my sandwich, Vanessa Carlos for cosmic exuberance, Polly Staple for emergency nuts, Trisha Baga for colour and acceleration, Ed Atkins for mutually merry filth, Vera, Tim, Laura and Kate Marten for all the love, Pip Fear, Bapcha and the Smaczylos for family, Bob and Angela Marten for books, Kasia Fudakowski for concrete comedy, Clem Blakemore for light, Richard Wentworth and Michael Archer for first showing me the abstractions of luck and craft, Vera Alemani for electricity, Patricia Lodeizen for your eagle eyes, and most of all, thank you Magali Reus, for holding this heart together, I love you. And for all the conversations, this is a better book for your friendship: Uri Aran, Pascale Berthier, Andrew Bonacina, Kristian Bodnar, Nicolas Deshayes, Tom Eccles, Josef Eisel, Tom Green, Katie Harkin, Maja Hoffmann, Mark Jenkins, Travis Jeppesen, Ruba Katrib, Oliver Kenyon, Dan Kidner, Laura Lord, Sarah McCrory, Marianne Morrow, Eileen Myles, Michael Ringier, Lewis Ronald, Ryan Sullivan, Adam Thirlwell, Caragh Thuring, Adam Sinclair, Jeffrey Rowledge, Alice Rawsthorn, Joseph Waller, Jordan Wolfson. Lastly, for all the happy pebbles and boiling cells, for the dreams traced by the tip of mind and dropped – thank you, I am so happy to know you.

( ) ( ) p prototype

poetry / prose / interdisciplinary projects / anthologies

Creating new possibilities in the publishing of fiction and poetry through a flexible, interdisciplinary approach and the production of unique and beautiful books.

Prototype is an independent publisher working across genres and disciplines, committed to discovering and sharing work that exists outside the mainstream.

Each publication is unique in its form and presentation, and the aesthetic of each object is considered critical to its production.

Prototype strives to increase audiences for experimental writing, as the home for writers and artists whose work requires a creative vision not offered by mainstream literary publishers.

In its current, evolving form, Prototype consists of 4 strands of publications:

(type 1 — poetry)
(type 2 — prose)
(type 3 — interdisciplinary projects)
(type 4 — anthologies) including an annual anthology of new work, *PROTOTYPE*.

The Boiled in Between by Helen Marten
Published by Prototype in 2020

 A CIP record for this book is available from the British Library.

Design by Traven T. Croves
(Matthew Stuart & Andrew Walsh-Lister)
Cover drawing by Helen Marten
Typeset in Bembo Book MT Pro & Bembo Std
Printed in Lithuania by KOPA

ISBN 978-1-9160520-6-2

( ) ( ) p prototype

(type 2 – prose)
www.prototypepublishing.co.uk
@prototypepubs

prototype publishing
71 oriel road
london e9 5sg
uk

This is a wildly, joyfully creative journey into the tenderness of being human, frail, together and apart. A remarkable debut from a keen eye and a deft, lyrical hand.
AL Kennedy

Helen Marten has always produced intricate, ricocheting systems, and now she has expanded this system-making into writing. She uses language in this novel like a bricoleur, where words acquire their own sticky, glued substance – brilliant explorations of ugly feelings that are also exercises in how clotted and wayward sentences can be, as well.
Adam Thirlwell

An incredible work of literary art.
Max Porter

The Old Victorian is new again and the dramatic poem is prose... or, in the words of at least one of the Brownings, 'As goes the empire, so goes the formatting.' Helen Marten strives, seeks, finds, and does not yield in any of her media; she stands in her integrity as the burning deck becomes a darkling plain.
Joshua Cohen

I love this book in all its wit and inventiveness.
Hans Ulrich Obrist

Each with their startling similes and swerves, their alarming and tender moments, I have begun to read Helen Marten's sculpture through her writing, her writing through her sculpture. With The Boiled in Between *Marten has become an insistent voice in my head, tying knots and undoing them, never the same way twice.*
Adrian Searle

( )

The Boiled in Between is the debut novel by Turner Prize-winning artist Helen Marten, an ambitious literary work full of beauty and sorrow. It is a novel told in the action of persistence and questioning: how the rhythms of a world built upon metaphor and symbolism can collide with relationships personal and domestic. Spliced between three voices, the narrative is a project always in movement, its characters traversing the in-betweens. The psychic excitements of wind, dust and weather merge with alchemical interior voices, all of them indexes of the universe's microscopic pornography, a fitful map of language and human systems. Philosophic and tactile, humorous and unrelenting, *The Boiled in Between* ignites new meaning for people and terms of living that have long ceased to astonish us.